Tales from
Hidden Basin

Tales from
HIDDEN BASIN

DICK HAMMOND

Illustrated by
ALISTAIR ANDERSON

Harbour
Publishing

Harbour Publishing
Box 219
Madeira Park, BC V0N 2H0

Cover painting by Diana Durrand
Cover design by Roger Handling / Terra Firma
Page design & layout by David Lee Communications
Drawings by Alistair Anderson
Author photo by Josephine Hammond
An earlier version of "Visitors" appeared in *Raincoast Chronicles 15*.

Published with the assistance of the Canada Council and the Cultural Services Branch of the BC Ministry of Tourism and Ministry Responsible for Culture.
Printed and bound in Canada by Friesen Printers.

Canadian Cataloguing in Publication Data

Hammond, Dick, 1929–
Tales from Hidden Basin

ISBN 1-55017-136-4

1. Tales—British Columbia. I. Title.
GR113.5.B7H35   398.2'09711   C95-910737-1

Contents

Dedication

This book is dedicated to my wife Josephine, whose suggestions were never without merit. She taught herself to type and use a word processor for its sake. Without her encouragement it would not be finished yet!

Acknowledgements

To daughter Patricia, for whose help, and her faith in the project, I am grateful. To son Erik, whose healthy skepticism made me try harder. And Mr. Allan Crane, whose erudition, and knowledge of matters literary, were freely offered and gratefully accepted.

Introduction

I BEGAN TO WRITE THESE STORIES some fifteen years after the death of my father, whose stories they are. I believe they happened very much as they are written, for the action is vivid to my mind. However names, dates, places, haven't fared as well, and are not to be taken as accurate. Even the sequence of events is not always as clear as I would like it to be. They are meant as entertainment, not history. I hope that you enjoy them.

Dick Hammond. October 1995

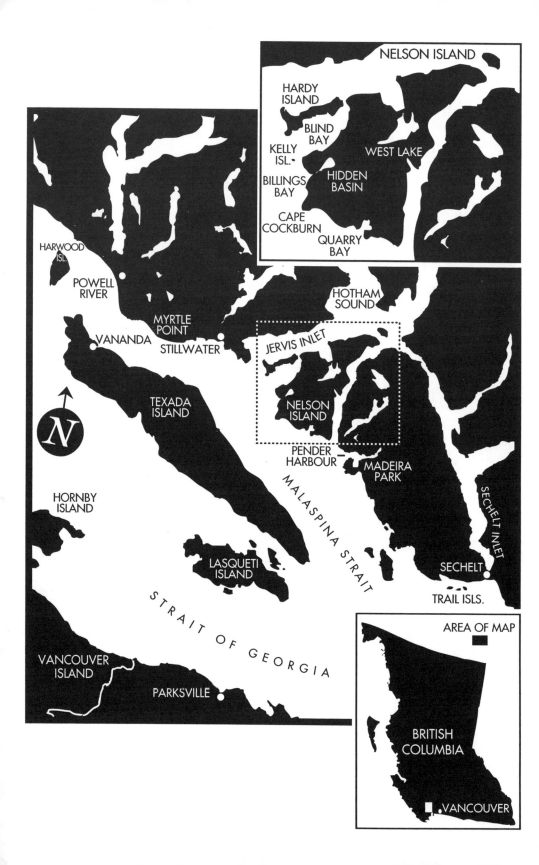

Chapter 1

In the Beginning

THE HAMMONDS OF OUR LINE came to America around the year 1500. When Britain lost the war of 1776, they were among those people, later known as United Empire Loyalists, who trekked north to Canada.

Some of them settled in Brandon, Manitoba, where John Latimer (later, "Jack") Hammond, my grandfather, was born. From a couple of uncles, he acquired a quite un-Canadian facility with weapons, and from his father, an equal skill with tools. Among the curious family traditions he carried on were songs and ballads in archaic English, one of which described a sea battle in the days when some ships were protected by armour made of brass plates. The names of the captains and some of the officers were given in full, to the great detriment of the metre. My father sang them—though he was vague on some of the names—but I neglected to learn them. I regret this.

Sometime in the 1880's, Jack moved to the BC coast, and eventually to the Nimpkish River valley on Vancouver Island. It was there, I think, that he built a sixty-four foot schooner out of wood from the local timber. He called it the *Crusader*.

There also he met the Mathers family, and married one of the daughters, May Mathers. Another daughter married one of the sons of Baron Lansdowne, and a third married a young timber cruiser called Eustace Smith, later to become one of the most famous men of his profession on the coast.

Jack was determined to carry on the tradition of life on the sea that ran so strongly through family history—though in fact it had probably not been a reality for several centuries! He decided to use the *Crusader* as a freight carrier to serve the isolated camps and communities of the mid- and upper coast. He was not then aware of the inconstant nature of the coast winds, nor of the force of the tides in the various narrows and inlets that would make this plan impractical.

He was a stubborn man, and he persevered far longer than he should have. During this time, he found many of the hidden rocks and reefs in the largely uncharted waters of Georgia Strait—found them the hard way.

Perhaps he could have made it work a couple of decades earlier, but now it was too late. The era of steam-powered ships was beginning, and even Jack had to admit that sails could not compete with engines.

He sold the *Crusader* and the Nimpkish property, relinquishing the sea forever, for he loathed the engine-driven ships that he knew were coming. He bought land on Texada Island, intending to go back to the farming that was also a tradition, though a more recent one. By now there was a family to provide for, sons and daughters born in the Nimpkish Valley. My father, christened Robert Henry, but always called "Hal'" was one of them, along with his older brother, Cliff.

The Texada Island property wasn't entirely to Jack's liking, though what his reasons were I never discovered.

Occasionally when his brother-in-law Eustace Smith was in the area, Jack would earn a bit of cash timber-cruising and land surveying. It was on one of these trips that he first saw the almost land-locked bit of water they called Hidden Basin, also known as Hidden Bay. It was about a mile in length, a quarter of that in width. Separated from Billings Bay by a narrow passage with a rock in the centre of it, even quite small gas boats could only enter it on high tide. Jack instantly fell in love with it, and acquired two parcels of land there, one on the shore, the other inland.

He built a big raft out of salvaged logs, and as soon as he could, he loaded his family and all of his livestock and possessions onto it, hired an acquaintance named Jack Deighton to tow them, and on a fine spring morning—I believe the year was 1902—they set off for their new home.

They left early in case a wind rose during the day. The trip was about twenty miles. When they had made about half the distance, the engine quit and refused to start again. Its owner tried to make up with profanity what he lacked in mechanical skills. May herded her children to the far end of the raft and forbade them to listen.

They drifted. Fog began to form on the still water. Before long, they were surrounded by soft grey walls, and even the sun was lost to them. They drifted.

Jack had used his knowledge of the area to pick a day when the tidal current would help them along, having small faith in his friend's primitive one-cylinder gas engine. Vindicated, he checked his compass and announced that they were going in the right direction. Of course, he had no way of knowing this, but it served to comfort his family somewhat. That night the fog lifted, but was on them as thick as ever before daylight.

All that next day they drifted, and another night. The morning once again brought fog. The engine had been abandoned as hopeless.

Suddenly May called, "Jack, look, there's seaweed around us. And listen—"

They listened and heard birds singing. Land was only yards away.

Jack took his longest pole, and it reached bottom. Soon there was the dark loom of trees in the mist ahead, and the raft touched gently on a sloping beach. He jumped into the water and splashed ashore.

Picking up a handful of gravel, he announced, "We're between Cape Cockburn and Billings Bay. It's the only beach we could drift to in that time where the gravel looks like this. We're almost there."

They were less than a mile from the entrance to Hidden Basin. So certain was he of this, that he began to pole the heavy raft along the shoreline to their left, over the objection of Mr. Deighton, who said he'd be damned if he'd believe anyone could recognize a beach from a handful of gravel. Jack said that he would probably be damned anyhow, and to push harder. May announced tartly that neither of their souls would be safe if they continued to use language like that in the hearing of the children.

The light grew brighter, and a faint halo showed the direction of the sun. The fog thinned, swirled in a slight breeze from the land, evaporated. The blue sky, translucent green water, the more intense green of trees and bushes came as a shock to senses so long accustomed to grey. They stood still, almost unspeaking, rejoicing in the colours. Jack spoke softly, pointing along the shore.

"Around that point," he promised, "is home. And the tide is with us."

And so it was. The raft seemed almost to move on its own, as the rising water caused a current to flow through the narrows of Hidden Basin, moving them along almost as fast as the engine could have done.

Jack rigged two long oars out of some planks from the supplies, so that when their motion slowed as the basin grew wider, the two men were able to move the big raft along, with the tide still slightly in their favour. By noon, sweating hotly under a blazing sun, they moored the raft to a tree. They were home.

Jack Hammond was satisfied at last. He put away his dreams of a life at sea. Here he would settle, and here he would raise his family. It was an idyllic spot; open to the sun, yet sheltered from any storm. The soil was good and there was a little creek nearby. There were neighbours, not too close, in Billings Bay and Cockburn Bay. The McConville logging camp at the head of the bay would provide work for cash money, but was quiet and unobtrusive. No engines! And there were patches of trees not far away, perfect for hand-logging, where good Douglas fir timber might be coaxed down to the water by anyone not afraid of hard work.

On previous trips, he had cleared some land, planted fruit trees, and built enough of the house to provide shelter. It was a dry month. By the first heavy spring rain, he had finished the living room, and another bedroom. All the furniture was now under cover, including his boxes of books, sorted and shelved. He was an omnivorous reader, and encouraged his children to read by providing them with books of romance and adventures, some of them violent even by today's standards! Strangely, he never taught his sons to write, and so although my father could read fluently, his handwriting was that of an illiterate.

Grandmother fought bitterly to censor her children's reading fare, but finally conceded defeat where the sons were concerned. So the girls were raised in accordance with the rather Victorian notions of their mother, while the boys were left to the somewhat eccentric attentions of Jack Hammond, who had theories about everything, including the raising of sons.

One result of this was a maturity in the boys that was remarkable for their years. Their father told them how they should act, and so great was his air of authority, so complete his assurance, that they did as he said without question. Even in the matter of chores they were encouraged to think for themselves, to be self reliant, not to

come to him for help, save in an emergency. But he seemed to miss nothing of what they did, and pushed their practical education to the limit of their abilities. They were allowed a degree of freedom usually afforded only those who have been essentially abandoned, but it was guided, and they thrived on it. It led to their having—and surviving—a number of adventures. The first of these happened to my father, Hal, alone, and led indirectly to the boys meeting someone who would have a great influence in their lives.

Chapter 2

White Spring

IT WAS LATE IN AUGUST. The day was warm, the water as smooth as glass. A large school of herring had come into the basin, its presence betrayed by the gulls and diving ducks. Cliff was helping his father clear a field. Eight years old, he was strong enough to be genuinely useful.

Two years younger than his brother, Hal had lighter duties. His father handed him the herring rake, telling him to go out in the skiff and rake in a bucket of herring for supper. (A herring rake is a long thin piece of wood shaped so as to slip easily through the water. One side is studded with sharp bits of wire on which the fish are impaled.) This beat picking rocks and roots out of the soil by a large margin, so off he went, whistling merrily, conscious of envious looks from his brother.

The flat-bottomed skiff was heavy to row, but he hadn't far to go to where the gulls, noisily circling, betrayed the location of the herring. When he judged that he was over the fish, he lifted the oars from the thole-pins and set them silently into the places made for them. Then he looked over the side into the clear water. Under him, so close he might have reached them with an oar, was a shoal of fish, so dense it appeared solid. The mass of undulating grey-green backs flecked with silver flashes as individual fish turned briefly onto their sides, gave a strange impression of movement. He had seen the like before, but it was fascinating still.

He watched for a few minutes, then took up the rake and quickly filled his bucket. His efforts seemed to have almost no effect on the school of fish except in the moment he drew the rake through it. When he had finished, they were as before.

He replaced the oars, gave a stroke to set the skiff moving, and leaning once more over the side, watched the countless fish pass beneath him. He wanted to see how big the mass of fish was, and each time the skiff slowed, he gave it another push with the oars. Peering ahead, he saw a circular area about ten feet across where there were no herring, and as the skiff drifted above it, he saw why.

"At first, I thought it was a seal," he told me. "I'd no notion that anything that big could be a fish. But then I got nearer and realized it was a salmon. A spring salmon, from the big black spots along its back. I'd heard stories about how big they grew, and all that, but they were just stories. I never dreamed I'd really see one, especially right out there in front of our house!"

There was a coil of heavy cod-fishing line wound around a stick on the stern seat. Moving as quietly as he could, he tied a live herring on the big hook, then lowered it over the side, where it sank with erratic little movements.

The huge salmon darted suddenly into the school of little fish, and Hal's heart pounded as he thought it had gone forever, but it made a slashing pass at the wall of herring, then came back to the centre of the clear circle. Its gill-flaps opened and closed, its fins moved languidly. Minute sparkles from tiny fish scales glinted in the water around it.

He had stopped letting the line down when the salmon moved; now he let the hook sink a bit further. He felt foolish, trying to entice the big fish with so obvious a lure, when it was surrounded by tons of herring with no line attached to them, but its very difference must have made the bait interesting. The salmon swung lazily towards it, engulfed herring and hook, turned back to its position. With a yell of triumph, the boy jerked savagely on the line, setting the heavy cod hook firmly in the fish's jaw.

As the startled salmon lunged for freedom, it almost pulled him out of the skiff. He gave line, tried to hold on. The line burned his palms. Desperate, he let it go, grabbed the stick on which the line was wound and jammed it under the back seat, holding it there with braced foot. The last of the line ran out, came tight with a snap that swung the heavy skiff sideways, then fell limply on the water. Dreading to find a straightened hook or broken line, he cautiously drew it in. Suddenly, resistance! Dropping it, he drew the loose line through the ring bolt in the stern, tied a quick hitch. His prize was secure, unless the hook pulled out or the line broke. But the tough line would hold his weight and more, and the hook had stood that first strain.

The line came tight, cut through the water in a hissing arc. He sat down, put the oars between the pins, began to row for shore.

It took a while. The salmon had other ideas; it wanted to escape to the deep water. There were moments when he made no gains, even went backwards a bit, but the heavy skiff tired the big fish and it began to go first to one side, then to the other. Sometimes the line slacked, and he feared he had lost it, but always it came tight again. He pulled strongly, heading for where the beach was flattest. His father was standing there at the water's edge, having heard the

yell when the hook was set. Behind him, the whole family watched. As the bow touched, his father seized it and heaved the boat part way up the beach. They were all talking, exclaiming, asking questions.

Cliff splashed out, made to seize the taut line, but his brother shouted, "No, it's mine! I'll land it!"

He jumped in, pulled on the line hand over hand. There was a huge splashing in the shallow water. The girls screamed, Cliff shouted with excitement. For a moment, the struggle was equal, but the tired fish had used its last store of energy. It lay over on its side as its exulting captor dragged it out of the water and onto the beach, where it flopped helplessly. Jack picked up a piece of driftwood, killed it quickly.

They stood around in a circle, admiring. Cliff pried open the huge mouth, worked the hook out. It was partially straightened, and came out quite easily. They took the prize to the balance scales on the verandah, where it evened out at sixty-one pounds. The happy fisherman weighed just sixty. In a lifetime of trying, he would never land one that big again!

After they had admired it sufficiently, came the question of what to do with so much fish. It was a white-fleshed spring salmon. Jack said that they were too coarse for eating fresh, but that they made the finest smoked salmon of all. He would build a smokehouse especially for it. They would need one to preserve meat for the coming winter anyhow.

The boys cleaned the fish, and buried the offal under an apple tree. Their mother sliced the fish, and soaked the pieces overnight in a special marinade. Jack was a fast worker. By evening, the smokehouse was ready, racks and all. A fire of crabapple was set smouldering in the fire pit, its pungent fumes enveloping rack after rack of salmon. After everyone had examined and exclaimed, Jack closed the door reverently, and they all trooped back to the house, while the grey smoke behind them curled into the twilight sky.

Next morning after breakfast, Jack went to replenish the fire with more crabapple wood. His sons trotted ahead, hoping to filch a bit of fresh-smoked salmon. As they came up to the little building, they could see no smoke coming from under the eaves.

"That's odd," said their father. "There should have been plenty of wood to keep it going."

He undid the latch, pulled open the door.

"What the deuce?..."

They crowded in for a look. The racks were bare of fish; they looked greasy. The ground was covered with mounds of an ugly grey-yellow stuff like melted candle wax. The fire was out, the fire-pit full of the same strange substance. There were little pools of yellow oil in the hollows. The air smelled strongly of fish. Jack knelt, poked at the stuff on the ground.

"How strange," he mused thoughtfully. "How very strange. It melted, like tallow in the hot sun!"

And so it had. They shovelled up the remains of the fish, all forty-odd pounds of it, and buried it in the garden. Not one bite of the big salmon did anyone get to eat.

"At least" said their mother consolingly, "we have a smokehouse now!"

About a month after this disaster, the boys were helping their father in the field when they heard the wide-spaced explosive sounds that indicated a one-cylinder engine coupled to a big flywheel. Looking towards the entrance to the basin, they could see the boat that was making the sound.

Jack studied it for a moment, announced, "That's old Charlie's boat. Charlie, the old Indian. Wonder what he's doing here in the basin?"

Chapter 3

Charlie

CHARLIE IS A FREQUENT CHARACTER in my father's stories of his boyhood. He travelled the waters of the coast in a little double-ender fishboat (both ends pointed) about twenty-four feet long. He was very proud of it. It was powered by a remarkably primitive gas engine, and had a short mast that would carry enough sail to get him home on those frequent occasions when the engine broke down or ran out of gas.

Charlie lived mostly on his boat; hunting a little, fishing a little, trapping in season—and sometimes out. He had a tolerant outlook on life. If the European newcomers wished to make laws, fine. He didn't mind at all. But it never seemed to occur to him that he should be obliged to take any notice of those laws.

His name was Charlie, but he had an odd way of referring to himself in the third person, as "the old Indian." He spoke to the boys in sort of shorthand English, with most on the non-essential words omitted.

Father told me, "Looking back on it, that first time we met him, I'm pretty sure he spoke normally when he said hello to Dad and Mother. But later, when he talked to us, he sounded just like the Indians in our story books, and it sounded so right, so natural, that I guess we just forgot we'd heard anything else. That was the way we wanted him to speak, you see. I've often wondered how he knew. I guess he read the same books!

"You know," he mused, "sometimes a person forgets because they don't want to remember. I was coming around the corner of the house, about a year later. Charlie and Dad were sitting on the

verandah talking. I stopped to listen for a moment, and I realized that Charlie was speaking just like anyone else. I turned around and walked away. It didn't really bother me, I just didn't think about it, and in a little while I'd pretty much forgotten about it. I never did tell Cliff."

Jack and his sons went down to the float to greet the visitor. The older girls watched from the verandah. Their mother tended to have reservations where strangers in scruffy boats were concerned, and Charlie's pride in his boat didn't involve keeping it painted. As it drew near, they could see that the cabin showed large areas of bare wood, and the hull wasn't painted at all, but tarred. The slow *Puff—Puff—* of the engine exhaust slowed even further, then stopped as the craft made a sharp turn and slid broadside against the float, bumping it gently. Jack explained that Charlie's engine had no reverse. The boys ran to tie the bow and stern lines, and Charlie stepped lightly onto the float. They were so awed at seeing a real Indian that they scarcely heard his greeting to their father. He had on the usual wool pants and grey flannel shirt, but also wore a fringed leather vest, darkened with age and grease.

"Look," whispered Cliff in exultation. "Moccasins. He's wearing moccasins!"

Charlie heard, turned towards them. There was grey in his hair, but his face was almost unlined. Deep-set eyes almost as black as his hair regarded them intently. When he spoke, his voice was deep and rich.

"Boys tie up boat for Old Indian. Good knots. Maybe good boys? What names have boys?"

"I'm Cliff."

"I'm Hal."

A wide grin turned sternness into friendliness; their apprehensions vanished.

"Hello, Cliff. Hello, Hal. My name Charlie."

He turned away to accompany their father to the house. They followed happily behind. A real Indian!

The old man enchanted their mother and the girls, and it was soon settled that he would stay for supper. Of course, the story of the big fish and the disaster in the smokehouse, so fresh in their minds, was told. Charlie was much impressed.

"Hal catch fish bigger than him. Even The Old Indian have hard time beat that!"

But what really got his attention was the part about the smoking of the salmon. His face became totally impassive, as if he was trying hard to conceal something. He said, "Show Charlie smokehouse."

So off they went. He stopped in front of the smokehouse, eyed it up and down, went to the door, opened it, peered inside. They saw his shoulders start to shake, and they heard strange sounds. He backed out, turned. He was laughing. He tried to speak, failed, tried again.

"You...ho-ho-ho!...you smoke big...ho-ho-ho!...big white spring in hot smoke?"

Tears ran over his cheeks

"And it all melt all over and put fire out? Ho-ho-ho!"

Suddenly his expression changed, became mournful. "And you lose all that good meat. Oh, that awful!"

He shook a large finger sternly.

"No hot smoke big white spring. Never! Too oily, too fat. All melt. Cold smoke big white spring. Not hot smoke. Cold."

Shaking his head at such incredible ignorance, he led the way back to the house. But what amazed the boys most was that their father, a man of pride and quick temper, took the ridicule and laughter of the old Indian so meekly and without protest.

That evening, Charlie quizzed the brothers on their knowledge concerning the things of woods and waters. Their answers plainly didn't satisfy him. At last, he leaned back in his chair with a deep sigh. Despairingly, he said, "Boys know nothing. Nothing! Father smart man, but head too full of books, and things white men know."

Startled, they looked at Jack, who was sitting listening with a book on his lap and a smile on his face. Charlie was saying: "Guess it up to old Indian to teach boys." He shook his grey head gloomily. "Boys probably too smart to learn anything anyhow."

He got up stiffly, said goodnight, went out into the dark and his boat. The brothers didn't know whether they had been complimented or insulted. They had a strong suspicion it had been the last!

Next morning, when they expected to be told what their duties for that day would be, their father said instead, "I won't need you today. Go and see old Charlie, and do as he tells you."

Off they went, feeling apprehensive. The old man was sitting with his back against the cabin, drowsing in the morning sun. As they approached, he opened one eye slightly, like a cat, and peered at them. Then he rose lightly to his feet, said firmly, "Well, old Indian try. Untie boat, we go on little trip."

He ducked into the cabin, and after a few preparatory wheezes, the engine began its slow-paced *Puff—Puff—Puff—* and the boat began to move slowly away from the float. Charlie came out, and taking the wheel, pushed a tarnished brass lever forward. The engine speed increased, and the old boat moved out into the basin, leaving almost no wake behind it. Their education was about to begin.

The old man was a good teacher, though his lessons very often began with an admonitory: "Boys know nothing."

But they soon realized that it in no way suggested they were stupid. It was simply Charlie's way of saying "Now listen carefully, I have something to tell you." And listen carefully they did.

There were no great revelations, no arcane knowledge revealed, nothing not known to other fishermen and hunters—just good practical advice and example, illustrated and driven home with stories and anecdotes. He showed them how to make a cod jig from a piece of lead, some strips of cod skin, or any other flexible material, and a shiny bit of tin cut from a can; he showed them how to use it, and where and when. He took them through the narrows, into Billings Bay, among the rocks and little islands nearby. They lit a very small fire, and roasted fresh-caught fish over it. All too soon, it was time to go back. Just past the narrows, they came on a little flock of mergansers. Charlie reached through the doorway, took out a rusty old single-shot twelve gauge, aimed briefly, fired. Shot slashed the surface of the water, leaving two ducks where it had passed. The boys were shocked.

"What'd you do that for, Charlie?" asked Cliff. "You can't eat sawbills. Dad says you shouldn't kill things you're not going to eat."

"Yeah," seconded his brother. "He says sawbills are tough, and their meat tastes fishy. Ugh!"

Charlie made no answer, but steered the boat towards the floating birds. He took a big dipnet from the roof of the cabin and expertly scooped them up as they slid by the boat. Then he reversed the net and dropped the ducks onto the deck at his feet, still wordless. He drew his sheath knife and began to skin and gut the birds with swift sure movements, tossing the unwanted parts back into the water, where the gulls squabbled noisily over them. Finally he spoke, his manner that of exaggerated patience.

"Boys know nothing," he sighed. "Nothing!"

They grinned. By now, they knew he didn't really mean it. Charlie shook his head again. "But that not stop them telling poor old Indian what ducks he can eat, and which ducks he can't eat."

He put the second carcass neatly beside the first, then shook the bloody knife at them. "All meat good to eat," he told them sternly. "All meat. Rats good. Snakes good. Frogs good. All meat good. Sawbill ducks very good."

Cliff and Hal made faces and disgusted noises.

"How about slugs Charlie?" asked Hal suddenly. "Are slugs good?"

Charlie was nonplussed. He pushed his lower lip out, finally admitted reluctantly, "Slugs...not so good. But all other meat, good."

"But Charlie, fishy old sawbills?" asked Hal, by far the fussiest of the two brothers about his food. Charlie reached through the door, brought out a good-sized iron pot.

"Boys like to eat fish, hah?"

"Well, yes."

With a dipper, he poured salt water in until it was about one-quarter full.

"And boys like to eat duck, hah?"

"Well, sure, but..."

He dropped the two ducks into the pot.

"Then what wrong with duck and fish together?"

Triumphantly, he went into the cabin, came out with two potatoes, two carrots and an onion, all of which he quartered without peeling and put into the pot, then put the pot on his little stove with a solid clunk. Back on deck, he corrected their course a bit, wiped bloody hands on his wool pants, said with considerable satisfaction, "There. Stay on stove until this time tomorrow. Maybe later. Cook long enough, not too hot, make toughest meat fall-off-bone tender. Then old Indian have meat stew with fish. Or maybe fish stew with meat." He beamed happily. "Same difference."

Of the two brothers, Cliff would adopt Charlie's "eat anything" attitude. Hal, however, rejected it almost entirely, most especially regarding the edibility of fish-flavoured duck. And, so great is the sensitivity of children in certain matters that though the subject was rarely mentioned in our house, I dislike the taste of fish with meat.

Chapter 4

The Blind Man

FATHER, AS I HAVE SAID, was a story-teller born. This became evident to his family when he was still quite young. The two brothers were very different in many ways. Cliff, if asked, would give a quick and concise account of where he had been and what he had done. But his younger brother would volunteer the information at the slightest sign of interest, or even none at all, and his recital would be teeming with descriptive detail. This ability was to lead to an unusual episode in his life.

It didn't take long before the people living in that area discovered that their new neighbour was so skilled with tools that he could build almost anything that could be clearly described, and that he was willing to take time to help whenever he was asked. This seldom brought in much money: first, because few people had any, and second, because he was reluctant to ask for payment. But people were grateful, and there are other forms of payment.

One day, a neat and tidy little gas boat, paint gleaming, came in to tie up at their float. The engine was well-muffled, and it was there almost before anyone noticed it. Out of it jumped a man of about average build, who moved like someone in a hurry. He had a wild beard and wilder hair, bright red, both. A strong Scottish accent coloured his words. Jack walked out into the yard to meet him and, after a few minutes, returned to the house, saying there was a chance of a paying job. Taking his hat from its peg, he went down to the float where the red-haired man already had the engine running and the ropes untied.

The boys were home when Jack returned. The first words he said when he came in and put his hat back in its place were, "That man has more books than I have!"

He was jubilant. He had met a man whose interests were similar to his own. There was carpentry to be done at an excellent wage. And there were all those books! Surely, if he worked it right, he would be able to borrow some of them.

But the books were a disappointment. Almost all of them were in Latin, Greek, Hebrew, none of which Jack could read. Oh yes, and the old man was blind. What was a blind man doing with so many books? It seemed that the wild-looking Scotsman was fluent in all these languages and more, and his chief task was to read to his employer!

Jack announced that he would start on the job the very next morning, at which May commented, "Well, we can certainly use the money."

After breakfast, while getting tools and materials ready, Jack told his wife, "I'll take the boys with me. It might do them good to see someone different."

That was welcome news! No chores, and a chance for a trip in their new boat. For their father, bowing to necessity, had recently become the owner of a boat powered by a gas engine! It was long and slim, with the hull shape of a yacht, and a cabin that ran almost its full length. He had, of course, immediately installed a mast so that it could be sailed if need be. He renamed it the *Lady May*, and very soon grew quite fond of it. Though he never overcame his dislike of engines, he promptly became an authority on "The Internal Combustion Principle," and lectured his sons upon it. The *Lady May* was still new enough that a trip on her was dearly sought after by the whole family, but especially by the boys.

When they were well on their way, Jack called his sons down from the roof of the cabin into the wheelhouse, where it was quieter. The engine was far behind them, and enclosed, and there were walls between. Their father would not abide a noisy engine or one too close to him. He signed for them to come near, and they stood one on each side of him. He spoke idly of unimportant things. They wondered apprehensively just what particular escapade might have come to his attention. Perhaps the incident of the chickens...?

"Now, pay attention," came the command. "I've something important to tell you. The man you will be meeting is a Jew."

They looked at him in bewilderment, and no small relief.

"You will have heard," he went on seriously, "visitors speak of Jews from time to time."

They searched their memories for the word "Jew," and found nothing. Hal had a notion that it might be something you might call someone to insult them.

"I had meant to speak to you boys before about this. Disregard what you may have heard. The Jews are a much-maligned people. Those I have known were honest, intelligent, and hard-working."

"They wrote the Bible; it is said that they killed Christ." His tone became speculative. "If the Book is true, then he was meant to die. It seems hard that they should be blamed..."

With obvious effort he shook off the temptation to lapse into religious philosophy.

"They are accused for loving money overmuch. I have not observed that others love it less. What hurts is that we are, on the whole, usually less skilled at obtaining it. They are a cultured and sensitive people, and they've given far more than their share of great thinkers and great musicians to make the world a richer place. But they are hated, in spite of it."

He was silent for a bit, then: "Now, remember, this man you'll be meeting is a bit different, but I think that he is a good man. He's certainly a learned one, though that's not necessarily the same thing. Pay attention to whatever he tells you."

Taking this for dismissal, the boys regained their perch on the cabin roof. The lecture had greatly impressed them by its serious tone. What sort of strange creature, they wondered, were they about to meet?

At last, they rounded a point and there was the neat little boat tied to a small dock of floating logs. There wasn't much room in the narrow bay, and Jack approached very cautiously; the *Lady May* was long and didn't manoeuvre well, but he eased her in until they could tie the bow, and then they ran out a stern anchor. The Scotsman had been watching, wearing a ferocious frown, perhaps fearing a possible scratch on his beautifully painted boat, but he greeted their father civilly enough, although he disdained to notice the presence of the boys. He led the way to the house they could see among the trees. It wasn't large, but neatly painted, like the boat. He knocked, and a deep voice replied, though he had opened the door without waiting.

They followed him into a fairly large room. Facing them in a high-backed chair of strange design sat an old man with a shawl drawn around his shoulders. A much-lined face with a great fierce beak of a nose dividing long grey hair and a bushy grey beard. By his side, on a table of dark wood, were two machines to play the two types of recordings then in use, cylinder and disc. The boys stared curiously, for they had never seen flat records before. Every other available surface and parts of the floor were piled with books, many of them in beautiful bindings.

The old man greeted them in a youthful-sounding voice that came strangely from someone who appeared so frail. "Welcome, Mr. Hammond. It is good of you to come so soon. I see you have brought your boys with you." Thin lips drew back in a gentle smile. "You will perceive that I use the word 'see' figuratively."

For wrinkled lids covered the blind scholar's shrunken eyes. He held out a thin blue veined hand. "Introduce us if you would."

First Cliff, as the oldest, then Hal, took the hand, which was warm and surprisingly strong, and each was questioned in his turn. They tried to avoid looking at the eyes, but were fascinated by the beard, which was by far the largest and bushiest they had ever seen. And that nose. Like an eagle's beak. It made him look like some ancient king. They were dismissed kindly, and the work was discussed in some detail. There were to be cabinets for the books. Not just shelves, but proper cabinets suited to the task of guarding such rare treasures. The task had been delayed for too long. Something had been spilled...it must not happen again.

Jack took measurements. As they were heading to the back room

where the work was to be done, the old man said, "Excuse me, Mr. Hammond, will you need your sons to assist you?"

"Perhaps one, to run errands. Did you want them for something?"

"Just to talk with, sir. At my age, youth is precious, even if it belongs to someone else. Perhaps a bit of it may linger here, when they have gone."

So they took turns, answering the old man's questions, soon talking freely with him, for he had the gift of making them feel at ease.

For over a week, they came back to the island every day. The job took longer then it should have, for Jack's questions soon revealed his interests, and lunch times were often several hours long as the old man engaged him in philosophical argument. Cliff became bored at being questioned, and an unlikely friendship started between him and the Scot, whose name was Dougal. But Hal felt sorry for the blind old man, and prattled on about everything he knew, and more, as some children will.

At last the job was done, the tools stowed, and Jack was having a few last words before he left. Cliff was already on the boat, impatient, but Hal was always interested in what adults had to say, and was loitering unobtrusively by the door. At the words "Those are two fine boys you have, Mr. Hammond," he came fully alert. His father acknowledged the praise complacently.

"The younger one, Hal, has a gift, as I'm sure you realize."

There was a noncommittal response.

"What I refer to is his ability to observe accurately, and more important, to report what he has observed, so that others can see it in their imagination. He has a wonderful memory. It is a rare gift, and with your permission, I would like to take advantage of it."

Jack must have indicated puzzlement, for the old man said, "I can understand your doubt, sir. But think you, I am blind. There are for me only the scenes of memory, and they fade sir, they fade. But your son has the gift of making the mind see, and that is very dear to me. I would like to employ him. What I propose is to have him visit me here one day every week. Dougal will fetch him and return him. For this service I will pay him one dollar each time. No, no, I insist. It is worth far more to me than that."

The listening boy couldn't believe his ears. A whole dollar for going on a boat ride and just talking. There had to be a catch!

But there was no catch. Every Sunday, weather permitting— and the Scot was a hard man to discourage—the boat arrived to take Hal to the island. There, the old man would listen intently to what he had done and seen during the week. His interest was relentless; he wanted to know the size, shape, colour and distinguishing character of every bush, tree, bird or animal, of every rock, stump, stream or field.

Father told me, "It was the best thing that ever happened to me.

I've never had anyone listen to me like he did. I learned to see things—really see them. And how to tell about them to make someone else see them. But you can't do it with just anyone. It has to be someone who can listen, who knows how to listen, like that old man listened. And when I got older, and began to hunt, it made a hunter out of me, because I knew how to look at things."

When he asked about the little flat records, and the machine with the little tapering horn that played them, the old man played some of them for him. He wasn't much impressed. The sound wasn't as good as that from their Edison machine, and there was a lot more hiss and scratch. The music was opera and classical, instead of the comic songs he liked.

In the end, the old scholar proved something of a disappointment to Jack. His books were unreadable, and the discussions of philosophy unsatisfactory. For the old man's faith in the existence of the God of his fathers was unshakeable, while for Jack it was the point most open to debate. But he liked the old man, and visited him fairly often. On one of these occasions, Hal was sitting on the little porch, looking at a book filled with grotesque drawings that he found fascinating. The two men were talking in the room of books, quite unaware they were being overheard.

"Your sons are very different, Mr. Hammond. They look so alike, one would not suspect it. Clifford is quite content with his life here. He wants nothing better. But Hal's mind wants to spread its wings. He could be a scholar where his brother would not."

Jack acknowledged the truth of this.

"He should go to school, to a good school. To do otherwise would be a waste, a sad waste."

"You may be right, I have sometimes thought it myself. But there is a problem with the doing of it. We have hardly enough money to get by. There is none left over for schooling, nor do I expect there will be."

"But, my dear sir, that is exactly why I mentioned the matter. I am fortunate, you see, in having more money than I will ever need. I would be very grateful to you if you would let me send him to school when he is ready."

The boy whose future they were they were deciding sat there in shock. Leave Hidden Basin? He wouldn't do it! He'd run away, hide in the hills. He heard his father say he'd think it over. There was nothing to think over. He wasn't going, that was all there was to it. He returned the book to its place in one of the cabinets, said good-bye numbly. The trip home was not a happy one. Neither one spoke. It would not have occurred to Jack to discuss the matter with his son.

That evening, his parents talked with lowered voices for a long while. He tried to eavesdrop, but the girls were making too much noise.

He needn't have worried. For a couple of weeks there were storms, and he didn't go to the island. Then one day, not a Sunday, the boat came into the dock. Dougal came striding up to the house, hair and beard wilder than ever. He seemed distraught, and began to speak while he was still a dozen paces distant.

"He's just sitting there, Mr. Hammond," he gasped.

They saw that his cheeks were wet.

"I just went out for a wee while, and when I looked in on him, he was just sitting there. It's uncanny, for, d'ye see, he never drew the lids back from his eyes, not while I knew him. But they are open now, and he sits there, with them all white and shrivelled, as if he is looking out the window. And he is as dead as dust!"

The house on the island stood deserted for a few years. (There were many people who would not have felt comfortable there after dark!) Then one fall it was destroyed by fire; no one knew how.

Chapter 5

Cougar Hunt

COUGARS HAVE ALWAYS held a fascination for the people of the Coast—native or European. Whenever hunters gather, tales of the secretive cats, of their strange mix of daring and cowardice, of rashness and cunning, are sure to be told.

There are no cougars on Nelson Island, but to the two brothers, they were the most interesting of all animals—even more interesting than the great bear, the grizzly. For just about everyone who hunted had seen those, but some men had hunted all of their lives and not seen one of the big cats.

Cliff and Hal's greatest ambition was to go on a cougar hunt with the old Indian, an event he had hinted might be in the future. But when they heard the familiar *Puff—Puff—* of Charlie's old engine one November morning, they weren't thinking of cougars; they were just glad he was there for a visit. Charlie's visits to the farm were welcomed by everyone. His kindness and sense of humour endeared him to the girls and their mother. His knowledge— which he was always willing to share—was valued by Jack, who liked the old man, and was impressed by his practical wisdom. And the boys could never get enough of his stories of hunting and fishing, and of the old times. For his part, Charlie relished the good food and appreciative audience.

But certain chores had to be finished, so by the time they got to the float the boat was tied up, and their father and Charlie had been talking for some while.

"Charlie, hey Charlie!"

The grin on the face of the old man disappeared. He said

severely, "Lazy boys. Boys no good. Not come down to meet Old Indian. Probably sleeping."

"We weren't sleeping. We were working. Ma wouldn't let us go 'til we'd finished."

"Yes. That's right, Charlie. You know we'd have been here if we could!"

"Well-ll, maybe Old Indian believe you. He not very smart. Try to make hunters out of farm boys."

"Farm boys! We're not farm boys. Just because we live on a farm..."

They were almost speechless at the insult. Charlie grunted, "Hmph. Real hunters eat'm fishy duck, like it."

"I like fishy duck, Charlie. It's good," said Cliff.

"Me too," lied his younger brother manfully.

Their father spoke. "Charlie thought you might want to go on a cougar hunt with him." His eyes twinkled. "I said I didn't think you would be interested, but that he could ask you himself."

He watched with amusement their frantic attempts to correct this second monstrous misapprehension.

"Well, perhaps I was mistaken. If you're going to go, you'd better hurry and get your things. The tide's dropping."

There wasn't much to get. Coats, hats, hunting shoes. Gun.

As they turned to go, Charlie said, "No gun. Old Indian have gun. One gun enough."

"Aw-w, Charlie..."

"No gun," firmly. No gun it was.

It all happened so fast. One moment doing chores, the next gliding over the smooth surface of Hidden Basin, with the *Puff— Puff—* of the boat's engine echoing from the rocky shore.

"Where's the cougar, Charlie?" "Where're we going Charlie?" "How long will we be gone?"

The old man ignored them, his attention on the tricky business of guiding his boat past the rock in the rapids leading out of Hidden Basin. That done, he condescended to notice his passengers. He looked them over, stern-faced.

"Noisy boys. Worse than seagulls. Like crows with owl. Cougar hear, he run away, never come back."

"Aw-w Charlie. You know we don't make any noise when we're hunting."

He relented somewhat. "Maybe so. Maybe could be worse. We see how quiet boys be when tired, hands cold, shoes full of snow." His voice lost its bantering tone. "Cougar go after old lady's chickens in Pender Harbour. Old lady's dog bark, cougar go into hills. Dog follow, not come back. Old lady call police. Cougar hounds all away somewhere. Police remember Old Indian, say, 'Get cougar.' Old Indian say 'sure.' New snow, easy track cougar. Come get boys."

There was no wind. The boat slipped easily along, making about four miles an hour—the speed that Charlie found most fuel-efficient. It seemed that he wasn't in any hurry. At the rate they were going, it would take about three hours to get to Pender Harbour. The land slid by, looking like a picture postcard of Christmas with the still, reflecting water and the dusting of snow on the trees, which became thicker as they rounded the point and turned north. Time passed quickly as the old man—stimulated as ever by an appreciative audience—told them stories of hunting and the old times. All too soon they arrived at the dock.

As the old boat had no reverse, docking could be an occasion of some excitement. You had the choice of making a one-eighty turn to kill momentum, which took a good deal of water, or stopping the engine, gliding up to the dock and leaping out to "snub" the line on whatever was convenient. As Charlie's lines were almost as old as his boat, they tended to snap under tension, giving added drama to already tense proceedings. This time, having deck hands, Charlie chose the second method. The ropes held, the boys knowing enough to let them slip a bit to ease the strain.

Safely docked, Charlie donned his wool jacket. Sanctified by many hunts, the wool retained traces of every odour with which it had ever been in contact. Then he took his old gun from its corner. Smelling heavily of the ratfish oil he kept it soaked with, it was loaded, hammer cocked, ready for any emergency—such as a potential dinner presenting itself within range. The boys were horrified. They had been taught, with great firmness, that one never kept a loaded gun around, much less one that was ready to fire!

Cliff said hesitantly, "Ah, Charlie, do you always keep your gun like that?"

"Like what?"

"You know, with a shell in the chamber, and cocked."

"Sure. Why not? Who going to pull trigger? Come around point, see seal, click of hammer maybe make dive. Boys know nothing."

They subsided. This would take some thinking about.

Years later, father would say, "You know, it's a funny thing, but I found out as I got older that people who really use guns, and have lived with them all their lives, are the most careless with them. You see someone doing all the right things, checking the chamber, safety on, that sort of thing, chances are he's a weekend hunter. I don't say it's right, mind you, but that's the way it is."

As they started off, Hal—always the practical one—asked, "How about food, Charlie?"

The old man grinned. "Oh," he said enigmatically, "I think we find plenty of food for hungry boys."

He hung a rolled-up blanket over his shoulder by a strap, but it was obviously just a blanket.

They walked briskly along the shore on the trail which led to the old lady's house. There was about an inch of snow on the ground, but though there were many footprints, there was no other sign of life. A dog barked somewhere, and there was a faint smell of woodsmoke. They passed several houses, seemingly deserted, and came to a cottage with a red-shingled roof. Smoke drifted from the chimney. The snow in the yard and around was heavily trampled.

"Sh-sh," whispered Charlie, "This house of old lady. No spook-um."

He led the way to the back of the house where the chicken pen was. There were many tracks in the snow; dogs, people, chickens. Charlie pointed to a track like a large dog's.

"No claws. Cougar."

The boys were immensely thrilled. Their first cougar track! Charlie walked towards the chicken pen. The chickens, made nervous by the cat's visit, cackled and clucked at the strangers.

Immediately, a door opened. There was the old lady, an impressive-looking gun grasped firmly in her hands, the muzzle pointing more or less in Charlie's direction. She peered at them as they stood frozen.

Lowering the gun, she said, "Well, it's about time! I don't know what you men do, it takes you so long to do anything. It's been a whole day almost that my Hopsy has been lost, but does anyone care? They do not! What are you doing there scaring my chickens? Why aren't you out rescuing my Hopsy?"

With his inscrutable look firmly in place, Charley weathered the word storm. When it finally subsided a bit, he said with great dignity, "Old Indian come many miles to help find little dog. Travel over water, over land, never stop. Now we are here, not worry. Old Indian find dog." He finished gravely, "We go now."

"Well, I should hope so. My poor Hopsy out in the woods all alone. I don't know why someone couldn't have done something before this..."

Her voice faded as Charlie hastily led the way around the corner and up the trail. The words became indistinct, but her voice could still be heard until they went around a rock outcropping. When it could be heard no more, Charlie sighed, "Cougar fool to come here. Old lady talk 'm to death sure."

As they went up the trail, he pointed to the marks in the snow.

"Cougar come up here. Dog come after. Dog go 'yap—yap—yap.' Cougar not like noise. He not afraid of dog, not go very fast. Head for high ground soon."

They went on another hundred yards or so. The boys studied the tracks with great care, scarcely able to believe that they were actually following the trail of a cougar. Charlie walked steadily on, not bothering to look at the trail at all, or so it seemed.

The right hand side of the trail became steeper until the bank was almost vertical for the first fifteen feet or so. Charlie said, "Boys watch. Cougar's trail go away soon."

Sure enough, in a few more paces there were only dog tracks going back and forth and running around in circles. Then the single track of a running dog led up the trail.

"What happened, Charlie? Where'd he go?"

"I'll bet he jumped away off down there in the brush," guessed Cliff.

The old man shook his head sadly. "Boys use mouth. Not use eyes. Even dog not use mouth until he have something to talk about."

The embarrassed brothers kept silent and began to study the trail. In a moment they found, half obscured by dog tracks, two deep parallel gouges in the ground, with well-defined claw marks facing the steep bank. They looked up. There was a ledge about three times their height, but there were no marks in the light cover of snow on the bank.

"You mean it jumped up there and didn't touch the bank? Ah-h Charlie, you're joking. Nothing could jump that high!"

The old man shrugged. "Boys so smart, maybe teach Old Indian how track cougar? Maybe first go up bank, look for cougar tracks, eh?"

They looked up at the steep slippery bank. Hal said doubtfully, "If we try to go up there, we'll get all wet and muddy and make a lot of noise. Why can't we just follow the dog tracks? The dog knows where the cougar went, I'll bet."

Charlie grinned. "Maybe some hope for boys yet. O.K. We follow after dog."

The dog tracks led only a little farther up the trail, then disappeared into the brush as the bank became lower. Charlie turned to the right, back along the way they had come.

"But Charlie, the tracks go that way!"

"Boys come, maybe learn something."

So they stumbled along the slippery broken rock with its coating of wet snow. Strangely enough, it didn't seem to be as slippery to the old man, although he wore boots much like theirs. Soon they were at the ledge above the marks on the trail. Charlie pointed, and there, plainly to be seen in the snow, was the mark where the big cat had lain. It had crouched there above the trail, watching the dog.

Charlie said, "What cougar thinking about? Why not jump on dog? Maybe too close to house. Maybe just not hungry enough!"

The boys looked at each other. They'd had visions of finding the lost dog and bringing it back to the old lady. But suddenly the woods didn't seem quite so friendly, nor the prospect of a happy ending so certain.

They were both wishing right then that they had the nice comforting heft of a gun in their hands. Hal was sure Old Charlie knew just what they were thinking. Why else would he have been grinning like that?

Back they went to follow the dog and cougar tracks. It was hard going. The trail headed almost straight up the hill. The ground was rough, and covered with thickets of salal and salmonberry brush.

They had turned north around the shoulder of the hill and the snow was now about four inches deep. They were soon sweating under their wool coats. Snow found its way down their necks, up their sleeves and into their boots. They were forced to make the most heroic efforts to keep from gasping or panting, for Old Charlie was strolling along as if he was on a good level trail, his breath coming and going silently, his footsteps almost as silent. This was a humiliating experience for two boys who prided themselves on their woodscraft! They began to watch how the old man walked. He never seemed to be looking at the ground just ahead of him, but he never slipped. Always his step took advantage of some foothold, a rock or a root, a stem or a branch, or a bit of log. They began to study the ground ahead, to plan their steps. (Thirty-odd years later, Hal's teen-aged son would experience exactly the same difficulty following his father as he strolled easily along a snowy trapline, or on an afternoon hunt!)

Several times the tracks showed that the cougar had leaped to a high place and watched as the dog came trotting busily along his trail. Suddenly, Charlie put up his hand in the signal to stop. He spoke very quietly.

"I think we find dog very soon. Maybe cougar too. Boys stay here, make no noise."

He looked at his gun, slid the lever enough to see the shell in the chamber. Though the barrel showed rust, the action worked smoothly and quietly. He took off his wool mittens and put them in his coat pocket, then he moved off. They thought he had moved silently before; now he was like drifting smoke. It seemed impossible to the boys that a human could make so little sound, even in snow.

About a hundred feet ahead, a good-sized fir tree had blown down many years before. Though almost prone, it still lived. The top was against a rock bluff, the middle some twenty feet from the ground. Charlie went up to the root of it where he stood still for a long time. The boys were in an agony of excitement. Finally he moved, just a shadow in the falling snow.

He was gone only a few minutes, but the boys had never known minutes to last so long. He reappeared and beckoned for them to come. He stood patiently as they slipped and scrambled up to him, all caution forgotten.

"Did you see the cougar, Charlie? Do you think he's around here? Maybe it's watching us! What did you see? Why'd you make us stay back?"

The old man raised his hands in mock horror.

"Boys not need guns. Old Indian right about that. Bad as old lady, find cougar, talk 'm to death!"

They subsided, waiting for him to tell them in his own time.

"Well," he said matter-of-factly, "anyhow, we find old lady's dog. Old lady's dog find cougar."

He pointed to the tracks. Those of the cougar had disappeared.

Alert this time, they looked at the fallen tree. Not near the root, but well up off the ground. Cliff pointed. The snow was disturbed. Charlie nodded approvingly, led them further on. He said, "Dog find cougar, cougar find dinner."

There was blood on the trampled snow, and drag marks leading to a dark shape already whitened with new-fallen snow. It was the dog, partly eaten.

"We camp here," said Charlie.

The boys looked around them. In the excitement of the hunt, they hadn't paid much attention to anything else, even discomfort. Now reality came back to them. It was late in the afternoon, perhaps four o'clock. Already the shadows under the trees were growing dark. Everything was covered with wet snow. It hung on the branches and clung to the trunks of the trees. The whole woods were wet. The boys were soaking wet, their wool Mackinaws heavy with water. These famous coats were supposed to protect the wearer in all-day rain. Indeed, they were very good. The raindrops caught in the dense wool, and trickled down to drip off the lower edge. The wet wool kept its wearer warm and absorbed sweat. However, the brothers' coats were old, thin hand-me-downs, and their shirts— also wool—were soaked. This didn't matter while movement kept them warm, but as soon as they stopped moving, they felt the damp. There is an old Irish saying about wool which goes, "No matter how cold and wet you get, you're always warm and dry." It has some truth to it, inasmuch as you will probably never, in our coastal conditions, die of exposure while dressed all in wool. But you can get very cold and uncomfortable.

And uncomfortable the boys were. Their wool pants were sodden, their boots full of partly melted snow. They had eaten nothing since breakfast, but if Charlie had any food, it was well hidden. They had no tarp and no blankets. Charlie had the tightly rolled blanket on his shoulder strap but it was small and very wet. Wet snowflakes were coming down quite fast now and there was no shelter in sight that seemed the least bit adequate. They looked at each other.

"Well," said Cliff, "now we'll see how a real Indian Woodsman builds his camp."

"I hope," said Hal, "That we'll see how a real Indian Woodsman finds dinner!"

Meanwhile, Charlie had been ambling about the line of broken bluff against which the tree had fallen. Now he called to them.

"Boys, come."

They scrambled up to where he was standing in the partial shelter of a slanting rock face. He was scuffing the snow away from an area about two feet square.

"We build fire here. Come," he ordered.

He led the way back to the fallen tree where, taking the little hatchet that he always carried from his belt, he walked along until he found some dry ribs of fir bark to his liking. Splitting off some of the cork-like bark, he handed the pieces to Cliff and indicated the direction of the fire-to-be with his thumb. Finding a pitch-soaked place by a knot, he gouged out a handful which he gave to Hal. He then walked back to the root where there were some bushes of leafless huckleberry, cut several bunches and gave them to the waiting boy. Again, he indicated the camping place with his thumb.

The boys delivered the loads, and seeing Charlie walking away, rushed to join him. They didn't want to miss a thing. Father could stand it no longer.

"Charlie, what are we going to eat? Why didn't you tell us to bring some food?" (They thought this hardly fair, for he had told them at the boat not to worry about food.)

"Well, never mind. Old Indian know there be food here."

Charlie led them over to where the dead dog lay, now just another white mound in the snow. He took out his big clasp-knife, reached down and, seizing the dog's hind leg, rolled it over. Its entrails flopped about messily. The cougar had eaten the soft underparts.

"Cat lazy, eat soft bits, leave good meat for boys."

Expertly, he cut away the hind leg he was holding.

Hal felt his stomach flop over and try to slip up to his throat. He looked at what was left of the dog.

"Charlie," he stammered, "We're not going to eat that dog, are we? Not really? Dogs are pets. We don't eat our pets!"

The old man looked at him, his face showing no expression at all.

"Boys listen. Dog NOT HERE. Dog go away someplace. Indians tell lot of stories, but they not know where dog go. White men say they know, but they lying. They not know. But Old Indian know one thing. Dog not here. What is here is dog MEAT. That good to eat. Okay?"

Back at the rocks, Charlie put down two pieces of bark with a bit of pitch between them. He fished a tin of matches out of a pocket, extracted one, and put the tin back in his pocket. He struck the match on his thumbnail and applied it to the pitch, which blazed up quickly, then he carefully placed a few more bits of bark on the little fire. In a few minutes, he had a small, hot, almost smokeless fire going.

Cliff asked, "Do you want us to get some armloads of bark, Charlie?"

The old man laughed. "Just like a white man. Build big fire, stand away back, carry wood all night. Indian make small fire, stay close."

With a few quick knife strokes, he skinned the leg, sliced the meat and cut out the bone. Handing them each a slice, he then took the bunches of huckleberry and cut off three of the biggest stems. Taking a third slice, he shoved the end of the stick through it and held it over the fire.

"Boys eat," he said.

In a moment there were three dog steaks sizzling in front of them. It didn't smell all that bad. In fact, the smell of roasting meat made Hal's mouth water.

At length, Charlie said, "Enough cooking. Too much cooking, all good gone from meat." He sniffed his meat appreciatively. "Dog meat, good. Make boys strong. Not get very often."

He handed them each a bunch of the huckleberry stems, and taking one for himself, put a bunch of tips in his mouth and stripped off the dormant buds with his teeth. "Boys do same," he commanded. "Buds good for you, all meat no good. Next year's leaves good for you. Taste good too."

Hal contemplated his piece of charred dog steak. He looked at his brother. Cliff had just taken a large bite and was chewing strongly, swallowing the mouthful as his brother watched. Cliff wasn't fussy about food. He would eat just about anything, usually with great enthusiasm. But Hal had always been very critical about what he ate, and he was very doubtful if dog meat came under the right heading.

He thought, well, if Cliff can do it, I suppose I can.

So he took a bite of dog. Years later, recounting the moment for my benefit, he still had vivid memories of the sensation.

"I knew I was in trouble as soon as I took the first bite. As soon as it touched my tongue, it reminded me of wet dog. I made myself chew on it, but the more I chewed, the bigger it seemed to get until my mouth was completely full of this lump that tasted like wet dog."

He decided to swallow it whole, but distinctly heard his stomach say, "You send that down here and I'm sending it right back up again."

He slipped it out of his mouth into his hand, and flung it under his arm onto the snow behind him. He looked over at Charlie. He was watching with a wicked little grin on his face. Hal's mouth still tasted like wet dog. He took a handful of the huckleberry tips and suddenly there was a taste that reminded him of spring and fresh berries.

Cliff threw away a bit of gristle.

"Aren't you going to eat your piece, Hal? Can I have it?"

Wordlessly, Hal handed the piece of meat to his brother. His supper consisted of huckleberry tips. Nothing else.

It was now dark. Small as it was, the fire of bark gave out quite a bit of heat which the sloping rock face reflected back at them. Their wet clothes were steaming a bit and the boys realized that they weren't nearly as uncomfortable as they had expected to be. Charlie picked up his blanket from beside the fire and unrolled it. It turned out to be three small wool blankets about five feet square. He handed one to each of them and folded the other around his shoulders. Then he began to talk. He told them stories of the days when there were no white men, of tribal wars and sudden raids, of warriors and hunters, gods and demons.

Father said, "I sat there on a rock, soaking wet to the skin with an empty stomach and wet feet, and dozed off into a sleep as sound as if I was in my own dry bed at home."

He woke up once about midnight. Charlie was carefully putting a small piece of bark on the fire. Cliff was lying on his side curled up towards the warmth. He was covered with about half an inch of snow. It was warm and comfortable under the blanket. He went back to sleep.

He woke to a gentle pressure on his arm. Embers glowed where the fire had been, and there was just the faintest trace of light in the morning sky. Cliff was rubbing his eyes sleepily. Charlie spoke, his voice just audible.

"Boys stay. Be quiet. No move, no talk, no breathe."

With this somewhat impractical admonition, he stalked off as silently as any ghost, carrying his rifle ready for action.

The minutes dragged endlessly. They huddled there in damp clothes on rocks that seemed to have grown much harder overnight, with wet snow on and about them. They were cold, stiff and hungry but daren't whisper so much as a word to each other about it. Just as they could begin to see around them in the growing light, they heard footsteps in the snow as Charlie crunched up to them making much more noise than usual. He was talking to himself, using guttural words they never heard before. He leaned his gun against a rock, and not saying anything to the boys, picked up the rest of the pitch and put it on the still warm ashes. When it began to smoke, he blew on it and it burst into flames. The air became filled with the smell of burning pitch. He put dry bark on the pitch and in a few minutes he had another cheerful smokeless fire. Reaching into his coat, he pulled out the other leg of the dog and with a few deft moves, had it skinned, de-boned and sliced.

"Eat," he growled.

Cliff was never one to be slow to speak. Even though Charlie's manner gave him little encouragement, he dared to ask, "What happened, Charlie?"

The old man looked at them from where he squatted by the fire. For a while, they thought he wasn't going to answer. His face appeared as if carved out of a piece of hard dark wood. Finally, he growled, "Old Indian getting too old. Bad as foolish boys. Forget to throw out shell when last shoot gun. Try to shoot cougar with empty shell!"

With the meat about half cooked, he kicked the fire apart and began to eat, Cliff following his lead. Hal hadn't even pretended to want any. Charlie picked up his gun.

"OK. Boys ready? Had nice rest, good breakfast. Should be able to walk fast."

He watched sardonically as they scrambled to roll their blankets with muscles half paralyzed by cold and soreness. They were ready quickly, but he started just soon enough to make them scramble to catch up. Running uphill in the snow did have the very salutary effect of getting their muscles warmed up and ready for work.

And work it was to keep up with the old man. He cut diagonally up the hill, apparently with a definite goal in mind. He didn't speak, and the boys couldn't, needing all their breath to keep up. After travelling for almost an hour, Charlie stopped. The boys threw themselves down on the snow, their wet clothes steaming from the exertion. After a few minutes' rest they got up and went to where Charlie was standing, his back towards them.

He was looking down a steep narrow draw. They could see about a hundred yards down it through scattered old-growth fir trees. There were a few small clumps of salal, but the ground was mostly clear.

"Why are we stopping here, Charlie?" asked Cliff.

Charlie looked at them. His face was relaxed and when he spoke, his voice was mild.

"This our last chance. This draw has deer trail that lead up hills to cedar swamp. Deer winter there. Eat cedar branches to keep belly full. Cedar no good food. Deer get weak, easy to catch. Cougar know this. Old Indian think he head for there by easiest trail. This trail. He not here yet. We wait."

He hunched by a fallen tree where he could see down the draw with only his head showing, and rested his rifle on the log.

"Boys find place to sit," he ordered. "Can look down trail but only with one eye," he chuckled. "Now we see what kind of hunters boys make!" His voice became stern. "No move, no make noise. Breathe slowly through mouth. If itch, no scratch. If cramp, no move. If nose run, let drip, no sniff. Blink eyes quietly! If cat come up trail, then turn and run away, Old Indian go home with two skins instead of one!"

He puffed out a cloud of breath which drifted slowly off to their right and up the trail. He pointed to it. "Wind right. Now we wait."

They waited. Remembering it as a grown man, Father said, "I never thought just sitting could be such misery. Cliff and I had done this sort of thing before, watching deer, but we didn't have old Charlie watching us then! I had got myself into what I thought was a comfortable position, but pretty soon my 'comfortable position' seemed like the worst sort of torture. I knew I had to relax, but I itched, especially my back and arms. If you can scratch when you want to, you never even think of it, but when you can't... and we were wearing wet wool! My nose started running, but I dassn't move a hair to stop it. I could see Cliff's face out of corner of my eye. He looked as a man might, sitting on an anthill. That made me feel a little better!"

He was so wrapped up in his misery, he almost missed seeing the cougar. Suddenly it was just there, about twenty feet from where he should have first seen it. It was all he had imagined one to be, and more. It belonged there in the woods more than anything else he had ever seen, and he had a feeling that they didn't. He had never felt that way before. He wondered why Charlie didn't shoot, then he figured he had the gun pointed at a certain spot and wasn't going to move it. All of a sudden Charlie made a quiet sound, something like a low whistle. The cougar stopped in its tracks, looking up toward them. Charlie fired, and the cougar turned and leaped, all in one movement. It soared through the air, all grace and wildness. It hit the trail about twenty-five feet down, but it was dead when it landed, and it hit all limp and crumpled. Charlie had shot it right through the heart. It was a good shot, about eighty yards, and downhill. The boys hadn't thought that either him or his old gun had it in them!

Before the echo of the shot had come back, Charlie was up and trotting down the hill. Cliff and Hal followed, but Hal's legs were so cramped he thought he was going to go down the hill head-first. Cliff was staggering as badly as he was. Charlie was by the cougar before they were more than halfway there, but they soon limbered up and ran down to him. He was kneeling by it, having first made sure it was dead. He stood up. His left hand was cupped, and the boys saw that it was full of blood. He stepped over to them, dipped two fingers of his other hand in the blood and drew them across Cliff's forehead, then down both cheeks in a sort of pattern. Then he did the same thing to Hal. As he did it, he said something in the strange language he had used that morning.

Then Charlie put his hand up to his mouth and licked the blood out of it. All of it. Hal felt a bit squeamish, but somehow he felt it was right.

Charlie said, "Old Indian forget exact words, but good enough. Spirit of cougar satisfied. Boys not be full hunters, but got good beginning. Old Indian think might be hope for them yet!" He pulled out his knife, went over and squatted beside the cougar. He looked back at them.

He said, "Now boys build fire. Old Indian skin cat while still warm." He grinned. "Small fire," he said.

They got pitchy bark from a fir tree, split some wood from a cedar windfall with the hatchet. Then they found a flat spot, brushed away the snow and carefully built a fire between three rocks as they had seen Charlie do. A small one.

Hal said, "I don't think we should use cedar. You know how it sparks and crackles."

"I think you're right. Charlie wouldn't like that, would he?"

So they went back and got more fir bark. Charlie called, "Bring hatchet." He took it and cracked the thigh bone after slicing the meat around it. They looked with awe at the huge jumping muscle of the hind legs.

Cliff said, "I wish I had muscles like that."

Charlie looked at him, his face impassive.

"Boys' legs make pretty good meat just like they are." He cackled at his own joke. Charlie was in a fine mood. He had guessed correctly. He had made a fine shot. The bounty for the cougar plus the hide would bring a fair bit of money. And they had fresh meat!

These were much bigger steaks than the ones from the dog. They toasted them on forked sticks of hemlock, peeled so the bark wouldn't give the meat a bitter taste. Hal had no qualms about this meat. It was dark and wild tasting, but at the first bite, his stomach informed him, "Yes, you can send some of that down, and the sooner, the better."

While they were eating, Charlie picked up a handful of the split cedar and threw it on the fire.

"Cedar make nice crackle," he remarked. The boys regarded him silently. The only thing you could predict about old Charlie was that he would be unpredictable!

After they had eaten, he chopped off the other haunch.

"Too good to leave."

He sliced a hole between the bones of the lower leg and shoved a stick through for a carrying handle. Then he rolled up the hide, tying it in such a way that the legs formed carrying straps. Tossing it to Cliff, he said, "You carry hide."

He tossed the rest of the meat from the haunch they had cut to Hal. Then he put the stick with the untouched one on his shoulder and started off down the draw.

When they had gone a little way, Hal remarked to his brother, "It seems kind of a shame to leave all the rest of that meat to go to waste."

Charlie heard. "Meat not go to waste. Listen."

They listened. A raven croaked not far away. Another answered from the flat below.

"Nothing go to waste in the woods."

They went a bit further. A raven called almost over their heads.

"Raven say thanks. Maybe even send good luck."

The grey sky began to send down a fine mist of rain, and though it wasn't enough to make them really wet, it made the snow more slippery. But the way back seemed short, as the way back always does. They reached the trail in less time than they would have thought possible, and soon enough, there was the house of the old woman. Charlie went to the door and knocked. Her face peered out of the window suspiciously. Then it disappeared and the door opened. She was talking as it opened.

"Well, you're back. About time too. Where is my Hopsy? Did you find him? You've been gone long enough!"

Charlie backed off a few steps.

"Ah-h-h—" he said, then stopped and looked desperately around at Cliff and Hal. They looked back at him silently. Suddenly Hal was inspired. Perhaps it was the adventure stories he had read. He spoke out boldly.

"Ma'am" he began, "we found your Hopsy but we were too late to save him. He died fighting that savage cougar. He put up an awful fight but it was too big for him. Mr. Charlie buried him and put a cross on his grave. He carved 'Good Dog' on it. He thought you would like that."

Cliff and Charlie were looking at him with awe. He almost began to believe it himself, it sounded so good. He continued, warmed by their appreciation, his voice solemn.

"Mr. Charlie swore he would get that cougar to revenge poor Hopsy. We tracked it all that night. In the morning it climbed a tree and Mr. Charlie shot it, and there is the skin!"

He pointed to Cliff's shoulder. The old woman was actually speechless. There were tears in her eyes. Finally she spoke to Charlie.

"I knew he was dead. I could feel it. But it was so good of you to do what you did, I'm going to give you a special reward."

She turned and went into the house. Charlie's eyes glittered brightly in his impassive face. He hadn't expected this! In a moment she was back, carrying an envelope in her hand. Cliff whispered, "I wonder how much she's going to give him."

She pulled out a square of cardboard, handed it to Charlie.

"This is a picture of my Hopsy. You may have it to keep."

The two boys looked at Charlie's face. Then they looked at each other. It was too much for them. They ran across the yard, down the trail, and on around the bend. There they stopped. They had to—they couldn't run for laughing.

Charlie came around the corner, walking with great dignity. He looked with disapproval at the boys. Cliff was lying on the wet ground, out of breath from laughter. Hal was trying unsuccessfully to remove the grin from his own face.

Charlie said sternly, "Foolish boys. Boys know nothing." He shook his head sadly. "Poor boys. No one teach them sense. Only Old Indian, and he think maybe too big a job for him!"

He took the picture out of his pocket, handling it with great care.

"Indian would know that this is great thing. Old Indian hang picture in cabin of boat. Spirit of dog be glad, bring good luck. Even foolish boys know that good luck is best thing you can have!"

He headed down the trail. The cougar hunt was over.

Chapter 6

Visitors

ONE FINE DAY toward the end of summer in 1907, one of the girls came running up from the beach. "Mother, Father, someone's coming in a boat!" Everyone stopped what they were doing and in a few minutes the whole family was on the floating dock watching a strange boat approach.

Visitors to Hidden Basin were few. Strangers rarely found their way through the narrow entrance channel. When someone did, it was an occasion of considerable excitement.

They saw a rowboat about fourteen feet long with one man sitting in the stern while another rowed. The boat slipped cleanly through the calm water, as boats did when they were built to be rowed fifty miles or more. A double row of swirls made by the oar blades stretched out behind.

"Nice lines," said their father approvingly. "Looks like an Andy Linton." (One of the best boat builders of that time.)

As the oarsman eased the boat alongside the float, they saw that he was a youth of only about fourteen or sixteen years, but tall and well-built. He didn't reply to Jack's greeting, but smiled at them all in a friendly way. He jumped lightly onto the float and knelt to tie up the boat, still without a word. Jack held out his hand to the older man in the stern seat to assist him onto the float, but he was completely ignored. The man just sat there with a slight smile on his lips, his eyes oddly unfocussed. Cliff and Hal watched with a mixture of delight and trepidation. Their father was not a patient man; certainly not one to be treated like this on his own float. His face was beginning to redden with that temper which they all feared. Just then, the youth uttered some weird bird-like chirps and whistles, at the same time snapping his fingers in a sort of pattern, and just in time the older man turned toward them and spoke.

"Friends," he said in a gentle voice, "I can hear you but I cannot see you. The Lord has seen fit to take away my sight. I am Father _____, and my young companion and helper here is Jeremiah, or Jerry for short. We bring the word of God to those who wish to listen. Our aim is to visit every isolated homestead and cabin on the coast, if the Lord should see fit."

Jack Hammond was delighted. He had at one time been intensely religious, but his restless mind had led him to the works of Darwin, whose theories he had accepted with complete conviction. However, unlike their originator, he didn't believe that Darwinism and religion could co-exist. One of his greatest pleasures was to corner some man with strong religious beliefs and proceed to demolish them with the aid of copious references to the Bible, natural history and Darwin, on which subjects his knowledge was encyclopedic. Thus he greeted the unsuspecting priest with an enthusiasm to which he was probably not accustomed, insisting that he come for dinner and stay the night at least. There were, he confided cunningly, a few passages in the Bible that he would like to have clarified.

"My boys will take care of Jeremiah. Hal, Cliff, take the lad and show him around."

"Ah, you have boys; good. I'm sure Jerry will get along well with them. He is a most good-natured soul. There is just one thing I must mention. As God made me sightless, so he took away Jeremiah's voice. He can hear, but he cannot speak."

Surely no stranger pair has travelled this coast. A blind priest and a mute boy. Not quite the halt leading the blind, but close!

Cliff and Hal were horrified. Wary of strangers at best, they were appalled by the prospect of entertaining one with some sort of disability. They felt no sympathy, even less considering the other was several years older, a vast gap at that age. But under the watchful eye of their father, they had no choice but to beckon him to come along. They walked along the shore, glancing furtively at

Jerry, who followed a few paces behind. He was a head taller than them, with long black hair and a tanned face. His big hands dangled at the ends of long arms that seemed even longer, for his tattered coat was made for a much smaller man. About eight inches of wrist hung bare out of each sleeve. The same was true of his trousers, which ended about halfway between knees and ankles. With the ill-fitting clothes and the grin that he still wore as he looked around him, they were sure he wasn't anyone they wanted to know.

"Let's lose him," hissed Cliff to his brother. They walked a bit faster, increasing the distance between them and the strange youth. When they were out of sight of the house, they dashed behind some boulders and through the bushes, and cut away from the shore, running as fast as they could. Then they hid behind a tree watching the beach. Soon Jeremiah came ambling along, looking around for his companions.

Cliff took a rock out of his pocket. They were never without a few throwing rocks, always being on the lookout for good ones. "Watch this," he said. With an easy, practiced motion he flung the rock. It was a good throw; the rock hit the water not far from the stranger. But much to their surprise, instead of being alarmed, he looked up and grinned a great pleased grin.

They had concealed themselves behind the tree as soon as the rock took flight, so that little more than their eyes showed. They felt quite safe. Jerry looked slowly around him. He put his hand in his pocket. As he took it out again, he flicked his arm in a careless-seeming way, and there was a loud *thwack* from the tree behind which Cliff and Hal thought they were hidden. A piece of bark flew from a spot about a foot over their heads and dropped into the bushes.

The boys were profoundly shocked. The ease and accuracy of that throw presented a challenge such as they had never imagined. They were vain about their rock-throwing. They had been at it since they were big enough to pick up a rock, and they threw at every opportunity at anything that presented itself. They threw until their arms ached, and then they threw some more, until their accuracy and range with a good rock were phenomenal—so good that they hunted grouse and ducks with rocks with considerable success, and all the more remarkable because their father would not tolerate bruised meat and they must hit their quarry on the head. As for range, they had recently routed a gang of five older boys on an outing to Whaletown, whose youths were implacably hostile to strangers, without a single enemy rock landing near them.

So war was declared on the peaceful shore of Hidden Basin. Both sides were enthusiastic at first, but it soon became apparent to one side that they were badly outgunned. However stealthily they might crawl, when they raised their heads, a rock would whistle by their ears with a velocity they could scarcely believe. No ambush worked, no plan of attack came even close to succeeding. It was the most frustrating afternoon of their lives. Jerry had eyes in the back

of his head, an arm like a catapult and the ability to read minds. And to make matters worse, his face never for a moment lost that delighted, infuriating grin.

At last came the sound of the supper bell; an armistice would have to be declared. From a place of safety, Cliff called, "Come on, it's suppertime." They cut home through the woods, leaving Jerry to find his way back however he could, and his long legs brought him to the door at almost the same moment as they arrived. They watched him enter, feeling more than a little apprehensive, as well as a bit guilty. They needn't have worried. He appeared as friendly as ever, as if he had thoroughly enjoyed a pleasant and playful afternoon.

Dinner was the signal for the cessation of combat of quite a different kind, if no less hard-fought. The priest had proven a most formidable opponent for their father, whose absent-minded replies to any question at dinner indicated that he was using the truce to marshal arguments for the fray which would certainly begin again after the meal. But now, as they ate, there was lighter conversation: news from down the coast and gossip of all sorts, at which their visitor also appeared adept. The girls chattered, the brothers were almost as mute as their guest.

The evening passed quickly, and the philosophical discussion ended inconclusively, as they always do. At last, the sleeping arrangements were organized and the house was still.

After breakfast, the visitors prepared to leave. Provisions were pressed on them, and advice on what they would encounter, who would welcome them, whom to avoid or risk being shot at!

Down at the dock, there were a few last words of discussion. The priest said mildly, "Well, you have a point there, I must admit. But God can give as well as take away. Jeremiah, now, might serve as an example." Turning to the youth, he said, "Show them your skill, Jeremiah."

Jeremiah grinned his ready grin. He picked up a piece of bark about the size of a man's hand, and with an easy motion tossed it in a long arc high over the bay. As it rose, he put his hand in his pocket and threw again. A rock sped almost too fast to see. There was a sound like a handclap as the piece of bark exploded into fragments at the top of its trajectory.

"Show them, Jeremiah," said the priest again.

The youth dug into his pocket. Then he threw with that odd-jointed motion they had seen him use the day before. It was the first time they had seen him appear to exert himself. A rather large rock flew out over the bay. They waited for it to drop, but instead of dropping it continued to rise, and rise, until their eyes could not longer track it. In that sheltered windless bay, the water was glass-smooth, and to the astonished watchers there appeared no splash, no sound. Did it go—incredibly—right across the bay? They would never know.

Their father said slowly, "That is the most extraordinary display I have ever seen. However, I do not concede the point."

The priest laughed. "I didn't think you would!" he said. He offered his hand, which was taken very cordially. Good-byes were said, and in a few more minutes the boat was sliding smoothly down the bay.

The boys stood alone on the float after the others had left. They were stunned. It was quite apparent that they had been at the mercy of the incredible Jeremiah all during that day of mock war. Mock on his side, at any rate. They felt strangely humbled.

Father told me later, "You see, up until then we thought we could do anything that anyone could. That if we really tried, we could do better. But there on that beach, we knew in our hearts that we could never, with any amount of practice, do what he could do so easily. We were never quite the same, ever again."

The boat was by now about a hundred yards from the float. Jerry was facing them as he rowed. Suddenly, as if by the same impulse, Cliff and Hal both waved to him. As he completed his stroke, he let go the oars and stood. His arm moved and a rock sped humming between them as they stood there just a few feet apart. It smacked into the water behind them and went skipping up along the beach. As he sat down again, Jerry waved back at them gaily. They had a sense of something lost, that would never be found again.

Next day the weather changed, and that night the first of the fall storms sent southeast winds howling up the gulf. A week or so later, on a chance meeting with a settler from Texada Island, Jack asked for any news of the strange pair, as their intended route led his way, but the man had seen nothing of them. Neither had anyone else in the area, as Jack gradually met and queried them. Nor did he ever find anyone who had met them after they left Hidden Basin. As far as he could discover, they were never seen again.

Chapter 7

Pots and Pans

CRAFTSMANSHIP IS BY NO MEANS a lost art. You may find just next door someone who makes marvelously detailed cross-bows, for instance, or furniture by the old methods. Masterworkers in one craft or another—many of them self-taught—aren't that uncommon.

In the days of my father's youth, European craftsmen of the old variety were quite plentiful along the Coast. They had completed their seven-year apprenticeship, undergone their examination, become masters at their trade, then emigrated to the New Land. Many of them were surprisingly old, but still they came: shoemakers, watchmakers, tool-and-die makers, artisans of every kind—some of them masters of crafts even then fading into obscurity.

The year was 1905, early on a fine day in July. The family had just finished lunch. No one had been looking out of the windows, because the knock on the door startled all of them, even the old dog who tried to make up for his lapse by barking furiously. As Jack went to the door, he said "Quiet Max!" And Max went back to his corner with the satisfied look of one who has redeemed himself.

The open door revealed an odd-looking stranger on the veran-dah. He had taken a polite step back, so as not to confront the householder too abruptly. He might have been of average height, but was very stooped, and appeared quite aged, though his shoulders were thick and his hands large and powerful. He wore the usual brown wool pants and checked shirt, but what riveted the attention of Hal and Cliff was that instead of a hat, his head was wound round with a thin black silk cloth, and in one ear he wore a golden ring. He looked, indeed, the very image of a pirate, although to be perfect, there should have been a black patch over one eye. He had no beard, but a big drooping moustache of a kind they had never seen before, whose grey hairs matched those which had escaped from under the edge of the black cloth.

On being greeted, he gave his name, which they didn't remember, for it was foreign and unfamiliar, and then went on to say, with a heavy accent that Jack later told them was German: "Sir, I fix tings. Pots, pans, what haf you. Anyting, I fix. Whateffer you got. Anyting. Someting you got maybe, to fix?"

"No, No," said Jack. "I'm afraid we've got nothing like that. If there's anything I can't solder up, we throw it out; it's not worth fixing."

The boys felt sorry for the old man. Their father's manner had been unusually curt. Perhaps he was annoyed at being taken by surprise.

But the old man's response surprised them all. His eyes flashed and he stood straighter, as he answered contemptuously

"Sauder! I do not fix mit sauder. Bring to me someting dot you trow oudt. I fix. If you nodt like, nodt pay, unt I go!"

Miffed now at the implied criticism of his repair methods, their father hesitated a moment, then turned to his sons.

"Cliff, go to where we throw the garbage and get the old enamel pot." Cliff dashed off, and Jack, in a better mood now he'd thought of something impossible for the boastful old man to fail at, suddenly remembered his hospitality and inviting the visitor in, seated him and proffered a cup of tea, which was accepted with such gratitude that Jack almost regretted his revenge. Enamelled ironware was good and long-lasting, but when the enamel chipped off and the iron rusted through in a few places, it was commonly held to be unrepairable and was discarded.

Cliff came back carrying the big pot, and his father took it over to the old German who looked at it closely, turning it over and over in his hands. The sides were as good as new, but the rounded lower part where the side met the bottom was chipped and rusted, while the bottom itself had a hole in it you could put your hand through. It had been out near the salt water for several years.

He put down his teacup and went to the door.

"Goodt," he approved. "I fix."

Unrepentant, Jack suggested, "Why don't you bring your tools up and work here?" pointing at the bench and table on the verandah.

"Ya, iss goodt" approved the old man. He set the pot on the bench and went off to his boat.

When he was gone, Jack said to his family, "If he can fix that, I'll take my hat off to him. You can't cut or bend enamel; it chips. You can't solder it; that much heat burns it. There may be a way, but if there is, I'd like to see it!"

The old man returned carrying a big toolbox and a thick sheet of copper which he placed on the floor beside the bench. Taking the pot off the table, he sat on the bench and selected a tool from the box, ordinary enough angled tin-snips. Jack made a "humph" sound.

But the tool was only used to cut out the bottom of the pot, though it was done remarkably quickly and efficiently. Another tool was selected, but this one was obviously something new to their father, and the boys saw him lean closer and look at it, his black moustache bristling with interest.

It had jaws that cut a thin clean line through the enamel on each side. With it, he worked right around the base of the pot just above the chipped places. Although he used it freehand, the line ended exactly where it had begun. No mean feat, that! Next, a short-jawed snips cut cleanly along the line, and the enamel-cutter was used again to cut another line around the bottom of the pot. Then, working quickly, he went around it with a crimping tool bending a fold toward the outside. They couldn't see very well, but their father said afterward that the tool he used seemed to stretch the metal so that it made up for the difference in circumference. The enamel cracked as the tool was used, but that didn't seem to concern him. He set out the pot on the copper sheet and used a scriber to draw a circle around the inside. Next, he used a small T-square to find the centre of the circle and a big pair of brass compasses to scribe another more accurate circle outside of the first one. Through all of these operations, his hands moved so quickly they seemed at times to almost be in two places at once. He was so intent on his work that no one spoke to him, and they spoke only in whispers to each other, though his concentration was such that it seemed doubtful that he would have noticed if they had shouted.

With heavy shears, he cut out the circle, bent the edge up all the way around, placed the pot on top of it, and with a very strange looking tool indeed, folded the two together, once, and then again.

Jack muttered to himself, "Double-crimped. Amazing!"

With a little hand-held anvil, much like the one used when sharpening saws, he reached inside, and tapping rapidly with a small hammer along the folded metal, made the fold tighter. As he tapped, he turned the pot, held now between his knees. The tools went back in the box, and he started to set the pot on the table, but as quickly, drew it back again. He tested the handles; one was loose. Driving out the rivets, he selected two from a little tin box and replaced the handle.

At last he was satisfied. Putting the pot on the table, he gave it an odd flick with his hand, and it spun there like a top.

Later the boys tried for hours to make it do that, but all they did was spin it off the table.

Their father took the pot in his hands, examined it closely.

"Cliff," he said. "Bring the water bucket."

The old man chuckled good-naturedly.

"Yah," he laughed "bring the bucked. It vill nodt leak."

Jack put the pot on the table and carefully filled it with water. It didn't leak. From start to finish, the work had taken no more than twenty minutes. The water was poured out, and everyone took turns admiring the new copper-bottom pot, proclaimed by their mother to be better than the original.

Jack went into the house and came out wearing a hat. To the old German he said, "Sir, I told my family that if you could repair that..." (pointing to the pot) "I would take my hat off to you. And I do so." Sweeping the hat off ceremoniously, he continued, "I have never heard of anyone repairing enamelware with any success. I didn't believe that it could be done. But then, I have never claimed that I had nothing left to learn!"

Their mother, always practical, asked what they owed him.

"For de vork, nodding. For de copper..." and he named a sum so low that she felt she must have misheard him.

She asked again, "How much?"

When the price was established, he leaned back and asked again, "Do you haf tings for me to fix? Anyting, I fix."

And this time they believed him!

It is surprising how many things needed repair. Repairing household utensils wasn't one of Jack's virtues. Tasks such as that weren't to his taste; they needed skill and patience, but required little or no creativity. Handlogging, running a farm, and all his other activities took up enough of Jack's time that I suppose he should be forgiven for such a slight lapse. So they looked and they found pots and basins, pans and lids and handles. And almost as fast as they were brought, he repaired them. Cliff and Hal searched the barn and outbuildings, and tried to remember where they had seen some utensil or other, for in those days very little was actually thrown out.

But at last there was nothing more to be found. By this time, the girls had tired of the game, their mother was cooking the evening meal, and only Jack and his sons still kept the old man company on the verandah. He looked quizzically at them. "No more?"

Their father shook his head, but Cliff suddenly remembered. "The old bucket?" he asked; and then Hal said "what about the baby bath we threw out?"

"The old bucket, yes," he approved, "but the bath, no. Too far gone," he explained. But their guest was alert instantly.

"No, no, might be not. Bring it me."

The brothers ran to the clump of bushes where things of no possible further use were discarded. They called it "the tin graveyard." In moments they were back, each with his prize. Cliff's bucket was chosen first, the bottom cut out and a new one of galvanized iron fitted, done very quickly, for he only crimped it once. Then he soldered the joint. As he lit the blowtorch, he looked up at Jack, blue eyes twinkling. "Sometimes, we sauder," he chuckled. Setting the bucket aside, he reached for the bathtub, turning it over carefully in his hands. It was in sad shape. The bottom was almost entirely missing, and the curved bottom edge was eaten with rust. Jack shook his head.

"Surely not worth fixing? With that double curve?" The old man didn't answer immediately. He wiped the inside surface with his thumb. It was an unusual shade of enamel, a light greenish blue.

He turned it over, ran his thumb over it. This side was a very deep royal blue, with greenish flecks in it. He looked at Jack.

"Can fix. Nodt easy." He tapped it lightly. "Dese colors, I never see. Nodt trow away."

Jack went to the door, opened it, called "Molly!"

She appeared, face flushed. Stove tops radiated much heat in those days. She looked at him questioningly, then at the object in the old man's hands, "Oh, my old baby bath. Surely you can't fix that?"

Before he could answer, Jack spoke. "Do you need it?"

She smiled a very small smile.

"I don't know that, do I? But I'd love to have it back. The colours are so beautiful. I'd forgotten how beautiful."

"Then you shall have it," he promised.

She flashed him a wide smile as she turned back to the door, calling back, "Supper in ten minutes."

The old man stood. "For dis I vill go to my boat."

But Jack would have none of that. "First, you will have supper with us," he said firmly, which, after a few protests, purely for politeness, he did.

In spite of the accent, he was a good talker, and told amusing and interesting stories of the people he had worked for or had met along the coast.

Finally, the meal ended. After the most exaggerated compliments (as the boys thought) to their mother, the two men went back to the porch, where their father insisted that his guest, as he was now obviously regarded, have a glass of homemade wine. As they were sipping it, he said, "I've never seen anyone handle metal like that. I've seen tinkers mend pots, and so on, but this is quite a different skill."

"Iss nodding" said the old German, making a dismissive gesture. "A few tools, somevun to show to use, practice ten, maybe twenty years." He shrugged. "If you have in de blood..." He was silent for a moment. Then, "Mein fader's fader, he vorked in de castles und homes of Europe. In gold, in silver. Mein fader vorked fixing de tings made by de great artists in metal. Und I? I fix pots, and pans."

His teeth flashed under his drooping moustache as he spread his hands wide. "Iss nodt so bad life."

He took the little bath and his box of tools and went to his boat. For an hour or so, they heard the intermittent sound of hammer on metal. Then there was a time of no sound, save an occasional tapping. At last, he came to the door, just as dusk was spreading shadows under the trees along the shore. He tapped at the door, and they all crowded out.

He held up the bath, glorious in hammered copper, with four gracefully curved little copper legs to stand on. A rolled rim went around where the metal joined the enamel. Two rusted holes in the side had been filled, then covered with melted glass, almost the colours of the original. He handed it to May, who took it in her hands with a cry of pleasure. Even the boys were impressed by its beauty.

They offered him a bed on the couch, but he declined it, saying he was used to sleeping outside in the boat.

"Dere iss no roof," he told them "like de sky."

Next morning, Cliff was sent to ask him to come for breakfast. He came, but would not stay long. He wanted to move on in the morning calm. Jack asked him what they owed him. He seemed curiously reluctant, as if the thought of taking money for what he did somehow embarrassed him. Finally he named a sum, which their father immediately dismissed as ridiculous. But he would accept no more.

"De bath," he said firmly "iss a gift for the lady."

They pressed food on him, which he accepted with obvious pleasure. Bread, a jar of the wild berry jam he had praised. Some bacon, some early vegetables, and Jack managed to slip an extra dollar into the box.

But at last he was gone, his long clinker-built rowboat sliding quickly through the calm water, the oarblades leaving a trail of little whirlpools as his powerful shoulders made the shafts bend. They all stood on the shore waving, and he dropped one oar for a moment to wave back. He caught it again without missing his stroke, and was soon out of sight round the bend.

Chapter 8

Wealth

FOR ALL HIS SKILLS and learning, his philosophy and his active brain, Jack Hammond had no luck with money: perhaps it was because of them. Making money was a game he thought he could play, but perhaps he never took it seriously enough. To be fair, most of his failures weren't of his making. Such as, for example, the timber claim.

It began with a visit from Jack's brother-in-law. Eustace Smith was a tall, powerful man with a craggy face, a sandy moustache and penetrating eyes. He had been for many years a timber cruiser and land surveyor, and was known for his uncompromising honesty, his professional skill, and his undeveloped sense of humour.

Maps of the BC coast at this time, and for many years after, were of wildly varying accuracy. The contours of the shores were mostly reliable, but once you ventured into the valleys and mountains, it was wise not to put too much faith in the official version of what was there. Not until the advent of aerial photography could these maps be trusted. Even the surveys by government engineers were only as good as those who made them.

Men of Eustace's profession were of great importance to the mapping process. They were hired to estimate the quality and quantity of timber in a certain area, to map the area and its surroundings, and to relate it to a known base previously surveyed. They were required to send a copy of this work to the survey office in Victoria, which would eventually incorporate it into their maps of the region.

Obviously, the accuracy of these maps depended on the competence and integrity of the individuals involved. The competence, naturally; the integrity, because there were many temptations. Various methods were used to ensure accuracy: astronomical observations, line-of-sight to two or more known points, actual ground measurement with surveyors' chain and compass.

But, how much easier to find a high place from which a map could be sketched than trudging through wet brush to relate the features to your base line! And on contract jobs, the sooner you were done, the more profit. And then, there was the matter of the bottles.

In the early fifties, I worked for a while as helper to a timber cruiser. Much of the job involved extending previously surveyed areas to include additional timber. To do this, the old corners had to be located. However, these weren't always where they should have been. But with the aid of "field notes" supplied by the forestry office and some guessing, the original base camp could be located. And almost always, when we found such a mis-placed camp, there were whiskey bottles—sometimes dozens of them! Which no doubt explains why some of our maps showed a mountain where there was actually a valley, and rock slopes where should have been a lake. One had two parcels of land some distance apart identified by the same lot number!

A marked corner was supposed to have nearby the name of the surveyor cut with a scribing tool on a blazed spot on a tree. Many of these were illegible, crudely cut, or simply scribbled on with a pencil, as if their authors didn't care to be identified. But on those corners where Eustace Smith had been, there was always a big "S" carved, plain to see, that would be there as long as the tree stood. And the location would be accurate beyond the capacity of our instruments to check it.

He had trouble finding helpers, for, impatient of human weakness, he worked them mercilessly, and word spread. If his duties took him near Nelson Island, he would often hire Jack to go out with him, as someone who could stand the pace he set. He never visited socially.

This then was the man who appeared in the Basin one day just before noon, driving the long slim rowboat that was his preferred form of travel with strokes that bowed the sturdy oars. May began to prepare a meal, because Eustace ate vastly when he visited. His driving energy required much fuel, but he ate like a Spartan on his trips to save carrying unnecessary weight—another reason he couldn't keep helpers. The boys watched as he came up the yard with his long measured strides. No one went to meet him. He had little time for children, and usually ignored them, seldom even remembering their names.

He had come from Parksville on Vancouver Island, a distance of some twenty-five miles. It had taken him just over four hours! While eating, he explained the reason for his visit. It seems he had found a valley of unclaimed timber on the big island.

"Best stand of fir I've seen for years that close to the water. Doesn't look like much when you go by. Guess that's why it's been missed. Five, six feet through, close together as teeth on a comb. But the best part is, whoever stakes the shore controls the valley. And that goes on for miles. Untouched. There's a fortune there, and I want you in with me."

Jack was pacing the floor with excitement. His family had never seen him so worked up about anything. This was the sort of thing he had been dreaming of. His ambition was to be a gentleman farmer, and to have the money to buy all the books he wanted. And to be able to give his wife a big house and as many nice things as she wanted.

"Why do you need anyone else?" he asked doubtfully. "I'll come in with you, of course, but you could handle it alone."

"There's enough there to make us all wealthy. Why shouldn't I share it with family? This is big. Too much for one man once it gets going. But there's a good reason why I need someone right away. The land office is as rotten as a week-old fish. I daren't show my face there; I'm too well known. If I register a claim, it'll be all over town in a day. There'll be a counter-claim sure as dogs have fleas, and I'll be tied up in court until my money's all gone. I've seen it happen. So, you'll file for us."

Jack scoffed at this. He refused to believe there was corruption in His Majesty's government or its deputies.

"They'd never get away with it," he declared positively. "But I'm with you, whatever the reason, and you won't regret it. We'll take the *Lady May*. We can be there before dark, set the stakes in the morning early, and be in Victoria before the Land Office closes." He rose, teeth gleaming under dark moustache. "Throw a bit of food in a sack, Molly. We're going to be rich!"

They kept to the schedule as planned, and the claim was all Eustace had said it was, and more. They were in Victoria well before the office closed, and Jack set off with the claim papers Eustace had given him.

He was to say later, "I don't take much stock in the idea that you can tell a person's character from his face, but I distrusted that clerk the moment I set eyes on him. He reminded me of a rat, and I don't like rats. His hair was all greased and slicked back and he had a sly little grin on him, as if he knew something that you should knokw but didn't. I felt like giving him a good swift kick in the pants!"

But he restrained the impulse, signed and filled out what was required, and handed over the filing fee. The clerk looked closely at the papers.

"Got a pretty good claim there, have you?" he quizzed, looking like a rat that smells raisins.

"Nothing much left in that area. Just pockets." Lying came to Jack with the greatest of difficulty. I doubt this effort was very convincing.

"It'll take a few days to process," sniffed the clerk.

They waited three, then Jack went to the office. The sly grin seemed more insolent than ever. Jack's foot itched for action.

"The maps for that area are missing," he was informed. "We had to send out for new ones."

Two more days. Jack phoned, rather than submit himself to the temptation the clerk presented.

"There's a problem with the survey."

The weekend passed slowly. Monday morning, Eustace did the phoning. After a few words of inquiry, his voice rose harshly.

"Say that again."

He held the handpiece in front of him, examined it intently. Then he replaced it on its fork. The impact tore the box off the wall. It smashed onto the floor, and pieces flew off it. He kicked it savagely.

"Our claim has been denied. There was a previous claim." He ripped open the door. "Let's go. I want that clerk to tell me that to my face."

The house Eustace maintained in Victoria wasn't far from the Claims Office. They ran up the steps of the building, the sound of their heavy boots on the stairs announcing their presence. As they strode down the hall, startled faces wondered who were these men in such a hurry. The clerk heard them, looked up. He went quickly to the gate in the counter and locked it, then went to stand behind his desk. His grin was missing. Eustace went to the gate. It was more a symbol than a barrier. He seized it in a calloused hand and tore it off its bolt. The two big men walked over to where the clerk stood cornered.

"Why haven't you filed this man's claim?" asked Eustace, his voice harsh with rage. Give the clerk credit, he had the proverbial courage of the animal he resembled when it is cornered.

"The area was staked before. You're just a couple of claim-jumpers. Get out or I'll call the police." At the look on their faces, he lost his nerve, squealing, "Help, I'm being attacked!"

"The police will be here all right," said Eustace grimly. "You can depend on that. And I wouldn't dirty myself by handling you."

"But I," said his partner, "am going to give myself the pleasure of kicking him through the wall."

He stepped forward and the clerk squealed again,

"Help, someone!"

But Eustace seized Jack's shoulder, saying: "Our case won't be helped if you're had up for assault. Leave the vermin to his filth. Come on, we've work to do."

Reluctantly, his brother-in-law followed him through the wrecked gate. There were watching faces everywhere. Most of them were grinning. It seemed the clerk wasn't very popular.

A bald headed man with glasses and a paunch came bustling importantly down the hall. "Here now, here now, what's all the fuss? These are government offices, you know. You are expected to behave with decorum here."

Eustace replied blandly, "I bumped into your gate back there," cocking a thumb behind him. "I think it may need some fixing. You know who I am. Send me the bill."

They went to the police. The officer in charge listened attentively. When they were finished, he shook his head doubtfully.

"Claim-jumping is a serious charge, and usually very difficult to prove. I'll take your names, but..."

"My name is Eustace Smith. You may have heard it mentioned," suggested Eustace. The officer looked up with new interest.

"Eustace Smith. Everyone's heard of you! That does make a difference. If a man like you makes an accusation, it should be taken seriously."

After a bit more discussion, he decided that the site of the claim should be examined for whatever evidence it could provide.

"I'll assign an officer to your case. Can you provide transportation?"

"Just name the time."

"How about tomorrow morning, eight o'clock?"

"We'll be ready," promised Eustace.

Next morning, precisely on time, a fresh-faced young officer, blonde hair short cropped, came striding down the dock. He was friendly, and obviously pleased to be going on a trip with Eustace Smith.

At the bay where the claim was, they anchored the *Lady May* and rowed ashore. They walked up the beach to where the line of stakes should be. There were stakes there, plain to see, but they weren't the ones they had placed. And there, tossed carelessly aside, were their stakes, plainly marked.

The young policeman couldn't believe what he was seeing. He went along picking up the discarded stakes, examining them, shaking his head.

"I don't see what they were thinking about," was his puzzled comment. "Why didn't they carry off the old stakes, or burn them or something? How did they think they were going to get away with it? It's the most obvious case of claim-jumping I've ever heard of. And you can be sure I'll testify to that in court. You'd think they'd be satisfied with what they own already, without trying to steal other people's claims."

For the name plainly marked on the new stakes was that of a well-known timber company with large holdings on Vancouver Island. Eustace's attitude was that of a man vindicated; Jack's a mixture of shock and indignation, for he had an unrealistic estimation of the world's honesty.

The trip back to Victoria was cheerful, though Jack was to say later: "My mind was a bit uneasy. Whoever was responsible was either stupid or knew there was no need to be careful. And that company hadn't got where it was by being stupid."

As he was leaving the boat, the young officer told them, "I'd get a lawyer, if I was you. They'll have one, and you never know what he may spring on you. Best not to take chances."

They thanked him most sincerely, but when he had gone, Eustace growled, "Lawyer! I don't see any need for it. Just complicate things. We'll go up there, lay a charge, all there is to it. They don't have a leg to stand on."

Off they went, full of righteous indignation, to the police station. A different officer was at the desk, large, impatient, brusque. He took down their names, gave them forms to fill out, papers to sign. At last, "All right, we'll look into it. You can go." Turning to go. Jack asked politely, "How long will it take, do you think?"

Without pausing, came the short answer: "As long as it needs to."

They waited and they waited. Inquiries were met evasively. They began to worry. Finally, Eustace conceded, "I guess the young fellow was right. We need a lawyer. I know a good one. Partly retired, takes a few cases. Knows everybody. Honest man, for a lawyer. He owes me a favour."

The lawyer greeted them cordially. A short man, heavy but not fat, bald and bearded, he looked and sounded competent. He listened intently to their story, asked a few questions. He leaned back then, tucked his thumbs into his vest.

"I don't see any problem," he assured them. " Open and shut case if I ever heard one. But that company has a name for playing dirty. Shouldn't take them lightly. I'll look into it, let you know."

More days went slowly by. They had been at it now for over three weeks. Weeks of lost work, of money spent, weeks of frustration.

At last, word from their lawyer. Would they come to his office?

As they were shown in, he looked up from the papers he was reading. Taking off his glasses, he placed them carefully on the desk, and ground the heels of his hands into his eyes. He looked tired. He said wearily, "My friends, I won't keep you in suspense. I can do nothing for you. You have no claim, and no case."

At their exclamations, he held up his hand, palm out.

"Hear me out. I know what you would say, and how you feel. I will explain the situation to you. It is quite simple. There is no record on file at the police station of a charge against the company. No one remembers that you were there. The claim is registered at the land office in the company's name. It predates your arrival in Victoria. There has been no protest, and no one remembers seeing you there. I sent a trusted man and two witnesses to the place of the claim. Your stakes were not to be seen, though they searched widely." He put his hands out before him, palms up. "I can do no more. It's one of the best cover-ups I've ever seen. Everywhere you turn, an impenetrable wall. It took money and influence."

"But what of our witness?" said Eustace.

"What of the officer we took...?" from Jack, simultaneously.

A bitter, angry laugh answered them. "I hope he likes snow! He's been transferred to a post in the Yukon Territories. As I have no case, I can't request his return. I can't even discover where he is. 'Internal Police Business.'" He sighed deeply. "Go home gentlemen. Try again if you will, but waste no more time here. Such as we are powerless against the forces of politics, the power of money, and corruption."

They thanked him, paid his bill. He charged only the expense of sending his men to the claim. They left, not speaking, too stunned by what they had been told to discuss it just then.

When they were back at his house, Eustace broke the silence. "Well, I guess that's that. Too bad, I thought we could sneak it through. Things up there—" indicating the government buildings, "—are worse than I thought. Time to get back to work. Guess you'll be leaving right away?"

"You're not going to give up? We can't let them get away with it!" Jack was profoundly shocked.

Eustace laughed mirthlessly. "It's not a case of 'letting them.' They have gotten away with it. You might as well face it."

"We can't quit. We have to take a stand. It's a matter of principle."

Eustace rounded on him.

"If you take a stand against those people on a matter of principle, you'll be like the dog that's just caught a skunk. People may say 'Good Dog,' but none of them will come near you. It would take more money than either of us have to even get started. Forget it. Go home."

"We can raise money. I can borrow some against the land. You must have some. You have this house, it should be worth a bit."

Eustace made a chopping gesture with his right hand.

"It's finished. Done. I'm not fool enough to throw money away for nothing, even if you are. Go home, I tell you."

They were both proud men, each in his way. It caused a rift that I think was never healed. Father could not recall that Eustace ever visited them again.

Jack went home. They were all down to meet him, except May, who stood watching from the porch. His manner told the news to their perceptive eyes. He sat wearily in his big chair, and May brought him tea. They clustered around him. One of the girls asked, "Are we going to be wealthy, papa? You don't act like we're wealthy."

He sipped the tea, considering the question. Sipped again. Pulled the little footstool over with his toe, put his feet up, leaned back. The temptation to be sententious confronted him. It was a brief contest; he lost. Slowly he said, as they waited breathlessly,

"We are wealthy."

His raised hand quelled their excited clamour. "We don't have much money. Not very much at all. Less than when I left here."

There were groans from his children.

"But we are wealthy all the same. We have our health, our farm, a beautiful place to live, here in the Basin. We have enough to eat. More than enough, and good things too. We're wealthy beyond the dreams of some folk. We don't need money. Tell me, any of you, what should we need money for? All we need, we have here."

"We can't make sugar," suggested one of the girls. "We need sugar."

"Honey," he said instantly, "We can find wild honey."

"Fishhooks," said practical Cliff.

"Make 'em. Easy."

"Clothes," said someone. "We need clothes to wear."

"Fur," he responded, "Leather, cedar bark, grass."

"Leather, yeah," enthused Hal. "I want a leather shirt, and pants."

There was a silent moment while each thought of what they must have that required money.

"Gas for the *Lady May*." Cliff again.

"We'll sail her."

Then May spoke one word.

"Books," she smiled. She knew his weakness. He considered this deeply, twisting his moustache the while. Should he argue that they had enough books, to maintain the position he had taken? They were all laughing at his indecision.

"Well-l-l," he conceded at last, "perhaps we need a little money from time to time!"

Chapter 9

Anno Mirabilis

NINETEEN-OH-SIX WAS TRULY A "year of miracles" for Hidden Basin. Four things happened, each of which burned its way into the boys' memories to remain there undimmed for the rest of their lives.

Spring

JACK WAS CUTTING fence poles high on the hill behind the farm. His sons were helping him, trimming branches, peeling bark, learning to use tools. It was one of those warm, sunny spring days, when it seems particularly good to be alive: the sort that, when recalled in later life, make you wonder why there are none like it anymore. The green water of the bay was like glass under the sun.

Cliff said, "What's that out in the bay?" and his brother and Jack turned to look.

"By Jove!" Jack breathed, then said solemnly, "Look well boys, look very carefully. For the rest of your days, you will be able to say that you once saw the great Sea Serpent!"

For a strange creature was floating idly at the surface about two thirds of the way across the water in front of the house. Not a serpent, although that was the impression it gave at first glance. The head and neck did look like those of a huge snake, but clearly visible in the limpid water was a bulbous body, tapering into a tail about as long as the neck. They could even make out two flippers, or fin-like feet, moving gently from time to time.

Jack held his hand out, measuring the creature's apparent length with thumb against forefinger. Then he transferred it to a bleached fallen tree lying on the far shore.

"Come on, boys, move!" and away he went down the hill to the house, his sons close on his heels. Into the house he rushed, and out, carrying his rifle and sketching pad. There was nothing to be seen on the water now, but scarcely pausing to look, he ran down to the float and jumped into the rowboat. Cliff and Hal piled in after him. As he propelled the boat with powerful strokes toward the narrow place that joined the bay to the sea, he told them, "Boys, that beast carries with it fame and fortune if we are able to seize it. If we can catch it in the narrows, in shallow water where we can retrieve it, the museums and scientists of the world will come to our door!"

They landed in a place they knew well, and concealed themselves carefully where they could see across the narrows. Minutes went by, then hours. The boys grew restive, and he sent them home. The long way, by shore, that they might not alarm the beast, bidding them keep watch for it as they went, and also to watch from the house until he returned.

He came home after dark. He had seen nothing, nor had they. He was off again before daybreak, but stayed only until noon. He sent the boys to watch for the rest of the day, with instructions to scare the creature back with noise should it appear. They waited in excitement, which soon enough became boredom. He didn't ask them to try again next day. But for days afterward, everyone glanced frequently out over the water. There were many cries of "There it is!" but it was always a seal, or a loon.

Jack rowed across to the tree against which he had compared the creature's length. After allowing for the extra distance, he announced that it had been thirty-nine feet long, give or take six inches. He speculated learnedly on what it might have been, and made many sketches, but he never spoke of it to others. As he said, "Without evidence, it would only bring ridicule." They never saw it again, or anything like it.

Summer

CLIFF AND HAL were thinning carrots when they heard it. The morning was fine and sunny, but a west wind was making sighing sounds in the trees, and they had heard the new sound for seconds before they were aware that it didn't belong. They looked, and there on the rippled water of the bay was a sight that made their hearts jump. A long streamlined speedboat was heading for their dock, engine rumbling with contained power. They rushed to the water's edge. Everyone in the family had heard the sound and was out in the yard or on the float to greet the strange new craft. It pulled up alongside the float, a thing of incredible beauty and strangeness, from its eye-dazzling white sides to its gleaming deck of polished brown wood. A space ship landing in a back yard today wouldn't seem as exotic to us as that craft did to them.

There were three people in it. One was the driver, a sort of sea-going chauffeur, although the boys wouldn't have recognized the term. The other two, a man of about middle age and a woman somewhat younger, stepped out onto the float after the boat was secured, and bumpers put down to protect the white paint.

Dressed all in white as bright as their boat, they seemed almost as exotic. They introduced themselves. It was a famous name; on a par with the Mellons, or the Rockefellers.

They had come from New York through the Panama Canal and up the Pacific coast, and were on their way to Alaska. However, the BC coast had proven so attractive that they had decided to take some time to explore it. Their yacht was at anchor off Billings Bay, while they took the launch to visit out-of-the-way places they had been told about, such as Hidden Basin.

They were nice people; unpretentious, and very curious about what life was like in this almost land-locked bay. They accepted with obviously sincere pleasure an invitation to come up to the house for tea. The boys would have stayed at the boat, but their father commanded them to "come along with us, you may learn something."

But what they learned they already knew, and that was that the talk of adults could be boring. The woman talked to their mother about children and clothes. For a few minutes, the talk of the men was interesting, as the guest answered questions about the Canal and things seen on their journey. But then he noticed the titles of some of Jack's books and seemed quite surprised to see such authors in such a place. Next, Jack discovered that the other held religious beliefs, and then they were deep in a discussion of evolution. This held no interest at all for the brothers, but did have one virtue. When thus involved, their father was totally oblivious to the presence or absence of his two sons.

They drifted quietly around the room and out of the door, and raced down to the boat, where the driver was polishing the already shining brass. They exchanged awestruck comments about the leather seats, the instruments, the steering wheel. They noted and discussed every smallest detail.

At last, encouraged by his amused expression as he listened to their chatter, they summoned courage enough to speak to the man. He was bored perhaps, and willing to talk. As soon as he thought polite, Cliff got to the important question. "How fast will she go?"

"Forty knots, maybe a bit more." They knew what a nautical mile was. After a quick calculation, Cliff said unbelievingly, "Forty-five miles an hour! Did you say forty-five miles an hour?"

"You heard right, youngster." Pleased with the effect of his words, and obviously proud of the craft he drove, he went on impressively,

"She's powered by twin five-hundred horse power Red Wing gas

engines." And he lifted a hatch to expose to awed eyes engines such as they had never dreamed existed.

"One thousand horsepower," he announced dramatically.

They felt they had seen all they could possibly assimilate, and must go now and discuss it.

An hour went by. Two hours. Feeling they might be missed, they thought it wise to return home. With luck, their father might not have noticed their absence. Just then the door opened. Out came their parents and the visitors, followed by the rest of the family. Jack eyed his sons balefully, but said nothing. Farewells were made. Their mother and the girls stayed just outside the door, as Jack went down to the float. The boys followed as unobtrusively as possible. Jack admired the boat, asked the same questions, got the same answers. This was reassuring. The thought had occurred that the man may have been exaggerating to impress them.

"Forty knots eh?" marvelled Jack. "That is very fast. Very fast indeed." Seeing perhaps, the expression on the faces of the boys, the man smiled.

"Perhaps you and your sons would like a ride?"

Their hearts leapt, then sank as their father said, "I thank you, but no, I think not. It is kind of you to ask, but no."

Father said, "At that moment, we hated him. I don't know why he said it. He must have known how much we wanted to ride in that boat. I don't think we ever really forgave him for that."

Jack continued, "But there is one thing you might do, if you had a mind to."

"Name it, we will try."

"It's just that I, we, have never seen a boat go that fast. Not nearly that fast. If you could just open it up for a moment, we would much appreciate it."

The man laughed.

"I had hoped it would be something more difficult."

The engine started instantly, and the boat glided out, then up toward the head of the basin. Jack murmured, as if to himself, "It's not possible. Not even those engines can move a boat through the water that fast. And yet, he wouldn't lie, and he surely should know..."

They watched the boat, its exhausts burbling, engines rumbling, as it cruised up the bay. It turned, the sound of the engines grew louder. The bow raised, and a V-shaped swell spread from the stern.

"See," said Jack, "it can't be done. So much power would sink her." And then the roar of a thousand horses unleashed shattered the air and came blasting back from the hillsides.

All the birds in the basin and in the hills around it took to the air. They had never known there were so many birds around. They all flew up. Even the loons flew instead of diving.

The boat shot forward like a stone from a sling, and hurtled down the bay towards them, leaving almost no swell, but behind it a solid column of tortured water. As it thundered past, the occupants waved, and as he waved back, Jack was saying, "I see! Now I see how it's done. Not in the water, but on it!" And he turned to his sons, "Look well boys. There you see the future. Look well." They looked. But though his words were prophetic, the future was quite a while in coming, and now that it is here, there are those of us who wish it had "tarried yet awhile!"

When the sound of the engines faded as the launch went out of the narrows into Blind Bay, Jack turned and called, "Molly, I think we'll go down to the narrows to see their ship. Would you and some of the girls like to come?"

Two of the older girls started to run to the float, but she called them back, replying firmly, "No, and if you have any sense, you'll stay here too." She turned and went into the house, calling on the two or three daughters who hesitated to follow her.

Jack stepped into the boat, saying, as the boys untied it, "Sometimes I just can't understand how your mother thinks," and they remembered how he had refused the proffered ride, and wondered.

They landed at their usual place, and walked to where they could see out across Blind Bay. There was a west wind blowing and there, across the blue sea with its white crested waves, was a ship such as they had never imagined. They must have seen pictures, but those hadn't prepared them for the sight that now met them. All in gleaming white, the ship dwarfed the Union Steamship vessels they had seen. At anchor, facing into the wind, the graceful bow curving into the sharp cutwater, as her lines tapered in wonderful symmetry to the angled stern, even the speedboat faded a little by comparison.

Fall

OCTOBER, AND THE BEGINNING of the season of storms from the southeast. The farm was on the sheltered side of the bay, and though the pounding of the surf could often be heard, and the roar of the wind on the mountain to the north, they weren't affected by storm winds. But there was no storm at the time of the strange occurrence. The sky was clear, though hazed, and the day was chill; there had been frost in the night. The water was as smooth as glass, which was its usual state most days. Around noon, they were all in the house waiting for lunch, when something, some sound not normal, made heads turn. Jack opened the door and walked out into the yard. They heard him call, "Molly! Everyone! Come quick!"

At the tone of his voice more than his words, everyone came running. He was pointing to the sky. "Look at that!"

They saw, about three hundred feet over the water, a huge tree branch, thirty feet long and as thick as a man's body, sailing majestically through the air, accompanied by a long cloud of smaller objects: sheets of moss, leaves, bushes, small branches. The surface of the water was speckled with splashes from small heavy objects that must have been stones, for few of them floated. The trees on the other shore were motionless. A strange moaning sound such as they had never heard before filled the air around them.

Cliff shouted, "It's the branch from the big tree down on the point!" and so, as they found later, it was, ripped from the tough old Douglas fir as if by a giant's hand.

They watched in amazement as it drove along through the air, seeming not to lose any height, but even perhaps, to gain it, although distance makes such judgements deceptive. They lost sight of it against the mountain at the head of the valley, but a few seconds later, a narrow strip of trees about two thirds of the way up the mountain changed colour, as if the finger of God had brushed it. A few seconds later, they heard an indescribable sound, a roar—whistle—crash, such that each one speaking of it afterwards, described it in different terms. There was no other occurrence. The weather for the remainder of the day was normal.

Jack and the boys rowed down to the narrows and climbed the slope to where the big tree was still standing, gnarled and contorted from its growth on the rocks and from centuries of wind. The place where the branch had been showed no trace of rot. Some immense force had torn it from the side of the tough old tree. Other, smaller branches were broken, but the far side of the tree appeared to have been untouched!

That section of slope showed evidence that some terrific force had struck there. The rocks were without moss, there was no debris on the ground; even some of the less stable boulders had been tipped over. Jack shook his head in bafflement. Nothing in his books, or that he had heard of, could explain this.

Of course, at that time, the "jet stream" was still unknown. Could a finger of it be fined down so narrow, yet retain its force?

"Ten or fifteen years later," Father said, "I was hunting along the face of the mountain where the wind had hit. There had been a fire there, some fifteen or twenty years before we came to live in the basin. The regrowth was as thick as hair. The wind had blown a swath through it, had laid every tree over on the ground. It didn't completely uproot them and most of them kept growing. But they didn't ever straighten up, so they grew with a kink in them. It was the queerest patch of trees I ever saw in my life."

And as if that wasn't enough for any year, there was to be yet another strange happening. Brief in the event, brief in the telling, but lingering in memory for a lifetime. Same month I think, about an hour after dark. There was a rumbling, like thunder, a flash of light that wasn't lightning, for it grew brighter. There was time to run to the window, even out the door. Once again, a sound never heard before, a tortured wailing sound. Something bright flashed overhead, filling the basin with a ghastly, lurid light. They heard a dull boom from the north, from the mountain, an echo, and nothing more.

Early next morning, Jack was out with his telescope, hoping to see some sign of where the thing had landed. A wisp of smoke perhaps, or a scarred spot on the mountain. Two days they spent combing the slopes, for Jack would dearly have loved to examine the "visitor from the stars" as he called the meteorite. But his luck with strange visitors was no better then it was in matters financial, and they found nothing, although the boys made other attempts as time allowed. But even a small mountain is a large place on which to find one particular rock.

Chapter 10

The Canoe

ONE OF FATHER'S earliest memories was of the farm on Texada Island. Jack was digging a drainage ditch. His older son was in the house with a cold. It was a hot day in summer, perfect for three year old Hal to wade in the muddy water, following Jack as the ditch was deepened. He was getting a bit bored, for they had been in the same place for quite a few minutes. Finally, his father moved on. Hal splashed along, muddy water up to his knees, pushing a bit of stick for a boat. Suddenly there was no bottom, and he was up to his nose in ditch water!

Jack leaned on his shovel handle, watching his son yell and splash in the hole that had been dug for him. Finally he reached down and hauled out the thoroughly frightened boy. Sitting him on the edge of the ditch, he said sternly, as he wrung out the soaked shirt,

"Now maybe you'll remember: if you can't see where you're stepping, walk carefully."

How cruel, you may be thinking.

There had been an elder son. He and his sister had been playing on a tidal flat in about a foot of water. She came to the house crying.

"Bert is being mean. He just lies there in the water and won't play with me."

When they found him, it was too late. He had apparently stepped into a hole, fallen on his face and sucked his lungs full of water when the shock made him take a deep breath.

The brothers, I have to admit, didn't think of humor as having a practical side at all.

The children were encouraged to read when they were very

young, by being read to as soon as they could understand, if not sooner. Their father would read them the comic strips, popular novels of the day, historical romances or whatever took his wide-ranging fancy. Hal was particularly fond of the series of stories about the arch-villain "Bigfinger," and the Inspector who pursued him so relentlessly. Also a comic hero named Ned, whose much quoted saying when someone finally caught on to the obvious, "I knew the moment that sack was pulled over my head that there was dirty work afoot!"

But the brothers' favourite characters were "Peck's Bad Boy," and "The Katzenjammer Kids," whose exploits they read avidly and whose trouble-making they longed to emulate. Unfortunately, Jack made sure that their opportunities to do so were extremely scarce. But they did their best, and at times the result of disobedience was unexpected retribution.

One winter, Jack began a project to occupy the long winter evenings. The previous summer he had found a cedar log with particularly fine and even grain. Most of it went into the making of shakes and fence-posts, but some of the choicest wood was split out and put in the loft to dry. Now the brothers learned what he planned to do with it. He was going to build a canoe.

"There's always a sale for a good canoe," he explained. "Might as well use these long evenings to make a bit of money."

They were enthralled. They had read about canoes in the stories about Indians and woodsmen, but they had never yet seen one. And now one was being built before their very eyes! Of course, it wasn't made of birch-bark, as they were convinced all *real* canoes must be.

But the glories of birch-bark soon faded as the canoe began to take shape under their father's hands. For Jack Hammond was not only a craftsman, but an artist. Whatever he made, people remembered. One winter, he had made a mechanical bird that hopped about the floor and pecked at grains of wheat.

He split long strips of cedar from the dry billets, and tapered them with a plane to proportions which he had worked out in his head. Then he drilled holes from edge to edge and joined the strips with dowels of seasoned crabapple wood and a waterproof glue of his own making. The shape of the strip determined the shape of the canoe. It is a method of building a boat which I have never heard of elsewhere, nor did father himself ever meet with it again. I doubt it would be practical for anyone but a master woodworker. The result was a canoe without ribs, unless you could think of the tough dowels as a sort of internal rib.

When the strips were all in place, he planed it inside and out until the flat surfaces took on a smooth flowing roundness. The boys were given the job of sanding and varnishing under Jack's critical eye, while he made the seats of edge-grain fir, and two paddles of fine white spruce.

The finishing touch was a half round strip of fine grained fir, so straight that it split like a piece of cedar. One was attached to each side of the gunwales. They too were fastened with glue and dowels. There was no metal anywhere in the canoe.

Started in the last week of October, it was finished by mid December.

The boys couldn't stay away from it. They had never even imagined anything could be so beautiful. Under the gleaming varnish, the red cedar seemed almost translucent. Just sitting there, it seemed to be moving. Almost alive even.

Now Christmas was just a few days away, and the boys tried to find in themselves the usual excitement of anticipation. But something was wrong. Never before had they needed to try. Cliff voiced it.

"You know," he said, "I just can't stand the thought that someone is going to buy it."

His brother knew quite well what "it" was.

"Me neither. But we do need the money."

"I suppose so, but still..."

And then it was Christmas morning. Everyone—as usual—was surprised at how many presents were under the tree. This year especially, for they were, in truth, very short of money at that time.

But everyone had made something. One of the girls had baked cookies. Another had made fudge with honey from the farm, not sugar. Their mother had knitted stockings and mittens for everyone. She had also found time to paint, as a present for the whole family, a beautiful picture in oils of the bay as seen from their farm. Their father had not only made something for everybody, he had painted a picture of his wife that was so life-like that everyone shouted in surprise and pleasure.

The boys gave their mother a prime mink skin, the best that their traps had produced that winter, carefully tanned in accordance with their father's instructions. For their father, a book on evolution, chosen and ordered by their mother long since and laid away until now, paid for by their hard-won trapline money. And finally, for each of their sisters, a perfect squirrel fur; soft, silky and delicate, very difficult to preserve without damage.

At last it was all over, and the string and wrapping paper carefully put aside for another year.

The boys were unusually quiet. As they looked at their small piles of cookies and so on, they felt that they had been most unfairly treated.

"Well," said their father with unwelcome joviality, "It seems that Santa Claus didn't bring you boys much this year. What have you been up to?"

They were silent. They didn't believe in Santa Claus. They had expected one of their father's usual gifts, a marvellously detailed toy boat perhaps. They would sulk.

"Say, Molly," he called. "Isn't there something else for the boys?"

Their mother pointed to the canoe. There was a bit of folded paper hanging over the side on a string.

"I think that paper will tell them where to look."

Cliff went over to the canoe, his brother right behind him. The paper was tied to the seat. It read, *To Cliff and Hal. Merry Christmas.*

That was a memorable spring and summer. The canoe proved to be just as good as it looked. It rode on the water surface like a duck feather. Just twelve feet long, it was so light that either boy could lift it easily with one hand. They treated it with the most fanatic care. The soft cedar was never allowed to touch rocks. When not in use, it was waxed and kept out of the sun. Even their father, a hard man to impress, was impressed.

Never were chores done so quickly! Every possible moment was

spent on the water. Even trout fishing was neglected as they explored the shores of the islands.

And now they could indulge in one of their favorite sports: rolling rocks down the steep slopes into the water.

This was forbidden them in Hidden Basin, and as the noise carried a long way over its calm water, they didn't dare disobey. But now they were no longer confined to the basin, and they soon found higher and steeper slopes than they had ever dreamed of.

Thus, one day in midsummer, they had anchored the canoe off a likely-looking prospect which they had never tried before. Swimming ashore, a steep climb of about a hundred feet put them amongst a fine collection of moveable boulders. The canoe was protected by the shoulder of the ridge they had climbed, and also by the slope of ground below them. But soon a mere hundred feet became too tame.

"Let's go further up," suggested Cliff. "There's some real big ones up there."

Up they went along the ridge to where an endless supply of

boulders of all sizes was waiting. How they worked! Heaving and straining, they would tip one over, then watch with awe as it leaped and crashed down the steep slope to plunge into the calm green water with a satisfying splash.

Down the hill they sent a big one. It smashed into an even bigger one part way down, and split in half. Great! One half went cartwheeling off to the right. The other...

"I think my heart stopped dead," remembered father, years later.

The other half hurtled off to the left, over the shoulder of the ridge, down the other side. Frozen, they listened.

"I knew what would happen," father said. "It was as if it had already happened. It could only end one way."

At last came the sound they were waiting for. Not just a splash, but a splash mixed with the sound of breaking wood.

They didn't speak. Couldn't speak. Numbly they descended the slope. Soon they could see the canoe. What was left of it. Two hundred pounds of rock—more or less—had hit it squarely between the seats.

They swam it home, one pushing while the other rested. It took a long time. They didn't mind. The longer the better. When they got home, their father would be there. Better perhaps if they never made it home at all! But make it they did at last, assisted by an incoming tide.

Jack had seen them from afar. He was waiting on the float as they swam wearily in. As they climbed out of the water, he reached down and, flipping the ruined craft over with a twist of his wrist, slid it upside down onto the float. He looked at the hole. They looked at him. He swung around to face his sons. I imagine it would have been very difficult to find two more miserable-looking boys. Tired, scared, heartsick at the loss of the canoe, they waited.

"Been rolling rocks, eh?" His voice was calm. He might have been asking them if they'd caught any fish. This terrified them even more. They looked at each other. Both spoke at once.

"Yes sir."

He turned to go. Glancing over his shoulder, he said, "Take it up to the house. When you've eaten, I need you up in the field."

That was all. I suppose he thought they had been punished enough. He was a strange man. In two weeks, working in the evenings, he made the canoe almost as good as new.

I would like to say that Cliff and Hall never rolled another rock, but I am afraid it wouldn't be the truth!

Chapter 11

Devil Thing

LOGGING CAMPS AND THEIR CREWS were a part of life in Hidden Basin for quite a few years. The first one was owned by a man named MacConville. It was a useful source of income for Jack Hammond.

When they needed bridges, or timbered sections of road around the lake edge, they called on Jack's skills to provide them. His constructions, using only wooden dowels for fastenings, were stronger, and more durable, than those using iron spikes. In fact, parts of his roads are still solid eighty years later, when spikes would long since have rusted away.

This camp had gone by the time the boys were old enough to have adventures. The next camp was called "Rat Portage" and was on the edge of their property, and for it, also, Jack Hammond's skills were useful at times.

To his sons, the camp was a challenge of quite a different sort, for the camp boss, a large and irate sort of man, had no patience to spare for boys. If he saw them around the bunkhouses or cookhouse, he would threaten them horribly. "Get away with you, and stay away, or I'll take a stick to you," was one of his milder threats.

But their real disappointment was with the Chinese cook, a bad-tempered and excitable man who must have been teased by boys at some time in his life, for he hated them implacably. This was unfortunate, for the cookhouse was a potential gold mine of exotic foods, as evidenced by the cast-out cans and bottles. Things like canned peaches and tomatoes, and sauces they had never even heard of. In their experience, most things were homemade.

When the boss was in the woods overseeing his crew, the boys would often hang around the cookhouse in the hope that the cook would take pity on them and offer them something good. But he would have none of them. He would open the door, stick his head out and shout, "Boys go home. Boys no good. Bad boys go home!"

"Aw, we don't mean any harm," Cliff would say. "Can't we do some chores or something?"

"No. No chores. Go home. Tell boss, boss fix boys good. Go home!"

They might have put up with this. They weren't vindictive, and their father had warned them to stay out of trouble with the loggers. But then the cook made his big mistake. One day, to the surprise and delight of the brothers, he called, "Hey there, boys. Like cookie?"

At last, their perseverance had paid off. They raced over to the door where the cook was standing, holding out two large and luscious looking cookies all glistening with sprinkled sugar. Eagerly they took the bait, not forgetting to thank him politely.

"The first bite was just delicious," remembered Father, "moist and sweet and tasting of molasses and ginger. But we'd no sooner chewed and swallowed that first mouthful when the inside of our mouths and throats began to burn like fire. We thought the skin would peel off our tongues. We were certain we were poisoned."

They ran to the creek to wash their mouths out with cold water, their eyes watering with pain, and as they ran, they heard behind them a gleeful, "He-he-hee! Bad boys go, stay away!"

Now they had a feud to pursue, revenge to take.

The next morning before daylight, they placed a pole against the end of the cookhouse, and Cliff shinnied up to the roof. He stuffed the stove chimney with an old sack they had brought from the barn and with wet moss that Hal threw up to him. Then they removed the pole and hid in the trees to watch.

Soon the light of the kitchen lamp showed that their enemy was astir. A few minutes later, the door was thrust open, allowing clouds of smoke to escape from the blocked stove. The cook was speaking Chinese and clearly in a foul humour. Of course, he would have no means of knowing what had happened until he discovered what was blocking the chimney.

"Let's give him a scare," whispered Cliff.

They each searched out a couple of fist-sized rocks and hurled them onto the shake roof where they made a most satisfying clatter. But the cook wasn't a man to scare easily. Out he came, waving a huge cleaver in the best comic-strip tradition, cursing in a weird mixture of English and Chinese. The only words they could make out clearly were "bad boys" repeated many times. By now, the men were beginning to appear to see what was causing the commotion, and then the boys could hear the loud voice of the boss over all the rest. It was time to fade quietly into the woods.

For a time, that was the highlight of their feud with the cook. There really wasn't much more they could do. They spent a great deal of time planning daring raids and elaborate stratagems, but none of their schemes was very practical. The best they could manage was to lob more rocks on the cookhouse roof from time to time. Soon though, their enemy hit on an effective counter. He simply ceased to appear at the door with his cleaver, thus robbing them of their chief satisfaction.

Life went on at the farm, and their feud receded into the background of their minds. Not forgotten, just dormant.

Planting time arrived and with it the hated jobs of digging the field, weeding vegetables, and hilling potatoes. Especially resented were the potatoes, for their father insisted on having enough stored to supply at least three families. Perhaps it was a response to some memory of famine back on the Prairies or perhaps it was simply his nature to overprovide. At any rate, each spring saw the dumping of about half a ton of excess potatoes as food for the stock.

It was just this knowledge which had gotten the boys into trouble that spring. Their assignment had been to plant the potato field. Endless rows of potatoes. They had been given permission to go trout fishing when the planting was done, but by noon there was still one whole box of potato "starts" to plant. There would be no time left for fishing that day if they had to put all those in the ground. What was worse, they knew that the rest of the week would leave them no other time to fish. They stood there looking at the box full of cut potatoes, each with its "eye" ready to sprout, which had to be placed right side up in each carefully dug hole.

"I don't see why," said Cliff, "we have to plant so many potatoes, anyhow. They'll only go to waste next spring. We have more than enough in the ground now. We'll never get to go fishing today."

"Well," said his brother, "there isn't much we can do about it, is there?"

But Cliff was thinking.

"Oh, yes, there is. Come on. Help me carry this box down to the end of the field." And then, "Now, let's get our shovels, and I'll show you what we can do." Hal had already guessed Cliff's idea.

"I don't think we ought to do this," he muttered doubtfully.

"Why not? Do you think he's counted them all?"

Hal considered this a distinct possibility, but forbore saying so. He did so much want to go fishing. So they dug a big hole and dumped the whole boxful into it, covered them up and scattered the leftover soil. Then they went to report that the potatoes were all planted. Their father looked somewhat surprised, said something like, "so soon?" but held true to his promise. Fishing they went.

"After all," said Cliff, " it's not as though we were lying. The potatoes are all planted."

Two weeks or so passed. The boys were weeding, with no premonition of trouble, when their father called to them from the upper field. They stopped what they were doing quite readily; they hated their job of pulling weeds. As they neared, Jack said, "Over here, boys. I want you to see something interesting."

They walked with him down to the edge of the field, now covered with rows of sturdy potato sprouts several inches high. They wondered what he had found that he wanted them to see. Suddenly, Hal felt apprehensive—of what he didn't quite know, but he felt a strong desire to be somewhere else.

Jack led them to the end of the field. "Over here, boys," he called cheerfully, for they had fallen quite a bit behind. They looked at each other guiltily. "Strangest thing I've ever seen in a potato field."

They went to where he was standing. They had guessed by now what they would see, and they were right. Hundreds of little potato sprouts jostling each other for room. Deeply buried though they had been, each one had striven for, and reached, the surface. There they all were, every one an accusation.

"Did you ever see so many sprouts from one hill?"

"No, sir," his sons mumbled numbly, feeling trapped and not understanding their father's jovial manner.

"Yes sir. Strangest thing. Just thought you should see it. You can go back to your weeding now."

They started off, feeling dazed with relief. They had gone about a dozen paces when they heard, "Oh, and boys, you might just oil your fishing tackle and put it away carefully. You won't be needing it for a while."

Spring became summer, and summer, as it always did, passed all too quickly. The weeding was done at last, and the harvesting finished. Now, as the leaves were falling and the nights were turning colder, the boys began to set out their traps. Squirrels, weasels, mink and raccoon would, with luck, put a bit of cash money in their pockets.

As they hated to leave animals in their traps any longer than necessary, they tried to make their rounds twice a day, as close to daybreak and dark as possible. Daytime usually produced little in the way of large animals, but was often good for a tally of squirrels which, if not collected, were apt to be eaten by predators before morning.

One evening, as they were approaching their last trap, a good "set" by a little swamp pool, Cliff stopped suddenly.

"Look," he said tensely, "over by that bush. There's something big. See, it moved!"

They peered warily into the shadows. They carried no weapons, only stout sticks with which to dispatch larger prey. They gripped these tightly as they edged closer.

"It's an eagle," shouted Hal as they drew near.

"We must have caught a squirrel in the trap and now he's eating it," guessed Cliff.

He ran towards the big bird, raising his stick and yelling, "Shoo! Go away!"

It lunged, not up but straight at them. Back they leaped, raising their sticks to fend it off, for an eagle is a truly formidable bird, but it checked abruptly and fell clumsily to the ground.

"It's caught in the trap!" both shouted at the same time.

And so it was, just by the tip of one toe. There it hunched, wings partly spread, hooked beak opened and threatening.

They considered what to do. They had no wish to kill it. Their father had impressed upon them that one only kills for a good reason, such as eating.

"Let's take it home and show it to everyone," suggested Hal. This was a great idea, with only one flaw. How were they to get this bad-tempered bird monster to go along with it? From the look in those glowing yellow eyes, it was just waiting for them to venture within reach, when it would endeavour to shred them into mouse-size pieces and devour them.

"We'll get a big sack," decided Cliff. "You stay here and watch while I run down to the barn."

Away he went, leaving his younger brother wondering just what he was supposed to do if the eagle did manage to pull its toe free. But it wasn't long before Cliff came panting back up the hill carrying one of the strong hemp sacks that oats came in.

"Now" he announced, "all we have to do is to get this sack over its head. You try first."

But his brother wasn't to be persuaded so easily to do something that rash.

"Try it yourself," was his reply. "I'll go get Dad to pack home what's left of you."

They finally hit on a scheme. Finding two poles, they fastened the bottom of the sack to them. Then they propped the mouth of the sack open with thin branches, and moving very slowly, suspended the contraption over the bird's head. For some reason, the eagle permitted them to do this without hindrance. It just stood there glaring, snapping its beak at any too-sudden movement, its wings almost folded. Perhaps it was confused at the three bulky objects—two boys and a sack—that confronted it, and couldn't decide which of them to attack. Also, by now the light was almost gone. Anyhow, when Cliff said, "drop it," the sack went over the bird just as they had planned, and they pounced on and pinioned their quarry before it realized what was happening, or had a chance to do anything about it.

"Just like Ned in the funny papers," father would comment at this point.

In the struggle, the bird's toe pulled out of the trap, taking care of what might have been an awkward problem. The only injury received was a talon rake on the back of Cliff's hand.

Down the hill they went in the gathering night, triumphant.

"Won't the girls scream when we walk in with this?"

"Yeah, but what if it gets loose in the house? Wouldn't that be an uproar?"

Hal stopped walking, struck by a thought so enticing that his brain forgot to move his legs.

"Cliff," he said slowly. His brother was walking in front carrying the sack of eagle. He turned around.

"What's the matter?"

"Suppose we were to let it loose in the cook-house?"

They considered. It was a fine idea, no doubt about that, but if they carried it out, they wouldn't have the pleasure of showing the captive to their family. In fact they wouldn't even be able to brag about it. That would be terrible. But the idea was so tempting! Just then, the eagle made a vicious strike with its beak in the general direction of Cliff's hand. He had relaxed his grip as they talked, and even muffled as the bird was, it almost got his fingers. Its power and ferocity awed them, and they thought of what could happen if it got away in the house.

"Let's do it," said Cliff. "We dassn't take a chance on its getting loose."

Now that the decision was made, their enthusiasm grew. They made plans. First of all, they must keep the eagle safe for the next few hours. What they intended to do wouldn't be possible until their family and the camp were asleep.

They took their captive to the barn. There they wrapped it in enough twine to immobilize the giant bird. There was no danger of it suffocating, for the coarsely woven sack would let in plenty of air. They scooped out a nest-like hole in the hay and tucked the sack down into it. Then they went home for supper.

What a long time it was until bedtime! It seemed that the family was never going to settle. But at last all was still in the house. They forced themselves to wait a while longer. Finally, Cliff whispered, "Let's go," and they were out of the window and down their escape route. A half moon in a clear sky lit their way to the barn. It was dark inside, and they had no light, but they knew their way around and went straight to where they had left the eagle. All they found was the hole in the hay that they had made for it.

"It's got loose!" Cliff said in amazement.

"There's no sack here," answered his brother. "Besides, it couldn't get out of all that cord we put on it. Feel around on the floor."

They groped about in the dark.

"Here he is," said Cliff. "I've found him. He's awfully still. I hope he's not dead."

But as he started to pick up the bundle, his solicitude was rewarded with such a vicious snap that the great beak actually broke through the heavy sacking. Their captive was quite healthy, it seemed, and in a foul temper! But it couldn't do them any damage, wrapped and sacked as it was, as long as they kept hands a safe distance from beak and talons.

Furtively, they made their way up to the camp. This was adventure such as they had read about! They skulked about through the stumps and bushes in the best traditions of the Red Indians of their dime novels. After all, the camp boss *could* be looking out across the clearing. Or even their arch-enemy the cook.

But they reached the cookhouse without raising an alarm, and sneaked softly around to the main door. The cook's bunk was at the other end, separated from the eating area only by a half partition.

Cliff had the bird. His brother eased up the big wooden door latch and pushed the door open a crack. The iron hinges creaked slightly. The boys froze, but there was no sound from the cook's quarters.

"Take off the string," Cliff hissed.

Hal couldn't untie the knots, so he got his knife out and cut through some of the turns until they all came free. The captive tried an exploratory jab with its beak. Cliff tried to get it out of the sack, but its talons were tangled in the weave, and its wings kept catching as it tried to spread them. There were sundry thumps and raspings. Hal was nervous.

"Come on, hurry up. Let's get out of here."

"What do you think I'm trying to do?" replied Cliff, just as nervous.

He grabbed the bottom of the sack and gave it a shake. The startled bird finding itself upside down, released its clutch on the sack and fell out onto the floor with much rattling of wings and beak. Cliff shut the door fast but none too gently, and they raced for their place in the trees. As they passed the end of the cookhouse, they heard the cook's voice saying loudly,

"Who there? What do?" Peering from cover, they saw the faint wavering light of a candle. There was the clatter of something overturning and a piercing scream echoed across the clearing. More clatters and thumps, then the slam of the door as the terrified cook charged out into the moonlight.

"Aiee, Devil thing! Aiee, Devil thing!" he screamed. Doors crashed open as men rushed out to see what was the matter. The foreman, ghostly in his long underwear, ran over to the screaming cook. Grabbing him by the arm, he shook him violently.

"What's the matter?" he roared. "What's going on here?"

But the poor cook had completely forgotten his scant English, except for the words "Devil thing!" as he pointed to the cookhouse.

"Aw, he's had a nightmare," said one of the men in disgust. He went to the cookhouse door and opened it. "See, there's nothing here, Chinee," he said as he stepped through into the cookhouse. Then he gave a great yell and jumped back, slamming the door shut.

"There's some great gawd-awful thing in there," he cried out. "It came at me through the air!"

"What are you talking about, you fool?"

The foreman strode to the door, shoved it open. Perched on the long table, its wings spread in menace, the eagle clacked its beak fiercely. He slammed the door. In the gloom, lit only partially by the moon's light, he didn't know just what he had seen, but he knew he didn't like it.

"Get a lantern. Get some pick handles!" he yelled. "There's something in there all right."

Strange fears, born of night and a land mostly unexplored, raised the hackles of every man there. They rushed to the toolshed, charged back, each one brandishing a pick or an axe handle. One carried a lantern.

"Come on, let's get it," someone yelled, and they rushed the door.

The man with the lantern reached it first. He lifted the latch, pushed the door open and held the light high. The others crowding behind him shoved him roughly through the door. He stumbled and dropped the lantern, extinguishing it and leaving them flailing at shadows in the dark, yelling to each other at the tops of their voices.

"Look out, there it goes!"

"Watch out, you fool. You almost knocked my head off!"

"What is that thing?"

The yelling was awful. There was a crash as the table went over, another smash and clatter as someone's club hit a lantern hanging from the ceiling. Someone knocked over a shelf of supplies, sending cans and bottles rolling across the floor. Someone else swung wildly and hit the stove pipe, which collapsed in a shower of soot.

Gradually it became quiet.

"Where did it go?" someone asked. Another answered with, "What was it? Get a light"

By now, the foreman and another were bringing lighted lanterns. They edged through the door, holding their lights high. Five men were standing in the wreck of the kitchen. Cans and bottles and broken glass littered the soot-covered floor. One man was bleeding from a gash in his scalp. Another was carefully examining his arm.

There was no sign of any intruder. The eagle had escaped. The watchers in the trees had seen it silhouetted for a moment against the pale sky. Eagles can fly at night, in the moonlight, though they prefer not to.

"There was something in here," the foreman said at last after looking for a while at the mess. "I saw it. Spread out, you fellows. See if you can see anything."

The brothers thought it was time to go. Their revenge had surpassed their wildest dreams. They eased quietly around the edge of the clearing towards home. Behind them, the men had gathered to talk it over. They showed no eagerness to leave the moonlit clearing.

Next morning while the family was eating breakfast, there came a loud knocking at the door. One of the girls opened it. There was the foreman, and he was not on a social visit.

"Hammond," he barked, "I want a word with you."

Normally he would have been invited in for a cup of tea, but Jack Hammond didn't like to be addressed in that fashion.

"I'll be out directly," he answered, his tone betraying his annoyance.

He put on his coat, not hurrying. The boys slipped out behind him. The foreman glared at them, and they thought it prudent to edge around the corner of the house where they could hear without being seen.

"Well, out with it, man. What is so important that you feel you have to miss work because of it?"

"Important!" roared the foreman. "My cookhouse is a wreck, my cook is leaving, and my men haven't had any breakfast. They won't work without eating, and no one wants to cook. I found eagle feathers in the cookhouse, and it didn't go in there in the night and shut the door after itself. And I found fresh footprints in the mud by the edge of the camp. Boy footprints, by God! Those boys have been up to their tricks again!"

They were mortified. They hadn't thought he would be clever enough to identify eagle feathers, nor to find tracks they hadn't even thought of concealing. This could turn out to be very unfunny. They listened apprehensively as his voice grew even louder.

"Now see here, Hammond," he shouted. "I want you to give those boys a hiding they won't forget. If you don't and I catch them around camp again, I'll do it for you!"

He opened his mouth to go on, but their father had heard enough. He didn't raise his voice, but it had in it a quality that made the other man stop short in surprise.

"Now you listen, and don't forget what you hear. Your camp is on my land. My boys will go there when they please. If they need disciplining, I will decide when and how much. If you so much as lay a finger on them, you'll discover what real trouble is. If you think they have broken something, tell me and I will ask them. They will not lie to me. If they say they did so, I will pay for it. As for last night, I don't know what happened, and I don't intend to find out. I will not be harangued on my own doorstep by any man for any reason whatsoever. Now go. You've wasted your time and mine. As to your men's breakfast, any fool can cook eggs, hotcakes and coffee. You might even manage it yourself! Good day, sir."

He went back into the house, shutting the door quietly behind him. The astonished foreman stood there with his mouth half open, but if he had words to say, there was no longer anyone to say them to. After a moment, he turned away and stamped up the path towards the camp.

When they could postpone it no longer, the brothers slunk back into the kitchen. Their father was seated at the table reading. He looked up.

"Been busy last night, have you?" he asked in his normal manner.

They mumbled something in reply.

"Better stay away from the camp for a while, don't you think?"

"Yes, sir."

The matter was never referred to again by their father. The cook was persuaded to stay, with the aid of a bottle of good whiskey kept for a special occasion.

The brothers were satisfied. Honour had been upheld. Peck's Bad Boy could, they felt, have done no more.

Chapter 12

Out of the Night

ALTHOUGH IT WAS ONLY seven or eight miles away from the communities of Lang Bay on one side and those around Pender Harbour on the other, Hidden Basin was peculiarly isolated. It wasn't on anyone's regular route, and no signal from there could be seen by passing ships or boats.

When the logging camp was working nearby, there was company, but for much of the time, the family had no near neighbours. This could be a danger in the event of an accident or sudden illness, but unless the weather was stormy, they were not much more than an hour away from help. No one in those days, no matter how lonely their situation, worried about humans as predators. Unless you were a misanthrope, strangers were welcomed, not shunned. But there are always a few bad apples in a barrel, and as human nature hasn't changed much, some of those could be very bad indeed.

The time was early November. It had been dark outside for an hour or so. Supper was over. The rooms were well lit, with a lamp in the kitchen and the wall lamp with its reflector, under which Jack in his big chair was carving something. He sat awkwardly, for his back was paining him. Cliff and Hal were at the table across the room, re-reading some comics.

Max, in his corner, began to growl. Then he got up and went towards the door, growling deep in his throat. This was most unusual. There are no predators on Nelson Island, and Max was a good-natured dog. Too good-natured, I'm afraid. He could have been the hero of this story, but having warned his master, and with nothing exciting happening, he felt that matters were under control, and stayed in his corner.

They heard the sound of boots on the verandah. All the family, except the very young, began to gather in the front room, eager to welcome visitors. Jack opened the door, only to be forced back into the room by a big man pointing a long-barrelled pistol. Two other men crowded in after him.

"Everybody just stay where you are, and no one'll get hurt!" commanded the man with the gun, harsh voiced. He waved the gun barrel at Jack.

"In the chair!" he ordered.

The boys observed all this with total fascination. From the moment they saw the pistol, they felt they were living one of the stories they loved so much. They had no sense of danger, only excitement. After all, they knew that villains never, without any exception, manage to win out. It was an article of faith, not to be questioned. And of course, there was no doubt that their father could handle any situation. So they sat there like statues, soaking up all the details.

The big man with the gun was their first interest. They had never seen a handgun before except in pictures, and they were impressed by their first sight of one. It looked quite suitably dangerous—and so, they realized, did the man holding it. There was something mean about his expression, something vicious. His face was pasty-white, without beard or moustache, and against it a quarter-inch black stubble of whiskers stood out in contrast. He was hatless, his black hair wild and unkempt. He kept turning his head from side to side, as if he feared something was lurking in the corners.

Jack did what he was ordered, somewhat to the surprise of his sons, who had expected him to wrest the gun from the intruder's hand.

The gunman, noticing the rifle in its rack on the wall, stepped over and took it down. Still holding the pistol, he moved the lever until he could see the shell ready in the magazine. Nearly everyone kept a shell or two in their gun; they might want it quickly. He levered the action back without letting the shell load, watching alertly all the while. Then he leaned the rifle against the wall, and turning to the other two men who had stopped just inside the door, he said, "Red, you stay where you are. Tex, check the other rooms."

The boys looked now—for the first time—at the other men. It was obvious which one was Red. He was built like a fire hydrant, short and thick, as sturdy as a stump. His hands were red, his face was red, with a stubble of red whiskers, and under his brown canvas hat, the hair that stuck out was bright red. He stepped aside to let the other by.

Tex! The name was a thrill to the brothers' ears. What cowboy tales the name conjured! He was a smallish man, lightly built. Under his black felt hat, his hair showed long and blonde. He had a small moustache of so pale a shade of blonde that it was scarcely visible in the light of the lamp, but individual hairs shone some-times, giving an illusion of cat whiskers. His alert look somehow reinforced this impression. Even his movements were catlike, fluid and economical. There was only one thing lacking.

"Where do you think he keeps his guns?" whispered Hal to his brother.

"I don't know, under his shirt maybe. Shh..."

Tex crossed to the kitchen, making a wide circle around the man with the gun, something which held no meaning for the boys, but they noticed that Jack's expression indicated intense thought as he took this in. As Tex approached, their mother herded the girls into the corner where the boys were, and stood protectively in front of them. He went into the kitchen, took the lamp, opened the door to the bedroom, looked around and came back.

"There's a kid asleep in a crib. Nothing else."

He went back to his place by the door, making the same wide circle.

"Bring food," the big man ordered. "Whiskey, if you've any."

"There's no drink in this house," Jack answered him. "It's against our religion. Food you would have been welcome to without waving a gun in our faces."

"I don't wait to be given. I take what I want." snarled the other.

"That's likely the reason you're on the run," Jack countered evenly.

"How did you know that?" The man's voice was dangerous as he swung the gun to point it directly at Jack's chest. From the tone of his voice and the look on his face, the boys thought he was going to shoot their father, and to Hal at least, it began to seem less like a story.

But Jack sat at ease, ignoring the gun. He replied calmly, "That's not hard to figure out." He looked away. "Molly, bring these gentlemen something to eat. Cliff, bring chairs."

They wondered why their father had lied about being religious and not having liquor in the house. They didn't know what alcohol can do to violent men.

Their mother went into the kitchen, face rebellious. Cliff brought the two chairs from the table where he and his brother were sitting, and one from the kitchen. He brought a chair to the gunman first, but fearing to come too close, placed it on the floor in front of him. The big man went to it, spun it around and sat, face to the chair back and to the room. He rested his gun on his right knee. Red took his with thanks, and sat down. Tex said, soft voiced, "Much obliged, kid," but stayed leaning against the door.

May brought food to the men. When that was done, she went over to her daughters, soothed their restiveness, then crossed the room to stand in the space between the wall and Jack's chair, resting her hands on the chair back. He turned his head and said something to her, keeping his voice low. She made no answer, and he turned again to face the room.

True to character, the big man wolfed his food down, making more noise about it than the family was used to, his eyes never ceasing their scrutiny of the room and everyone in it. The boys felt uneasy when his gaze rested on them, but he scarcely seemed to notice them, for which they were very glad. Red ate carefully and appreciatively, Tex slowly, eyes watchful.

Jack started to speak, but at the first words, the gun came up again.

"You shut up. If I want to hear from you, I'll tell you."

He tossed his cup carelessly to the floor, where it broke into two pieces. He said, "We need food. Everything you've got in the house. And money. If you hold out on us, I'll make you wish you hadn't."

Red broke in, protesting, "You said there'd be a camp here, that we'd raid the cookhouse. Not that we'd steal from folks that likely need it as much as we do."

"They may not need it as much as you think," came the answer, in a manner that implied something ominous. His tone changed, became commanding.

"All right now. Here's how we're going to fix it so's everyone's snug and won't do anything I wouldn't like." He pointed the gun at Jack. "Him we'll tie to the chair. I don't like the way he looks at us." At May, "Her, too. You can't trust a woman for a minute not to do something crazy." Next he pointed to the ladder leading to the boys' room. "The brats can go into the attic out of the way. Except her," pointing to the oldest girl, "she can keep me company for a while. It's been a long time since I had company like that." He leered, and for the first time in their lives, the boys saw the face of evil.

Father told me, "We didn't know what it was, but we knew something bad had come into the room. And the look on Dad's and Mother's' faces was something I didn't want to see again."

Impervious to the effect his words had caused, the big man continued, "You and Tex can do as you like," gesturing at the group of girls staring at him, uncomprehending. "There's enough there for everyone. Just stay out of my way, and keep where I can see you. We won't leave until a couple of hours before daybreak."

Red was looking at the man incredulously, shaking his head as if he couldn't believe what he had heard. He said slowly, but very firmly, "You can't do that."

"Oh yeah? What can't I do?"

"Touch those girls. It's not right. And you'd have every man on the Coast after you if you did. Tell him, Tex," looking over at the other man. "He can't do that, can he?"

"I reckon not," said Tex slowly. "But he's got the gun."

"And you'd better all remember that," warned the one with the gun. "And as for the rest of it, who'll be after us if there's no one to tell them who to look for?"

"Aw, that's crazy talk. I don't want to hear talk like that." Red picked up his cup, got up and walked towards the kitchen.

"That was a great cup of tea, ma'am, I'd sure like another one if you had it." He spoke directly to May, ignoring the big man who stood there irresolute. Red's manner didn't invite confrontation as he went towards May, holding the cup out for her to take. As he went by, almost within arms reach of the gun, he threw the cup directly at the big man's face. It was almost full. He had only pretended to drink. With the same motion he took a quick step nearer, grabbing the gun barrel with his right hand and aiming a blow at the other's face with his left, but he was pulled off balance and the blow missed. They staggered out toward the centre of the room.

Tex stepped quickly towards them as Red gasped his name. Jack said "Now, Molly!" and she ran to where the rifle leaned against the wall, with one quick one motion seizing it and throwing it to her husband. But excitement makes us stronger than we know, and it went high over his head.

The big man was too strong for Red, for a gun barrel is a hard thing to get a grip on. He ripped it free, clubbed the shorter man viciously on the head, then whirled to meet Tex, who was almost on him, but who now stopped short, and holding out his hands in conciliation, backed off a few steps.

Jack, hurling himself up by the strength of his arms, reached high over his head and caught the rifle in his left hand. As he fell back in the chair, his other hand flashed to the lever, slapping it open with the back of his fingers and closed with his palm, thus putting a shell in the chamber. His face was twisted with the pain in his back from the sudden movement, but the level gun barrel was steady as he held it waist high in front of him.

At the metallic sound of the rifle action, the big man turned, to find the gun's muzzle pointed straight at him. He stood frozen for an instant, then tensed a little. Jack spoke, voice steady, implacable.

"You're half a second from Hell. Put the gun down."

It seemed for a moment that the other might chance it, but there is much truth in the observation that this sort has no true courage. Perhaps he had imagination enough to think what the big lead slug from the gaping rifle muzzle would do to him. He stooped and placed the gun on the floor at his feet.

"Now," ordered Jack, "turn and take three slow steps towards the wall. A quick move may make my finger twitch. Remember, the only reason you're not dead is that I don't want your blood on my floor. But I could change my mind on that with very little effort." He shifted his position to ease his back. "Molly, that was quick of you. Now bring me the gun. Don't get in the line of fire."

She went to the gun, staying low so as not to give cover to the man scowling at her just a few steps away. Red was sitting on the floor, one hand to his head.

"Are you hurt?" she asked, concern in her voice.

He looked up at her and grinned. "It's just a bump on the head ma'am. Can't hurt this noggin with a gun barrel!"

"That was a very brave thing to do. We have a great deal to thank you for."

He flushed even redder with pleasure, and mumbled something

inaudible. She went to Jack and handed him the gun. He took it and with his left hand set it on the floor by his chair.

"Red, you look like you could pull a knot good and tight."

"I came over on a four-master out of Liverpool. Yes, I guess I can tie a knot."

"Good. Molly, get the coil of sash cord—give it to Red."

She came back with the rope, tossed it to Red, who caught it and rose to his feet. The big lank-haired man was glowering fiercely. If looks could have killed...

"If you come near me with that rope, I'll..."

Jack continued for him, "You'll put your hands behind your back. If you try anything, I'll put a bullet in your shoulder. I can hit a grouse on the wing with this rifle. Truss him good, Red, but don't get between us. You," he ordered the other, "turn so your left side is toward me. Hands behind you."

There was that in his voice that compelled obedience. Red tied the wrists together with the quick skill of a professional. Then he knelt, and using the same rope end tied the man's feet together, leaving only about eight inches of slack. He stood up then, saying, "I think we can sit more comfortable if he's hobbled."

The big man's face was livid.

"I'll get you for this, you little runt. I'll make you wish you'd hung yourself with that rope!"

"Only if you can sneak up behind me" said his captor, unimpressed. He took a chair, placed it, and pulled his man into it by the collar, aided by a kick behind the knee.

Jack sighed with release of tension, and leaned the rifle against the side of his chair. He picked up the handgun, hefted it, spun the cylinder expertly to check the load.

"Nice," he approved. "How did he come to get your piece, Tex?"

Tex looked surprised.

"Stupidity, suh. Purely stupidity. And how, suh, if I may ask, did you know it was mine?"

"Had to be. The front sight's filed off for a quick draw. He hasn't got the guts to face a man. He's a backshooter. And he didn't handle it right. Red isn't the sort to use a gun; he fights with his fists."

"I hate guns," agreed Red.

"That leaves you, and I think we can trust you with it, so here it is."

He held the gun out, hanging upside down from his finger through the trigger guard.

"Don't let him get it from you again."

Tex walked over, cat whiskers glinting.

"Suh, I surely won't let him get it again. You can bank on that!"

He reached for the gun, but Jack's hand twitched, it spun around his finger, so the butt slapped into his palm and the barrel pointed straight and level at Tex's belt buckle. He had scarcely time to look surprised, when it spun again, presenting the handle to his still outstretched hand.

He took it, saying in admiration, "Very nicely done, suh. Very nicely. I don't know that I have seen it done better."

"My sons, I know, have read about it, but have never seen it. I thought I might take the opportunity to show them how it is done."

Tex had taken a couple of steps back towards his place at the door, but when he heard that, he turned back. He said, "Then perhaps they would like to see this."

The gun in his hand became a blur as it spun. With his left hand he reached under his belt with two fingers just behind his hip, making a space into which the gun darted as if it was some live thing returning home. The whiskers twitched as the cat-man went back to the door. This time he sat in the chair, arms on its back, looking very relaxed.

All this, from the time Red had acted, had taken no more than ten minutes. The brothers had sat through it as if mesmerized, afraid to blink lest they miss something. Cliff whispered, "Did you see that? Did you see the way Dad handled that gun?"

And not for the first time, they wondered what their father had done when he was a young man.

His brother whispered back, "Yeah, but Tex made it spin faster. How could he make a gun do that?"

Cliff said, "I told you dad could handle things. I knew he'd win out."

His brother wasn't so sure.

"But he couldn't have done it without Red and mother."

"Oh," said Cliff confidently, "he would have come up with something."

Years later, father told me, "But I knew Cliff was wrong, even though he was older. I realized then that it's not enough to be strong, or good, or in the right. You can be all those things and still lose. It came as quite a shock. I didn't lay it all out just like that, but I knew it. And I think that right then, I wasn't the younger brother any more."

Their mother was bustling about, getting the girls ready for bed. The men were talking. Jack asked casually, "What are you running from, Red?"

Red blushed, stammered something. Tex answered for him.

"He was working in a saloon. The owner didn't take to him. Fired him after a couple of weeks, had the bouncers toss him out without his wages. Next day Red comes back with an axe, chases the bouncers out the window, wrecks the place. Owner calls the law. You can't fight guns with an axe. Owner has an in with the police. They're going to put Red away for a long time. But he gets lucky, and here he is."

"And you, Tex?"

"Well, suh, as for me, my gun went off when I was pointing it at a fellow. Not quite by accident, you know? And I'm kind of small, but fast. Slip away if you don't watch close." He grinned.

Red spoke up, fluent now the subject wasn't himself.

"I was there with him. It was down on the docks, bunch of guys off a ship. Drunk, with knives. I guess they were too drunk to be afraid of a gun. Of course, Tex usually wears a coat over his piece, and they didn't see it at first. He didn't shoot 'til he had to. Must have been a carload of cops near, 'cause they were right on us. The others all ran back to their ship, and one of them must have picked up the fella's knife that got shot, so we know the cops would say Tex'd shot an unarmed man. It was pretty dark around there, and Tex just sort of melted away in the shadows. I was slow, and a cop spotted me, so I pretended I was dead drunk." He grinned. "Wasn't too hard, you know? And when Tex got far enough away, he shoots off his gun, and away they go after him, and I don't wait around any more."

When he stopped talking, Tex added, "I didn't shoot to kill, just winged him. We figured him and his friends would give a pretty good description of us. The police knew Red of course, and I'd been in a couple of scrapes. Time to move on."

Jack indicated the captive.

"How did you come to hook up with him?"

Red answered shortly, "It's a long story, and I'm not too proud of it." He stopped, then seemed to feel the need to explain.

"He's got quite a line to string you along with. We didn't know what a snake he was until he got Tex's gun, but then it was too late."

"Couldn't you jump him?" asked Jack curiously. "He has to sleep sometime."

Red shook his head. "He's not as thick as he looks."

The big man snarled like a beast. Red ignored him.

"He'd put us off on some little rock or other, and he'd throw the anchor over and sleep in the boat. No way we could climb up on it without him waking, even if I could swim, which I can't."

Tex put in "Me neither."

May had been listening. Now she spoke to Red, pointing to the tied man.

"What did he do?"

Red looked uncomfortable, and with obvious reluctance, answered, "It's to do with a woman, ma'am. You'll excuse me if I don't go into the details."

She stared at the big man for a moment, loathing in her eyes. She said to the others, voice strained with hatred, "I don't want him in this house. Get him out of here as quickly as you can, or I'll shoot him myself." She turned quickly and went back to the kitchen.

Jack rose. He said, "I'd guess you'd better. She's a hard woman when she wants to be. I'll give you some provisions. Where are you headed?"

Red shrugged, "I thought I might try one of the big camps."

"I'm heading south, suh. I'm farther from Texas than I evah want to be again."

"You are rowing, I presume? Then I would suggest that you head for Stillwater, about three hours from here if you have a good hull. It is near enough to Powell River, where you can find work or transport. Pender Harbour is closer, but strangers will be noticed."

"I've heard that Powell River might be a good place to work," agreed Red.

"And what do you propose to do with him? You could leave him on one of the islands, I suppose, but it would hardly be fair to the unsuspecting passer-by who picks him up. As for releasing him on the Mainland, again he is sure to do someone harm. The best thing to do, of course, would be to take him about halfway across to the other side and leave him. The water there is very deep."

The man in the chair began to look worried.

"But," Jack continued, "I don't think either of you are the sort to go for that solution."

"Not me," agreed Red hastily. "He deserves it, but I couldn't do it. And Tex wouldn't hurt anybody that didn't come at him. I know that. But we'll try to think of something to clip his wings."

May brought a bundle of food wrapped in a flour sack.

"There's farm bacon and butter, and a loaf of bread. But you must promise me that you won't give any to him. I don't want that man eating my food."

Red took the sack and grinned.

"I thank you, ma'am. It's a promise, and it's one that will be easy to keep."

Jack took up the lantern and lit it. "I'll light your way down to the water."

And then they were gone.

The story has a sequel, which I'll call "Twelve Years Later," though the period is only approximate.

Chapter 13

Twelve Years Later

THE BLOEDEL, STUART AND WELCH booming ground at Myrtle Point, near the mill town of Powell River, was a difficult one to operate. Exposed to winds off the gulf, poorly designed, and too small to handle the volume of wood being dumped, it was a weak link in the operation at the time Father came to work there. Several times during his first couple of months, the operation of the camp had to stop while room was made at the dump for incoming logs. Then one day, following a heated exchange with the camp foreman, the head boom man quit, taking five of his best men with him.

Now the foreman was in real trouble. It wasn't just a matter of waiting until the remainder of the crew made room for more logs. The cause of the argument with the boom boss had been the dumping, against his wishes, of a trainload of logs on top of the ones already blocking the dump. There was such a tangle of logs on top of logs that the boom crew, armed only with peaveys and pike poles, couldn't move them. Another trainload was due within the hour, and wouldn't be able to dump its logs. A big logging camp is, in its way, a precision instrument; if one part fails, the rest of the machine will falter. At this rate, soon only the falling crews would still be working.

With their boss gone and the dump jammed, what was left of the boom crew, including Hal, joined the group by the dump machine. Suggestions, none of them very practical, were being offered freely, to be shot down by one or another of the participants as soon as they were flown.

The young man from Hidden Basin stood listening. In the last few years, he had worked in several smaller camps, and found that he not only liked to work on logs in the water, but that he had a talent for it as well.

Each booming ground is different; each has its own special problems. Tides, weather, lay-out, or design, and so on. Already, in spite of his youth, he had been boom boss of two small crews, but had become restless and moved on. Here was the situation that he felt he had been looking for. He had learned, if it needed to be learned, to use that quality in his voice that compelled attention.

He spoke, and the sound, though not very loud, cut through the other voices like a hawk through pigeons, "I can clear the dump for you," he promised confidently. "And I'll guarantee to keep it clear."

The camp supervisor looked at him skeptically. "And how do you propose to do that, young fellow?"

But his question went unanswered for the moment. Hal continued, "Ever since I've been here, this dump has been a problem. It's laid out wrong, and it's been worked wrong. And it should be on contract, not wages."

"Maybe so," returned the foreman, "but no one wants the contract."

"I do. On the same terms as the camp at Fanny Bay. Give me four men to replace the ones that walked off, that machine for a day (pointing to a steam donkey waiting to go back to the woods), and an operator. I'll have the dump clear for you by this time tomorrow."

"Done," said the boss. "I see what you're going to do and I like it."

He went off to see about getting a machine operator and some men, and the group broke up, leaving Hal with the crew of boom men. They stared curiously, some with hostility, at this youth who had only minutes ago been one of them, and by no means the most important. And now they were to take orders from him? He spoke, and they recognized an indefinable air of authority.

"No one has to stay. When we get this mess straightened out, I won't need as big a crew as we've been working. But for those that stay, there'll be a pay raise, starting now."

They all stayed. He gave directions to make room out in the storage area for the logs that would be coming, then took the four new men the boss had sent down from less urgent jobs, and went to supervise the moving of the steam donkey. (For the rest of his life, he never worked as part of a crew, but as a foreman.)

His scheme worked splendidly. The machine was placed, and its line run through a block hung on the other shore. The logs were dragged by brute force out of the tangle into open water, where they were sorted and taken to where they would be boomed. The dump was clear sooner than anyone expected, and the routine of the camp resumed. Father was duly praised, and given the contract as promised. The dump was never blocked again while he was there.

In the next couple of months, he began to make the changes he wanted. He re-designed the grounds so that each operation led naturally into the next. But most of all, he redesigned his crew. He hired and fired ruthlessly until the crew was down to fourteen men plus himself, each man picked for skill and stamina. And he used the money saved as the size of the crew dropped to pay higher wages to the others. The word spread, and soon he was turning good men away.

The most important thing that he looked for, after ability, was pride, the quality of scoffing at obstacles, and, of course, the knack each man must have to get along well with the others. And finally he had the crew he wanted, one that functioned like a well-designed machine. But these were men, not machines. Young men mostly. And because he liked pranks and jokes, the men he picked were of the same stripe.

Sometimes a prank could backfire.

One afternoon, just before quitting time, he chanced to pass near the walk-log that led to the boom shack where tools and spare clothes were kept; the last stop before the way to shore. This walk-way was a big slab—half a tree—four feet wide and fifty feet long. The dropping tide had left it balanced precariously just out of water, one end on a sunken sloping log, the other on a taut chain. He put one foot on it, and could tell that it was just about ready to flip completely over, pivoting on the end of the log. He studied it for a moment, then placed a chunk strategically so that it would prevent the slab from moving but could be easily knocked out. Then he went about his business.

Came quitting time, and the crew headed for the boom shack, fourteen men, one behind the other, tools in hand, talking, joking. He made sure he was the last. They came to the walk slab. The first in line noticed how it was suspended on both ends, tested it cautiously. It felt solid. He stepped onto it, walking in the centre just in case. The others followed. When they were all on the slab, father, last in line, knocked out the block with a jab of his pike-pole. Then he leaped on, putting all his weight first on one edge, then on the other. It was enough; the slab tipped upside down, and put all fourteen men in the water. Father, being prepared, had no trouble staying on it. He took a few steps, stood there with hands on hips.

He said mockingly, "I thought you fellows were supposed to be able to stay on logs. Fine bunch of boom-men you are!"

Someone said, "That was no accident. I heard a block being knocked out."

And another, "So did I."

One of the men pulled himself onto the log and crouched there, grinning. Father decided it might be better for him to take the long way back to camp. He turned, but there were two on that side of him. Recognizing the inevitable, he dropped his pike-pole and jumped in the water. But, as he always said, "It was a good trick, just the same!"

There is another anecdote from this time and place that I like, illustrating the effect father's voice could have. I heard the story from his brother-in-law.

There was a building in the camp, in part of which the saw filer worked. The rest of it held various tools and supplies, along with a big foot-powered sharpening wheel, where you could sit and sharpen axes or other edged tools. It was also a place to sit and talk, and there were always a few men there after supper. This particular evening, Hal had taken his turn at the stone, and was putting an edge on his axe. Some of his crew were there, and a few fallers with their axes.

There was a pecking order in the camps. It varied according to the personalities involved, but the head faller and his men were usually, though not always, at the top. The position of the boom boss and his crew was ambiguous. Though not considered "real loggers" by the men in the woods, they were tough, independent, and just as essential to the camp's functioning.

Father was giving his axe the final touches when the door was thrust open and the head faller strode in, followed by two of his men. They all held axes. He stood there for a moment, a big man and a rough one. There was no doubt in his mind who was the top dog here. Father ignored him, concentrating on his axe-edge.

The head faller said loudly, "You there, I want the stone."

The silence in the room grew tense. Father made no answer. Not used to being ignored, the big man flushed darkly.

He said again, more harshly, confident in his size, "You there, are you deaf? I said I want the stone. Now move!"

From the first word, father's temper, never all that far from the surface, began to rise. He had no intention of fighting the man for something so trivial, but rage burned in him at such stupidity. He jumped to his feet, a picture of cat-like power, small though he was. His heel caught the stool he had been using, sending it rolling across the room. Raising the axe over his head as he turned, to avoid hitting the stone with it, he said, "You want it so bad, you can have it!"

Bill, his brother-in-law, said, "I was his friend and on the other side of the room, but when I heard that voice, I wished I was somewhere else."

The faller took one horrified look at the razor-sharp axe, backed by a force—that voice—such as he had never before encountered. He turned, still holding his axe, and went through the door so fast the leather hinges broke, and it went clattering out onto the path.

Father looked around him at the awe-struck men. He said mildly, "I wonder what got into him? I was going to let him use the stone, he wanted it so bad." Of course no one believed him.

Next day, the "super" stopped him. He said, "Hal, you've got me wondering if I ought to laugh or curse."

"Why is that?"

"You've cost me my best team of fallers. They called in for their time this morning. Seems there were smirks on a lot of faces in the cookhouse at breakfast, and no particular reason for them. He wasn't all that well liked you know."

And the young boom boss began to notice that there was a new note of respect in people's greetings, and the boom crew walked with a bit more strut in their step.

Once at work, the crew was all business, but getting from the boom shack to the job was a time for high spirits and horseplay. This particular morning one of the men was in an unusually frolicsome state of mind. He was well liked, but he had mood swings, being sometimes rather quiet, or as now, quite rowdy. He tried to trip up the man in front of him by bumping him behind the knee, but that didn't work. They were passing a "dolphin" (a group of pilings bound together) and reaching up with his pike-pole, he hooked the top of one of the pilings and climbed his pole like a rope, caulk boots walking up the piling. But when pilings are driven the old way with the big hammer, the ends are often split and weakened. The piece he was hooked into split off, and he hit the water on his back with a tremendous splash. If he had fallen on the log they were walking on, he could have broken his back, but luckily there was a space of water between the log and the dolphin, and only his pride was hurt. But that was enough.

He climbed out on the log. Everyone was grinning or laughing outright. His mood turned to rage. Looking around for something on which to vent his fury, he picked up his pike-pole, slammed it down again violently. "Damn you!" he cursed. "Pull loose on me, will you? I'll fix you for that!"

Of course, it wasn't the pike-pole's fault. If anything was to blame, it was the piling, but there was nothing he could do to that.

He grabbed the pole, and sticking one end between two of the pilings in the dolphin, began to walk along the log, meaning to break the end off the pole. Now in those days, poles were made of wood, not metal. They were chosen with care from the best of straight grained hickory. Each man made his own, oiling the wood regularly, and putting it on a rack to keep it straight when not in use. The tough wood bent, but it would not break. He turned onto the log that went at a right angle to the one he was on.

"Break, damn you!"

He leaned forward, straining with all his might. A bit of bark slipped under his caulks, he lost his balance, and the spring of the bent pole threw him into the water again. He climbed out, white-faced, looked around him wildly, then set off at a run back to the boom shack. Everyone stood waiting, wondering what he would do next. Back he came, carrying an axe. Placing the pole across the log, he chopped it into pieces a couple of feet long, picking up each piece as he cut it and hurling it out across the water as hard as he could throw it. The last piece, the one with the metal spike, sank before he could grab it. He stood there, both hands on the double-bladed axe, head hunched between his shoulders. He looked around him at the grinning men, and the grins all vanished.

He said, "I'll kill the man that laughs."

He stood there for a moment. No one laughed. Then he swung around and went back to the boom shack to change into the dry clothes each of them kept there. The crew went off to work without him.

After some time had gone by, and he hadn't shown up, father went to see what the matter was. The boom shack was empty, and his clothes were gone. Father went up to the bunkhouse. He was there, sitting on his bunk. He looked up as father entered.

"Don't ask me to go back there, Hal. I can't do it. Just don't ask me. I hate to leave you short-handed, but I can't work thinking they're all grinning behind my back. I'll spread the word that you need a good man."

And nothing father could say would change his mind. He left word at the office that he needed a man, and went back to work.

A few days passed. A good crew can make up for a man gone for a while. Then, when they were eating lunch out on the boom, a man came down from camp, carrying a pair of boots in one hand. He walked out to the boom shack, sat down to put the boots on, and headed for the group eating lunch. A short but sturdy figure, he seemed to father's critical eye very much at ease on the logs.

He walked up, and asked, "Who's the boss?"

Replied father, "You're looking at him."

Returned the other, "I hear you're looking for a man."

It was Red, a bit more weathered-looking, and heavier in the shoulders. What looked to be the same brown canvas hat was squashed down over his red hair. Understandably, he didn't recognize in the young boom boss the boy he had seen so briefly years before.

"We're short-handed, all right. Right now we need some sticks bored. Come along, I'll get the auger and we'll see what you can do."

And he did very well indeed. Using the big four-inch auger to bore holes was one of the least-liked jobs on the boom, but Red positively enjoyed it, and his thick shoulders and heavy arms never seemed to tire. He was also competent at any of the other jobs he might be put to, and his unfailing cheerfulness soon made him liked by the rest of the men.

And now comes a part of this story that makes me uncomfortable, for it involves one of those coincidences that no fiction writer would expect his readers to tolerate. I thought seriously of changing some of it, of inventing some more plausible scenario, but have, in the end, decided to leave it as father told it.

Two days had passed since Red had appeared. On the morning of the third day, he was again boring the long logs, called boomsticks, that would be chained together to contain the logs into booms.

The pocket, or area where this was done, was beside the big float the boom shack was built on. Hal was at some job or other on the float. A train-load of logs was being dumped; it's a noisy operation, and he didn't notice the approaching man, until the crunch of caulks on wood alerted him. He turned, and there, only a few feet away, was the big man whom he had last seen going through the door back at Hidden Basin, the man whose arms Red had bound with sash-cord.

"I hear this crew needs a man. Is that right?"

The harsh voice brought the scenes of that night back to vivid life. Father looked at him for a wordless moment. He hadn't changed much: face a bit puffier, lips a bit looser than memory had them. Not as big as he had appeared to the half-grown boy, but still, a big man.

In the intervening years, allusions that had been lost on the boy, had come to be understood by the man. Father felt the stir of anger. He said shortly, "Not anymore. Job's filled."

But the man wasn't to be put off that easily. He retorted, "Yeah. Well, maybe you haven't got the best man for it."

Father heard Red's footsteps as he came around the corner of the shack to get a chain from the pile nearby. Realizing a meeting was inevitable, he replied, "Here he is now. Why don't you ask him?"

And he stepped back so that he could see both of them. A wave of colour suffused the big man's face when he saw Red. He snarled viciously, "You little cockroach. Caught up with you at last!"

He picked up a length of two-by-four from several lying at his feet. "Now I'm going to beat your head off!"

He stepped toward Red, who had simply stood there staring at first, but who now darted to one side and wrenched a pike pole out of a log. Holding it like a lance, he faced the approaching enemy. Level-voiced, he ground out, "That's it. Come a bit closer. Come on. I'll ram this into your belly and yank your guts out on the logs. Come on."

Father cut in with his best drill sergeant's voice, "That's enough of that! You—" to the big man, "—get along out of here. I told you there's no work here for you."

It worked, as it usually did. Throwing the club down, the man grinned nastily, "That's all right. I can wait a few more hours." To Red, he said meaningfully, "I'll be seeing you!" And back he went in the direction of the camp.

"He doesn't seem to like you," Father commented.

"He'd do for me if he could," agreed Red. "Hal, I hate that man more than I can tell you. But don't ask me why." He picked up a chain, turned, then added, "I may not come to work tomorrow. If I don't show up next day, you better look for another man."

"Need any help?"

"Maybe so, but it's my hand, and I'll play it out. Thanks, though, just the same."

Red was in his place at the table for supper that evening, but was absent at breakfast. He didn't come to work that day, but the day after that he appeared at the breakfast table with a badly bruised and cut cheek and a split lip. He fended off questions with good-natured jokes, but no explanation.

As soon as they were alone, Red was first to speak.

"I'm sorry, Hal, but I guess I'll be moving along. I'll wait until you find a new hand, then I'm off. Too bad though, I like working here. Good crew."

"Stay then. You fit in fine. If it's that fellow after you, we'll make it hot for him around here."

"Oh, it's not him I'm worried about. No, he won't be any more trouble. It's just that I don't feel comfortable here any more."

"I'll hate to lose you," said father sincerely, "but it's your choice. That's a bad looking cheek you have there."

"Yeah, he was a dirty fighter."

"Was?"

"Slip o' the tongue," responded Red innocently.

In a week or so he moved on. Father never saw him again.

Chapter 14

Pitlampers

IT WAS A BEAUTIFUL September evening in Hidden Basin. The day had been windy, but now the air was still, and the surface of the bay was, as usual in the evening, like a sheet of glass. The family was scattered about doing evening chores. Jack was in his favourite chair by the door, reading.

Suddenly, a girl's voice rang out. "Listen! Visitors!"

Everyone stopped what they were doing. Sure enough, there was the unmistakeable *putt—putt—putt* of an engine in the distance, and in a few minutes a boat appeared around the point. No one recognized it, not even Jack, who knew everything worth knowing about every boat for miles around. It was of the rather old-fashioned double cabin design: a wheelhouse at the bow, some open deck, and a squarish cabin aft for the stove and bunks.

"Nice hull," Jack commented, "Doesn't leave much wake."

As it drew nearer, they could see that its best days were long past. Most of the paint was gone, the bleached grey wood showing it had been that way for some time. A wheelhouse side window had been broken, and some paper was stuck over the break. The paper was torn. Over all was that air of neglect and disrepair that indicated an indifferent owner.

Their father was disgusted. "It's a crime to see a good craft let go to ruin like that," he growled.

The brothers started to run down to the dock as the boat approached, but they stopped short as their father said sternly, "Boys! That woodbox isn't nearly full yet."

They turned back most reluctantly. Visitors were always an

event to be enjoyed, and they wanted to be the first to welcome them. They needn't have worried. These weren't visitors. The boat went on by without slowing. The occupants didn't even wave, although two figures could be seen through the remaining wheelhouse window. Soon the engine slowed, reversed, and then stopped as the strangers pulled in to the temporarily abandoned loggers' float further up the bay.

Much of the evening was spent in excited speculation as to the identity, character and intentions of the strangers, but none of them came near the answer.

The brothers went to bed even more reluctantly than usual, and sleep was long in coming, for they had their own somewhat lurid speculations regarding the newcomers which they had prudently kept from the rest of the family, who were critical enough already of their choice of literature. But sleep came at last, even to them.

Hal woke in the night, his nerves tense. He listened, but for what, he couldn't be sure. Had he been dreaming the sound of guns? He was a light sleeper, easily disturbed, unlike Cliff who was snoring gently beside him.

Suddenly, two shots, not far away. He poked his brother in the ribs.

"Cliff! Wake up. Somebody's shooting!"

"Huh? What's the matter? What are you talking about?"

"Someone is shooting, up in the bay."

"You're crazy. You must have been dreaming. It's the middle of the night. Go to sleep."

Bang! Bang! Another two closely spaced shots.

"See?" said Hal.

From downstairs came the sounds of movement, a flare of lamplight. They jumped out of bed, pulled on trousers, tumbled down the ladder. Everyone was awake, the girls chattering excitedly. Their father was standing at the window in his nightshirt. He was saying, "I'm afraid there's nothing I can do about it tonight, Molly." Then to the frantic questions of his sons, "You boys go back up to bed. Those men on the boat must be meat hunters. They're pitlamping deer." His words were punctuated by another shot.

"But isn't it against the law?" asked Cliff.

"Yes, it is. But the law is far from here, and won't be of much use to us tonight. Now back to bed, every one of you. Goodnight." And off he went, taking the light with him.

Of course there was little sleep now for the brothers that night. Pitlampers! They had heard of them, read of them. The name was supposed to come from the resemblance of the light to one used in the mine-pits of long ago. You took a shielded lantern with a hole cut in one side and a reflector behind the light. Then you went for a walk in the woods at night; up a road, or along the edge of a field. Animals come out in the night, and they aren't so quick to run away. They look at you, and their eyes shine in the light. An easy target, especially if you use a shotgun loaded with buckshot.

But it's not so easy to be sure of a kill, and there is no second chance. A wounded animal turns and runs, and you can't see to shoot again. Also, although some hunters can tell by the colour of the shining eyes what animal it is, most cannot, and shoot at whatever they see, be it horse or cow; coon, cat or dog—it matters not to pitlampers. It is a method often used by those who hunt for profit, who sell game to those who aren't too nosy about how it was obtained.

Farmers hate them, other hunters despise them, and the law proscribes them. Unfortunately they seldom operate where the law is, and now the peaceful bay was invaded by them.

The boys were up early the next morning. They couldn't wait to see what their father was going to do. Something dramatic, surely! A confrontation, certain of outcome of course. No two men could hope to stand up to Jack Hammond with his temper up.

But they were in for a disappointment. At breakfast, their parents discussed the matter at length. Their mother, who was afraid of nothing and no one, counselled caution.

Their father said finally, "There's not much I can do. I am not about to take the law into my own hands. Not for this. I would like to," he said slowly and thoughtfully, and his sons quivered with excitement, "but the consequences must be considered." Their spirits fell. He continued in a brisker tone, "The stock must be kept in. No one is to go near the head of the bay. Those men will sleep until about noon, then go and drag out whatever they killed last night...what they can find." He looked at his sons. "That kind of hunter may well shoot at anything that moves. Don't let it be you."

"Yes sir," they chorused.

All that morning they moped around. There was no sign of life from the boat up the bay. Bit by bit, their play drew them up the hill away from the farm.

Finally Cliff said, "Let's go spy on them."

"We can't," answered his brother regretfully. "Dad said we mustn't."

"That wouldn't stop Peck's Bad Boy," countered Cliff scornfully.

Hal considered this. "It certainly wouldn't stop Hans and Fritz."

Off they went, sneaking through the woods almost like the Indian scouts they were so sure they resembled. They knew the land almost as well as they knew their own yard, and headed for a spot that overlooked the boat. There they lay, feeling hugely adventurous, talking in terse whispers.

At last, out of the aft cabin came their quarry, the two meat hunters (a derogatory term used sometimes to indicate someone who hunted for gain, and wasn't too fussy about his methods).

The two men conferred at length. At last they headed up the logging road, taking no guns.

The two boys looked at each other. "Let's go see what they got."

They ran along a sort of trail that led from the farm to the head of the bay, where it met the road a hundred yards or so from the water. There was no sign of the men. They hadn't gone far when they heard the sound of voices.

"I think we'd better go back," said Hal.

"What for?" asked Cliff. "They've not got their guns, and nobody could catch us in our own woods."

His brother was easily persuaded. On they went, their hearts beating wildly.

The two men were crouched by the side of the road, their backs towards the water. Their bare feet noiseless on the soft ground, the boys drew near. The men were field dressing two deer; a doe and a yearling fawn.

The brothers had always been taught that this was not proper game to shoot. They were disgusted. One of them incautiously scuffed a pebble. Both men leaped quickly to their feet.

"Damn it," snarled one. "What do you mean sneaking up on us like that?" He held a bloodstained knife in front of him menacingly.

"Aw, it's just a couple of kids," said his partner.

They relaxed a bit. The first one said, "Go on kids, scram out of here. We don't want no kids around."

"And stay scrammed," added his partner. "Anything that moves around here is likely to get a belly full of buckshot."

To Hal's amazement and awe, Cliff replied defiantly, "This is our woods, and we don't want you around here shooting our deer. And besides, you shouldn't shoot at anything unless you know what it is."

The nearest man took a step towards them, slowly, ominously. He raised the hand with the bloody knife. He was bearded, dirty and unkempt, and he looked as mean as any villain in their adventure books. He took another slow step towards them. That was enough for them. Their nerve broke and they tore into the woods as fast as they could run. Mocking laughter followed them.

There was no sign of pursuit, and they soon stopped running, but they kept on towards home. It was time to be seen again, anyhow.

"Imagine," fumed Cliff, "the nerve of that gut-shooter telling us to scram off our own road. We've got to do something."

All that day they schemed revenge. Nothing seemed feasible. What, they wondered, would so and so have done, as each thought of a favourite hero. Not that they were naive enough to think that life was like a comic book. Still, there must be some way to get back at villains, even in real life. But they couldn't think of one.

That evening at supper, there was a bit of a commotion at the table. A wasp landed on the fruit bowl, alarming the younger girls, then buzzed around making everyone duck.

Hal stopped eating. Inspiration! He cornered his brother the first moment he could. Greatly excited, he said, "Cliff, do you remember how the cabin on the boat was? How the hatches looked?"

"Sure I do. Aft cabin is lower than the wheelhouse. You step down into it. That's so you can see over it from where you're steering."

"I know that. How about the hatch on the sleeping cabin? Did you see how it worked?"

"Sure. It was just like Charlie's. A sliding hatch, and a sliding door. The hatch can't open when the door's locked. What do you want to know for?"

"I just want to make sure I remembered it right. Now, you know the big hornet's nest on the beach?. . ."

Cliff's face lit like a beacon. He was never slow at catching on. "Tomorrow morning just before daylight," he said softly. "That is such a great idea. I should have thought of it myself!"

His brother glowed at such a sincere compliment from a source not lavish with them.

Again there was little sleep for the brothers. They lay awake until after midnight going over the details of their plan, and listening to the gunshots, more widely spaced now as the hunters moved farther up the road. Even so, they were awake two hours before daybreak. They listened a while for shots, but none came, and they decided it was time. They took only moments to dress, climb out the window and down the log ends that were their "escape ladder." On the way down to the beach, they retrieved the items they had cached the previous evening: a flour sack, a large funnel, its neck plugged with a wad of rag, and the meat saw from the barn, having agreed it would be too risky to try for one of their father's handsaws.

A couple of minutes later, they were at the hornets' nest. Big as a basketball, it was constructed around the forked branch of a cedar tree. Not a tidy sphere as it should have been, but all lop-sided and lumpy. This was the fault of the two brothers. All summer, since they had first spotted it, they had sneaked up and thrown sticks or stones at it. As they had to be quite close to get a clear shot, there was considerable danger involved. Hornets don't like their nest disturbed, and have ways of dealing with those who are so rash as to attempt it. The boys would get in a few hasty throws, then run for their lives, for the hornets had soon learned to fly straight for any moving form. By summer's end, anything on two legs was attacked without mercy, no provocation needed. Even as far away as the farm, sometimes a hornet would sting someone for no reason at all.

Father laughed as he told me, "Those must have been the meanest hornets on the coast. They just hated people!"

And around this nest of ferocious creatures revolved their plan. With sweaty palms and pounding hearts they crept along the big log. Hornets sleep, but there are always a few guards around the entrance hole, and they will both fly and sting at any time of the night.

They could see the pale blob of the nest against the dark branches. Cliff had the saw. Hal carried the funnel by the spout in his right hand; his left was holding the flour sack. Silently as weasels they crept up on the huge nest. Hal raised slowly from his crouch. With a sudden swift movement, he jammed the funnel under the nest, covering the entrance and any guards that might be lurking around it. At the same time he threw the sack over the top and pressed it down over the nest. "Quick!" he whispered urgently. There was an angry hum from the nest. Cliff needed no urging; he was already sawing at the support limb. It took only a few strokes. Jack's tools were kept sharp. He trimmed off the projecting ends and they were ready.

"Don't you dast drop it," warned Cliff, as if his brother needed that caution. Never did Hal take such care with his footing. It was the longest couple of hundred feet he had ever walked. He could hear chewing sounds as the hornets started to tunnel out. He was holding the flour sack down tight over the nest, and it was vibrating; he could feel their rage. He knew that if they got out to the sack, they'd sting right through it at the warmth of his hand, and he tried to just hold it by the edge. Hornets get mean in the fall, as if they know they're going to die soon and they don't like it, and these hornets were already about as mean as they could be.

Now they had reached the logs that made a walkway out to the float where the boats were tied. Daylight was approaching rapidly. Already they felt terribly exposed in the early morning light. They ran lightly along the logs to the boat, expecting a challenge every moment. All was still. With infinite care they eased onto the stern of the old boat. Door and hatch were open. They were counting on the men being in the boat, tired from their night of pitlamping, and it seemed that this was so. The sound of snoring from below was immensely welcome. Until they heard it, they couldn't know for sure the men weren't on their way back, and that they wouldn't be caught in the act.

They studied the set-up of the hatch and door. It was as they had supposed—the standard for this type of opening. The sliding hatch had a downward projecting rim. When the door slid closed behind this, the latch couldn't be opened. This saved using two locks. The door closed with a hasp, and a tapered piece of wood hung on a cord, to be put in the hasp so that the door couldn't slide back and forth in rough weather. A practical arrangement, and one exactly suited to the plans of the two brothers.

The hum from the nest was becoming frantic as its population found itself trapped, and there was a continuous rasping of jaws biting and tearing at the nest walls.

"Now!" said Cliff, and his brother stood up and hurled the nest through the open hatchway on to the cabin floor, then seized the hatch edge and pulled it closed. Cliff slammed the door shut and secured the peg in the staple.

"Run!" he gasped, and run they did. As the door had slammed against the stop, there had sounded a slurred, "Wha' the hell. . ." and a louder "Hey," and as they raced up the bank, a crescendo of yells that sped their flight as if their feet had wings. In seconds they were at their vantage point, hunkered down behind a log. In the locked cabin, the shouts had turned to screams. There was the sound of breaking glass and collapsing cupboards, of loud thumps and violent crashes. Suddenly the door burst open with a crash and clatter as the stove was thrown through it. Right behind the stove came the two men, both trying to exit at the same time. There was a frantic scuffle as in some wild farce, then one was flung back by his stronger partner, who scrambled across the deck and plunged into the water with a mighty splash, followed closely by the other. The boys watched gleefully as their enemies splashed and cursed, slapping at their heads and ducking under the surface.

But Hal was having second thoughts about what they had done. He said tentatively, "You know Cliff, those hornets might have killed them."

"Yeah-h-h!" said his brother raptly. Cliff never was one to waste his time on thoughts of unmerited mercy.

"But," said father as he told the tale, "I began to get a very strange feeling. This whole affair had seemed at first like something from a funny paper. But I was realizing that it was actually quite different, something real. It might not turn out the way it always did in the stories."

Tapping his brother on the shoulder, he said, "Cliff."

Cliff turned, his face one huge grin. "What?"

Hal said slowly, hesitatingly, "I don't think it was such a good idea. They'll know who did it you know. They looked awful mean."

Cliff's face fell a little as he considered this. He started to answer, but stopped as there came a metallic click from behind them. They spun around in shock. There, standing at the foot of a tree a few yards away and a bit to one side, was their father! He had just slid the safety shut on his rifle. Leaning against the tree, he said quietly, "You boys are up early, aren't you?"

They couldn't answer. They were paralyzed. How had he known?

He continued easily, "Seems like quite a lot of activity down there so early in the morning. Bit cold for swimming."

He paused, seemed to consider. "Say boys, is that big hornets' nest still down there on the beach?"

"N-no sir," stammered Cliff. "I think it might be in the cabin on the boat."

"M-m-m." Jack rose to his feet, tucked the rifle under his arm. "You know, when I was crossing the field this morning, I noticed a deer standing by the fence. It never moved as I walked up to it. It was that big tame doe that hangs around the apple trees. It had taken a charge of shot in the face. Blinded it. Wonderful how she found her way by instinct back to the field." He paused for a moment, then said firmly, "Boys, I want you to go home. Right now, and no stopping. I know that you sometimes interpret my orders in your own way. Sometimes I allow you to do so. This is not one of those times. You will go directly home. Now."

When he spoke in that tone of voice, it was no time for disobedience. They went. They looked back once, but he was gone.

At home, their mother was up, the stove going. They were in an agony of uncertainty. What was their father doing? Almost certainly he was confronting the hunters. What would they do after what had happened? They listened for shots. What would he do to them when he got back, they wondered guiltily. They went as close to the woods as they dared, waiting. After what seemed hours, they were called for breakfast. Their father was seated at the table holding his cup of tea. He must have walked up the road, then down to the house on the far side; he probably wanted to leave them in suspense for a while.

He was saying, "I don't think they'll be here much longer. Just long enough to load a couple more deer. No use wasting them. No, I had no trouble with them. They had been softened up a bit you see. Seems they had a bit of an accident with a hornets' nest!"

He looked at the boys standing there listening, a small smile under his big moustache. "By the way, boys," he said jovially, "How would you fancy a fishing trip today? I think we deserve a day off!"

Chapter 15

Sweeny

THERE IS NO boy-and-his-dog story from Hidden Basin. Max was definitely Jack's dog, and though he could be persuaded to go fishing if his master was occupied at something that didn't require his advice, he was a serious dog who got into no scrapes. There is, however, a story of boys-and-their-pig.

Jack was determined to make the farm as self-sufficient as possible. They cured and preserved their own meat and fish, stored and preserved their own vegetables, preserved and dried fruits from the farm, and wild berries. And most particularly appreciated, they cured their own ham and bacon. This required raising three pigs each year.

Now, pigs are intelligent animals, but their short lives don't usually allow much time for personality development. However, this year, one of the pigs was different. From the day he arrived, he wasn't interested in associating with pigs; he wanted to be with people. The pen that had served to contain pigs in other years proved no impediment to this one. He was a genius at finding ways over, under or around any obstacle. Then he would locate the nearest human, and try to assist them in whatever they happened to be doing, all the while conversing in pig language, which is quite eloquent.

Of course, when he found a way to freedom, the other pigs would tag along and get into trouble, something for which all pigs have a talent. The boys would herd the other two pigs back to the pen, where they would settle down comfortably enough. But the third one was playful and hard to catch. They began to let him follow them about, and very soon became quite attached to him.

They called him Sweeny. He proved to be remarkably intelligent, learning quickly not to root in the vegetable patch, but assisting with enthusiasm in any other operation that required digging. He followed them wherever they went more faithfully than Max, the old dog, who usually felt that his place was with his master. Max and Sweeny soon came to like one another and could often be found curled up together as closely as a couple of hamsters. Jack observed all this with an interested eye, and gave his tacit permission by not forbidding it.

Sweeny was not allowed in the house, to his evident disgust. The boys swore that he was housebroken, a matter which they took on faith, and which may well have been true, but their mother drew the line at a pig in her parlour. Besides, he couldn't be broken of a taste for roses.

The girls didn't like Sweeny. He was too rough when he played and his skin was all coarse and bristly.

By July, Sweeny was big for his age, and could have been too much for the boys to handle, but he knew his manners, and caused them no trouble at all.

One day, their Uncle Fred arrived on one of his twice-yearly visits. He always brought presents, often strange and inappropriate ones. This time, for the boys, it was an unseasonal but very welcome gift of firecrackers. They hoarded these as a miser hoards gold, using them judiciously to frighten the chickens, the cow, Max, and most of all, their sisters, although this promptly brought the threat of confiscation. Next they were forbidden to alarm the livestock, and finally, Max. Then, one hot July day, somewhat disconsolate at the lack of victims, they were idling about at the upper limits of the farm, when Cliff had an idea.

"Let's give Sweeny a scare."

I don't know why the notion had taken so long to occur to them, but when it did, it was instantly welcome. They flipped a penny to see whose firecracker would be used, and Cliff lost. He selected one from his dwindling stock, lit it and threw it at Sweeny. It landed right in the middle of the pig's broad back, and exploded. But the surprise fizzled, if the firecracker did not. Sweeny was by now used to explosions, and though this one was nearer to him than the others, apart from an irritated grunt and a slight shake of his head, he continued to root in the ants' nest he had found.

Chagrined at the waste of a firecracker, they were about to continue on their way, when Hal said, "Cliff, look, what's that?" He was pointing at Sweeny's back. In the middle of it, almost invisible in the sunlight, was a little ring of blue that seemed to flicker a bit. Cliff looked, took a step closer. Suddenly, he shouted in alarm, "He's on fire!" And so he was. The oil on the skin, volatile in the sun's heat, had been lit by the explosion.

Sweeny lifted his head in annoyance. He said, "Hrumph?" and then "Hrumph!" as the fire grew larger and brighter. There was now a tinge of yellow to the flame, and a wisp or two of dark smoke rose from it.

"He's burning. We've got to put it out," cried Hal.

"How?"

"Smother it," came inspiration "Like Dad told us to if the grease in the pan caught fire!"

Sweeny just then made a sound which I will not attempt to transcribe, but which meant the situation now had his full attention. He tried to reach his back with his mouth but the attempt made him spin like a dog chasing its tail. Cliff tore off his shirt and ran to the pig's side, but was promptly knocked head over tail by the pig's spinning hindquarters. By this time, Sweeny was screaming with pain and rage.

"Do something!" shouted Hal to his older brother.

"I can't get near him! What can I do?" Cliff shouted back.

They looked in helpless horror as the flame grew brighter, fed by its own heat. A stream of black smoke was coming from it now.

"We'll have to knock him down," decided Cliff. "Come on, both together..." But before they could act, Sweeny came to his own decision. He took off across the field, squealing with every jump as only a pig can squeal.

They ran after him hopelessly, for they knew he could run faster than they could. Sweeny disappeared in a dip of ground far ahead; the squeals stopped. They dashed on as fast as they could run, fearing the worst, terrified at what they might find ahead. But as they burst into the little draw, they heard the sounds that are made only by a contented pig. And there was Sweeny, covered in mud, lying on his back in a little swamp that he had remembered but they had not. Twisting his back and shoulders to and fro in the mud, he greeted them with happy grunts. Weak with relief, they waded in with him, until they were all so covered in mud that they looked like three pigs together.

When they finally got a look at it, there was a round raw spot the size of a saucer on Sweeny's back. It healed quickly, although if you looked closely, you could see a mark.

They kept Sweeny's back smeared with mud, and discouraged him from visiting the house, and as a result, their father never noticed anything amiss.

All things have their season, and none more so than farm animals raised for food. Fall came, and cold weather, in which meat would keep. It may seem callous to use a pet for food, but there is small room for sentimentality on a farm. Sweeny met his fated end. He had lived a happy life, and died without pain; his death justified his living. Would that more of us could be as fortunate, or claim as much!

When a pig is killed, it is dipped in boiling water to remove the dirt and bristles. When this was done, a strange round bluish-red mark was revealed on the pig's back, much to the puzzlement of Jack and the men helping him. They examined it with care. No one had seen or heard of anything like it. Jack was not a man to be easily baffled. He cut the piece out and preserved it, but though he showed it to many and various experts over the next couple of years, the problem of the strange mark was never solved.

The sides of bacon were prepared and hung in the smokehouse to cure. In due time, they were brought into the house, where they would hang in the loft with the rest of the meat until they were needed. Now the first slices of new bacon were cut, and the smell of their frying filled the house. When it was served, Hal sat there looking at his plate.

He told me: "There is no smell like it, and as a kid I could never get enough bacon. But this time it was different. I thought of Sweeny, and I knew if I took a bite of that bacon, I wouldn't be able to swallow it."

So he said, "I don't think I want any bacon."

Cliff looked up, said eagerly, "If you're not going to eat it, can I have it?"

I remember once when father had finished telling this story, a listener protested skeptically, "Do you mean to tell us that pig was so smart it knew enough to put fire out with water?"

"No," answered father, "I didn't say that."

"Well, how do you explain it then?"

"Very easily," countered father. "As anyone should be able to see, a pig's answer to any problem is mud!"

Chapter 16

Uncle Fred

JACK'S BROTHER FRED, who had been the cause of the problem with his gift of firecrackers, is himself worth a second look. It would scarcely be possible for two brothers to be more dissimilar. Jack was of average height, broad and strong, with dark moustache and hair. Fred was six foot four, and lean as a rake handle. His long skinny legs and arms, though surprisingly strong, seemed oddly stiff and awkward. He had sandy hair and a small tidy moustache. In temperament, Jack had a somewhat volatile nature, quick and unpredictable, with a wide-ranging curiosity. His brother took life much more seriously. I don't know which was the older, but it certainly seemed to be Fred. In fact, as father put it: "Uncle Fred was born old."

As I said, Fred took life very seriously. His views were narrow, but very concentrated. It was easy to imagine him as a religious fanatic, a great artist blind to criticism, a leader of lost causes. His honesty was proverbial. He was the sort who would walk twenty miles through snow to correct a mistake in change of a few pennies, no matter how the balance lay.

Uncle Fred's type seems to be fading out of humanity (or so I hope, for their unswerving conviction that they know what is right has been the cause of much misery). He used to visit us when I was in my late teens. By then, he was nearly eighty. Tall, thin as a stick, serious. A bit of grey in his hair, none in his moustache. Neatly dressed—I might say nattily—quite sure that he was attractive to any woman of sufficient discrimination. Some sense of humour, but what he laughed at no one else found funny. Unconscious, or unconcerned, that we had heard his anecdotes many times, and that few of them were of interest even on first hearing. They did not improve with age, nor vary by so much as a word.

He usually came once a year, perhaps twice, from his farm in the northern interior of BC, to stay for three days each time. On this particular trip, his purpose was to buy a new watch in Vancouver to replace the big silver one he had owned for something like fifty years and which he regarded as having become unreliable. Fred attached a peculiar importance to an accurate knowledge of the passage of time. I say peculiar, because with his lifestyle, one would think that the rising and setting of the sun would serve his needs. But no, Fred had to know the time to within a minute, at the very least. He wound his watch at precisely the same time, morning and night, and kept it on a stand near his bed (where the temperature was constant) when not in use. It was always placed with twelve o'clock pointing north, and he had it checked yearly by a watchmaker he considered reliable. But now it was showing signs of age, and he had bought a new one, guaranteed accurate, which he displayed to us with much satisfaction, along with a recital of its virtues.

The three days passed, rather slowly, and Uncle Fred went on his way, not to be seen for, we assumed, another six months—for in this, as in all things, he was invariant. Imagine then our surprise when he appeared at our door after only a little more than a month.

That he was in a state of indignation was immediately apparent, and Uncle Fred indignant was not someone to be taken lightly! He wasted no time in telling us the reason for his return.

"You know that watch I came down for last time I was here? Well, you won't believe this, I know, but it's God's truth just the same. The first month I had it, it lost thirty-seven seconds! Thirty seven. I checked it with the radio. Now, what do you think of that? A new watch, guaranteed accurate. Thirty-seven seconds!"

Our awed silence seemed to mollify him by an amount just barely perceptible. He could never have believed that we would have been content with a timepiece that lost no more than thirty-seven seconds a day!

His fury mounted as he continued the catalogue of his wrongs.

"Of course, I came right back as soon as I had given it a fair trial. And do you know what that fellow at the store had the cheek to tell me? He said that thirty-seven seconds lost was very good accuracy. He said that I couldn't expect much better than that. Well, I told him! 'Call yourself a watchmaker,' I said. 'I don't know how you could have the nerve to take the money!' Oh, I guess I put a flea in his ear. Watchmaker! There was a time when a man like that wouldn't have been allowed to repair a wheelbarrow. There's no pride in doing a job anymore..."

Well, I'll leave it at that. Fred didn't. We eventually learned that he had left the offending watch there, and that he was to be notified when it could be relied on. I presume the chastened watchmaker delivered a suitable timepiece eventually, for I can't recall hearing any more on the subject. But this should give you some idea of Uncle Fred.

Hal and Cliff were both awed and fascinated by him, for when someone takes themselves seriously enough, it often serves to convince others of their importance. Besides, Fred had joined the Klondike gold rush, and had actually gone down the Yukon River on a raft! To the brothers, this gave him an aura of adventure that more than made up for his faults, chief of which—in their eyes—was his complete inability to tell an interesting story. For though he had found no gold, and had come back poorer by far than he had started, he had had adventures, there was no doubt of that. But the tales he recounted had all to do with how he had pointed out this person's error in supplies packed, or that person's failure to do something else adequately. Or he would give detailed observations on the suitability of the land he had seen for farming, or the amount and kind of crops it could be expected to produce—all in a voice that neither rose nor fell, and which invariably produced yawns in his audience. But in spite of all that, his angular frame and sober demeanor commanded their respect. Until the day he decided to go fishing in one of the island lakes. Alone.

He made this decision at about three o'clock in the afternoon, which would give him six hours or so of daylight. Jack said, "Take one of the boys. He can show you around."

But Fred wouldn't hear of it. He was, in fact, indignant.

"Show me around! Do you think a man who's been to the Klondike needs 'showing around' a little piece of land like this? I will find my own way, thank you."

When he had gone stalking stiffly off, his brother growled, "Klondike! If he hadn't had someone to follow, he'd have ended up at the South Pole!"

His sons were shocked at such irreverence.

The afternoon waned; evening became dusk, then dark. There was no sign of Fred. Jack had forbidden the boys to go looking for

him, saying gruffly, "He asked for it. Now let him suffer the consequences." But he was worried just the same. He woke them at daybreak to go looking, saying, "He's just fool enough to have walked off a rock and broken one of those skinny legs of his."

They went first to the lake Fred had intended to try. There was a fairly definite trail, and then the old road. It seemed unlikely that he would stray far from them. It wasn't long before they saw the lake through the trees, and then the clear place by the lake edge, where grew only moss, small bushes and a few scattered pine trees. And there was Uncle Fred, about twenty feet from the ground, near the top of one of the little trees! With his long legs bent one way and his elbows another, he looked like some huge, ungainly insect from an alien star.

Jack walked towards him, stood with hands on hips.

"What," he asked in amazement "are you doing up there?"

His brother unfolded, and descended stiffly to the ground. He said accusingly.

"Well, I must say, it took you long enough."

"We came when it got light enough to see. Now, what in thunder were you playing at?"

Fred answered defensively, "I was not playing. When you are surrounded by wolves, a tree is the only safe place to be."

Cliff and Hal looked at each other in wonder. Wolves?

"Wolves?" said Jack, his voice incredulous. "What do you mean, wolves? There are no wolves on Nelson Island. What are you talking about?"

"I'm talking about wolves. Do you think I don't know the sound of a wolf when I hear one? They were howling all night. The sound was enough to make your flesh creep! I knew I couldn't make it back through the woods, so I..." He held up one hand. "Listen, there's one now!"

The long mournful cry of a loon echoed over the lake.

Jack roared with laughter, while his brother looked at him with increasing indignation.

"What are you laughing for, you fool? A pack of wolves in the night is no laughing matter."

"You greenhorn, that's a loon. Haven't you heard a loon before?" His teeth flashed under his dark moustache as he grinned broadly in derision.

His brother's face flushed brick red from collar to hairline.

"Are you trying to tell me some sort of duck made that noise? I don't believe it!"

"I'm trying to tell you," said Jack derisively, "that you spent the night in that tree because of a bird about the size of a chicken. Now come on home. We've wasted enough time."

The word "chicken," coupled with the look on Uncle Fred's face, was too much for the boys. They fled for the woods, but the laughter they had been suppressing exploded before they got there. It just was not humanly possible to hold it in.

Chapter 17

Fish Story

OLD CHARLIE PROFESSED to be contemptuous of trout fishing. "Little fish," he would say scornfully, "good for squaws to catch. A man fishes for salmon. One fish, enough for whole tribe to eat."

But the brothers soon found out that the old man was not only a most enthusiastic angler, but that in practice he took quite a different approach. But if they accused him of contradicting himself, he would explain disdainfully that the fault lay in their immature understanding, and that it would be a waste of effort to try to put them right.

For the fact was that the one drawback to fishing with the old Indian lay in his refusal to leave a pool if he had detected even one fish in it, however small. And to make matters worse, he ridiculed their obsession with catching big trout, completely oblivious to his pronouncement regarding salmon.

"Big trout," he would snort, "always the big trout. Foolish boys. Small trout better to eat, more tender. Eat bones and all. Big trout, probably wormy. Boys run about all day, catch nothing, come home tired, hungry. Old Indian come home, have frying pan full of nice little trout, good to eat."

This criticism conveniently ignored the fact that the boys, usually being the first to arrive at a new pool, almost always caught more trout than Charlie, due to his spending so much time at the previous pool.

In spite of all this, they passionately loved fishing with the old man, though the opportunity came far too seldom.

Their favorite place to fish was West Lake, the big lake at the north end of Nelson Island. About six miles long, approximately the same distance from Hidden Basin, it was full of fish, some of them of legendary size. There was a heavy old flat-bottomed skiff in the near end of it, once used by the MacConville camp, now abandoned. This allowed them access to the first third of the lake, which held quite enough places to fish, even during a long summer day.

They went there—sometimes the whole family on a picnic; usually just Hal and Cliff by themselves, as often as they could get permission.

They had never gone there with Charlie, though this was one of their keenest ambitions. Thus, late in the spring of 1907, when his old boat came chuffing up the bay to their float, they had already laid their plans carefully.

After an unusually short greeting, which caused their father to eye them speculatively, they left the two men to exchange news while they made their way quickly up to the vegetable patch. They didn't show up at the house until supper time; though responding dutifully to Charlie's jokes, they were obviously tired and preoccupied.

At last, their father swung around in his chair to face them, saying sternly, "All right now. You boys have been up to something. Let's have it."

Cliff spoke, as the elder of the two, compelled not so much by desire as by the perceived obligation of his extra two years.

"We hilled the potatoes, sir."

Lifted eyebrows, "All of them?"

"Yes sir."

"The carrots need thinning."

"We did them, and we staked the peas."

"Did you indeed! Of course, there are the turnips." His eyes were twinkling. He knew quite well what they were up to. Old Charlie was openly grinning.

The boys looked glum. There were a lot of turnips to be weeded and thinned. Many long rows destined to be stored for winter feed for the stock. Their father, having had his joke, relented.

"I don't suppose you would rather go fishing tomorrow instead?"

"Yes sir!"

"I think Charlie here would like to visit West Lake. He was showing me a lure he's made up, especially good for lake trout. I guess we can spare you for one day."

They could scarcely believe what they were hearing. This was a dream come true. Their father's leniency when it came to allowing them to spend time with their friend was probably not entirely without motive, for the old man was a mine of practical information about life on the Coast.

They spent the evening seeing to their fishing rods, sharpening hooks, repairing homemade lures, and listening to their parents' conversation with Charlie. And always, when they were near enough to overhear, he stayed in character.

Next morning dawned fair and calm. They were awake long before the rest of the family, and made themselves a hurried breakfast. Charlie was fast asleep when they peered through the cabin door, for he saw no cause to rise early without a good reason. He slept fully clothed, under a single blanket. He seemed to sense that they were there, for he was awake before they spoke.

"Hmf. Boys early. Fish all be asleep yet."

"Aw, Charlie," said Cliff, "you know that the best fishing is in the early morning."

"Old Indian know no such thing. Only fish know when fishing best. Might be noon. Might be anytime."

Cliff didn't argue. They all knew that both were right to some extent. They drew back to let Charlie out onto the deck. There was a bucket there, half filled with big purple-shelled sea urchins kept alive in salt water. They were easy to find at low tide around the kelp patches. Reaching down, Charlie took one out, broke the shell in half and sucked out the contents. He did this twice more, then noticing the expression on the boys faces, he picked out one more, broke it and—grinning wickedly—offered half to each.

"Boys want some breakfast?"

Cliff, always daring, accepted his, and sucked out the contents as he had seen Charlie do. But Hal took one glance at the bilious-looking mess in the broken shell and refused firmly. Nor could he be persuaded to reconsider.

"Come on" urged his brother, "it's not bad. It won't hurt you to try it."

"If you think it's so great, you can have my half too."

Charlie was listening, highly amused; but tiring of the game, he finished the last half himself, to the relief of the brothers. They never knew what the old man was apt to come up with in the way of strange things to eat. He had, at one time or another, offered them octopus, dogfish, skate, coon, dog, crow, and several varieties of ducks not considered edible by their father because their meat smelled and tasted of fish.

It is a strange fact that most of the early European settlers on the Coast were extremely conservative in their choice of wild food. They learned very little from the native peoples, and indeed, many of them came very near to starving, while living near beaches teeming with edible life!

Charlie picked up a stick around which was wound a few dozen feet of strong fishing line. From where it hung by a piece of string from the guy-wire, he selected one of several pieces of dried meat of uncertain origin, so unsavory of aspect that even the gulls weren't interested in them.

"Well, what boys standing around for? Let's go get fish."

They dashed back to the house for their tackle and the lunches their mother had left for them and set off after Charlie, already part-way up the shore.

The walk to West Lake along the MacConville ox-road was an easy one, for the saplings hadn't yet had time to grow, and they reached the lake without incident.

Well, almost without. The road went by the edge of Mackechnie Lake and as they were walking along, Cliff picked a salmonberry and tossed it into the water. A little trout swirled up after it as it slowly sank, nudging the bright orange berry. They could see it twitch in the clear lake water.

Charlie had almost to be dragged away from the spot. He could see no reason at all to go further when there were obviously fish to be caught there.

"Boys go. Leave old Indian here. Boys crazy. Walk miles, leave fish behind, go to big lake, too big, too deep, can't find fish. Boys go, old Indian happy here."

But they finally prevailed on him, using every persuasion they could imagine, plus the promise that they would stop there on the way back, but it was probably Hal's plea that turned the trick.

"But Charlie, we need you along to tell us how to get those big lake trout. We'll never catch any if you don't come!"

Now this was not strictly the truth, for they knew quite well how to fish for the big trout, but the appeal to Charlie's vanity was successful. He turned his back on the little lake—however reluctantly—and set off with them once more, but not without muttering imprecations about "big trout, foolish boys," and much else of similar import.

They found the skiff where they had tied it the previous fall, full of water of course, but that was easily remedied with the help of a couple of gallon fruit cans from the litter left by the loggers. The skiff had three seats: one in the bow, one for the oarsman, and a large stern seat which they conceded to Charlie as the seat of honor, being both roomy and comfortable.

They set off along the west shore, Cliff rowing. The morning sun was warm. The water was like a sheet of glass, only more transparent.

It held in it the green of the trees along the unlogged rocky shore, and in its depths was mystery, as the bottom sloped into regions unplumbed.

They got out their tackle and began to fish. The boys had poles for rods, carefully chosen from springy saplings, lovingly scraped and polished, stored for the winter in the attic. Charlie preferred to have his line in his hand, and scoffed at their rods as impractical.

"How you get big fish in boat on little thin sticks?" he queried, mockingly.

They each had their own can of worms dug from the rich soil where the lakehead camp had been, as well as various spoons and lures brought by the boys.

But the fishing was slow. Their lines looked like rope in the clear water. Surely no fish would be foolish enough to be deceived. They drifted along, propelled now and then by a few strokes of the oars. There were many places to try: rocky points, the mouths of little streams, enticing bays, rock faces where the bottom couldn't be seen an arm's length from shore. The boys spent much of the time talking of big fish that had been rumoured, seen, lost or almost caught. Charley listened to all this with skeptical toleration. Finally he had enough.

"Big fish," he scoffed, "always big fish. Boys don't know what big fish is. Just talk about little tiny minnows. Listen to Old Indian, boys learn about big fish!"

"Go on, Charlie, tell us a story."

"Yeah, Charlie, please."

The old man, settling himself comfortably on his seat, commenced: "Boys know that old Indian's tribe mountain people. Were very first people, before all others. Live in valley high in mountains, beside lake. What boys don't know, because Old Indian never tell them, is that lake is home of Fish-god, Uglukaluk.

"Uglukaluk live in lake. Lake very deep, so deep it go all the way down to salt chuck, so Fish-god can go back and forth when he want."

"I suddenly had this picture in my mind," recalled father, "of the mountain sort of sliced away, with the lake looking something like a funnel with a long spout going down to the ocean. And I realized from helping to pour things like milk or gas into funnels at home, that water won't stay in a funnel when the can is full."

"But Charlie," he objected, "wouldn't the lake water all run down into the ocean?"

"Yeah," echoed Cliff in sudden comprehension, "how would the water stay up there in the lake?"

Charlie's face lost all expression, and his gaze became unfocussed as he carefully considered this unexpected objection for a few seconds. But animation returned quickly and he gazed with ostentatious superiority over their heads.

"What did Old Indian do bad?" he appealed to the sky, "he get dragged away from nice little lake with schools of fish, all hungry, and have to sit here on hard seat on lake with no fish, and then not get to tell story without silly interruption?"

He lowered his gaze, eyeing them sternly. "Even foolish boys who know nothing, should know that if god say water stay in lake, it stay!"

And with that, he leaned back with the look of satisfaction that always followed a point scored.

They were properly humbled. When a few minutes had passed with no resumption of the story, "Aw come on Charlie, we're sorry we interrupted you."

"Yeah Charlie, we won't do it again."

When he was certain they were properly contrite, he recommenced.

"Well, where Fish-god live, even boys can see that there must be big fish. Bigger than anywhere. The people know this, but they can't catch. Fish too big. Now when Old Indian is young man, he strong, strong like bear. Smart too, like coyote. He make line braided from wolverine hide, can't break. Make hook from bone of bear. Bait with whole deer liver. Go to end of lake where creek go out, put down bait, right to bottom. Wait long time. Finally feel line go heavy, pull hard. Hook pointed sharp at both ends, swing in middle. Swing crosswise, dig into fish's mouth, can't come loose. Fish go fast, but Old Indian too smart, have line tied to tree. Water boil like Skookumchuck on big tide. Finally fish tired, pull him up. Big! Big as rowboat. Bigger. Old Indian untie line from tree, fish lie in water gasping. Throw loop of line over snout, pull into corners of mouth, take one end each hand. Jump on fish, ride him down lake, steer like a horse. Go right up creek by village, jump off, tie line to tree. People all come around, have big feast. Enough fish to last whole tribe for week. Now that—big fish."

He stopped, looked at them expectantly. Gradually, his expression changed to one of concern. Leaning forward, he asked plaintively, "Boys believe old Indian, don't they?"

Cliff said firmly "No Charlie," while his brother added, "Nope. Not a word."

For a moment the look of hurt surprise on the old man's face made them want to recant, but then it changed to a broad grin as he leaned back in the seat.

"Huh. Boys not as stupid as they look. Might be some hope yet!"

"Well, Charlie," encouraged Hal, "it was a great story anyhow, wasn't it, Cliff?"

"Sure was."

There was silence for a few minutes, then Cliff spoke. "Why did you leave, Charlie? Didn't you like living there?"

For a while there was no answer, as the old man carefully checked his bait, discarded it and replaced it with another. When he at last replied, it was quietly, in the tone of one who remembers things long past, seldom recalled.

"Not many people left. All killed in wars. Ones left, find valley, hide there. Learn to make fire without smoke, small fire. Keep no dogs. Dogs bark. Go different path every time leave valley. Make no trail. But valley small, only enough to eat for small village. The old people, the wise ones, decide how many people can live there. No more, not ever. If one die, young one can live. Others sent back where they come from."

From Cliff in horror, "You mean they killed all the babies?"

But his brother cut in, "You know what Dad was reading to us about last year? About that fellow called Malthus, and how people will have so many babies that they'll all starve to death? This is just like that, really." And to Charlie, "But how did you come to leave? You haven't told us that yet."

And the old man resumed his story in that same remote voice.

"When Charlie a young man, he have woman. And woman have baby. Have son. Too many now. No one ready to go. Charlie say 'Come, we leave,' but woman not want to leave. So Charlie leave so son can live. But swear mighty oath to never tell where village is."

The brothers were deeply affected by this revelation of their friend's past. It brought them new perceptions. They had never really thought of the old man as being an adult, as having had a family, or sorrows in his life. In spite of his knowledge and wisdom, he somehow had appeared to them as essentially an older version of themselves. Now this had changed, and they felt vaguely uneasy about it, but worse was yet to come.

"Did you ever go back, Charlie?" asked Cliff. "You must have gone back to see your son."

This time, the silence lasted so long that they thought he wasn't going to answer. His eyes were hooded, and he seemed to be looking inwardly at things best forgotten. Then, so quietly they could scarcely hear, he replied, "Old Indian go back many years ago. Stay away six, maybe eight years, then go back. In fall, weather good, berries ripe, fish in creeks, deer, goats, bears, everything fat, everything living. Climb up to valley, go along shore of lake. No sound of people, no tracks of people. Go to village, lodges all down, broke by snow. No people, just bones. Every lodge just bones. Someone go maybe, then come back. Bring sickness. Old Indian leave, not go back again."

They were horrified. They sat there silently. What was there to say? They wanted desperately to say something to comfort the old man. They were old enough to realize that they could not.

Charlie broke the silence. He stretched hugely, as if awakening from a nap.

"Boys look like they just lost biggest fish in lake. Or have bellyache," he said mockingly. Then, more seriously, "Not feel bad. Was a long time ago. Most be dead now anyhow. Everything die, sooner or later."

He took a leather pouch out of his shirt pocket, where it had been carefully buttoned in. Undoing the drawstring, he said, "Old Indian tired of sitting in the sun doing nothing. Time to catch fish."

He withdrew something from the pouch, held it out in the palm of his hand for their inspection. They had both been sitting on the middle seat while he had been telling the story, and now they leaned forward curiously to see what he held. It was a lure, but a lure such as they had never seen before.

"This," he announced proudly, "Fish-god teach Charlie's people how to make. Not easy. Hard to get right things. Not use until have to."

He pointed with a sliver of wood to various parts of the lure.

"This—feather from kingfisher. This—from head of sawbill duck (merganser). This—chest feather from crane (blue heron). This—from tail of fisher. This bit—from old shag (cormorant). And this bit—from dipper. Tips of otter whisker, and claw of mink. Tied with sinew from leg of crane."

He touched the hook lightly with the splinter.

"Hook should be carved from wolverine bone, but Charlie make improvement. Iron hook good; better than bone. Charlie modern Indian, keep up with times."

It lay there in his hand, looking rather shapeless. Much care had obviously gone into making it. Some materials were tied together, some linked with bits of fine sinew, so that they could move freely.

"Have you ever caught a fish on it, Charlie?" asked Hal.

"No-oo, not yet. But it work, you'll see."

"I think a fish would rather have a worm than dead fur and feathers," judged skeptical Cliff.

The old man tied it to his line very carefully, having removed the other hook and thrown its limp worm overboard.

He dropped the lure into the water, let it sink a few inches. Wrapping the line in his fingers, he began to move them slightly. And suddenly, it came alive! Each little bit of fur and feather, whisker and claw, moved in its own fashion. Some suggested gills, some fins. The brothers watched fascinated. They felt now that no fish could fail to want an object so enticing. Unwrapping more line from his fingers, Charlie began to lower it slowly into the clear water.

They had stopped in a slight cove just past a rockface where the water was black with depth. Beneath them, a bottom of broken rock sloped sharply downward. A big fir tree had fallen into the water here uncounted years ago. It was submerged for half its length; the bark was gone from it, and one bone-hard limb stuck out of the water a few feet away. A dozen or so feet down, others could be seen, reaching out like groping arms. A sunken tree offers shelter to fish, including minnows which serve as food for larger fish. It also offers a place of interest to the fisherman, a landmark on an otherwise featureless shoreline.

The sun was just high enough to provide the best conditions for seeing. At about thirty feet of depth, the bottom was still visible, but directly underneath the skiff, the slight greenish tinge of the water darkened to almost black, and they could not see bottom.

As the lure drifted slowly towards the bottom, Hal noticed the big sunken branch beneath them.

"Charlie," he cautioned. "Maybe we ought to move away a bit. If you get a fish on here, he might tangle around a branch."

"This good place," said Charlie firmly. "Line strong, hook strong. Old Indian have fish in boat before he know what happen."

Charlie didn't believe in the concept of giving the fish a chance, thinking it to be further evidence, if more was needed, of the essential foolishness of the newcomers. He fished to get fish, however much he may have enjoyed the doing.

The boys had pulled in their lines and laid their rods across the seats. The skiff was wide and stable enough that all of them could look over the same side without it tipping. They sprawled in the bottom, chins on the gunwale, eyes close to the water for the best vision. Charlie was kneeling on his seat, supporting himself with his elbows. They were all watching the lure intently. Hal was the first to see it.

"What's that?" he whispered. "That" was a strange white thing, roughly diamond shaped, that had appeared just then almost directly beneath the lure.

Then all three of them realized what it was, and said the same words at the same time: "Fish! Big fish!"

For the white object was the open mouth of a huge trout coming almost straight up out of the deep water, its black shape blending into the background, but the white inside of its gaping mouth plain to see. The lure disappeared as the fish swallowed it, and they saw its great black back and a flash of silver belly as it turned to go back into the depths. The power of its thrusting tail tore the loosely held line from Charlie's hand, and almost pulled the stick around which it was wound out of the boat. But the old man could move fast when he needed to, and a desperate grab saved it. He pulled strongly; for a moment the big fish resisted, then it turned and dashed up and inshore, trying to reach the shelter of the sunken tree. Charlie retrieved line frantically, but he wasn't fast enough to keep the fish from going over the branch. When the line came tight, the trout lunged for the bottom again, going under the branch this time. When the line again came tight, the fish's momentum sheered it to one side, and then over the line.

It dove again for deep water; the springy crossed lines stopped it, but didn't provide enough resistance for it to pull loose or break the line. It hung there thrashing about, alternately showing black and silver. All this took only seconds.

Charlie kneeled there, mouth open in shock. Then he said, slowly and distinctly, and without a trace of his "Old Indian" dialect, "That's the biggest trout that I've ever seen in my whole life!"

That was the only time they ever heard him refer to himself in the first person.

He realized his slip instantly, and flashed a glance at the boys to see if they had noticed, but they appeared to be totally absorbed in watching the struggles of the huge trout. He gave his attention to the line in his hand, and pulled it tentatively, but it had slid along the branch until it stuck under a sliver of wood; the only result was that the skiff drifted over until it was directly above the sunken branch and the fish. He let the line go slack, but it was now fouled so tightly that the pull exerted by the fish wasn't enough to free it.

The brothers looked at him expectantly, waiting to see what he would try next, but he simply looked back at them, shrugging his shoulders and spreading his hands helplessly.

In a flash of motion, Cliff shed his clothes and slipped over the side like an otter from a log. At this time he was the better swimmer of the two, equally adept on top of the water or under it. He dove in a cloud of bubbles which obscured the view, and they were forced to wait in breathless excitement.

At last, he surfaced, treading water, breathing deeply, and shook his hair back out of his face.

Charlie took a few quick pulls on the line, but it was slack. Hal said, "It got away," voice shaking with emotion. Cliff hesitated a moment, then, "Well, no, not exactly." He looked up at them and continued easily, "You know, Charlie, how you said that big fish aren't any good? Well, I got thinking about that, and I figured you wouldn't want that big old tough trout and that I'd better save your magic lure. So I slipped it out of the trout's mouth and let him go. I knew that's what you would want."

Rising to his feet, the old man looked down at him. He seemed to grow larger, to somehow expand as he stood there. His face darkened perceptibly.

"You lose fish? YOU LET FISH GO?!!"

Father reminisced, "I thought he was going to explode, that something awful was going to happen. We'd never seen him mad before. I mean not really in a rage. I sat there in awe, wondering what he would do to Cliff."

But just as Charlie opened his mouth to continue, Cliff held his hand up, the lure between his fingers. The curve of the hook had been pulled almost straight by the struggling fish. Instead of the tough steel a good hook should have, it had been made of soft iron.

Charlie glared at it, mouth still open. Then he relaxed, settled his features, resumed his normal size. Regaining his seat, he pulled in the line, held the lure in his hand, sat there looking at it in disgust. He shook his head.

"Fish-god punish Old Indian. Not like change. Should have been wolverine bone. That not bend. Old Indian lazy, not want to go find wolverine. Lose biggest trout ever have on line. Serve him right, know White man things no good!"

He looked at Cliff, who had climbed back into the skiff and was pulling on his pants. His face was grim as he said severely, "In old days, if boy played trick like that on Old Indian, he get cut up into little pieces, use for fish bait." He made motions with his hand suggestive of chopping something into small pieces. But then his eyes began to twinkle, the stern expression turned to a grin.

"Pretty good joke," he said approvingly. He began to chuckle. "Heh-heh-heh... good joke!"

The chuckle became a hearty laugh, so infectious that they joined in, and as they did, the sun seemed to shine a bit more brightly.

They talked over what had just happened, the boys excitedly, Charlie philosophically, each giving his version of the affair. Charlie put the point of the hook against the side of the skiff and bent it roughly back into a curve. He inspected it critically.

"Good enough" he pronounced. "Will catch fish. But no more treetops. Boys take Old Indian over top of tree, over branches." He accused, "not even he can catch big fish in branches."

They didn't defend themselves. They were used to Charlie's ways, and they knew that when he changed the facts around like that, there was no arguing with him. If they pointed out that he had said just the opposite only a little while ago or that he had things backwards, he would just look at them. His expression would make them feel that he was very disappointed in them, and they always ended up feeling that they were somehow in the wrong.

They drifted along the shore, giving a stroke or two of the oars every few minutes. Cliff caught a trout, a small one about ten inches long. Then another a bit larger. Then Hal landed one about the same size. Over the next half hour or so, they caught about a dozen more between the two of them. Charlie made disparaging remarks each time they hauled in one of the little trout. He had caught nothing. His lure was too large for fish of that size.

As Cliff pulled in another nice trout about a foot long, Charlie suggested, "Maybe boys have enough bait now?"

He had let his lure trail behind the boat at the full length of his line, using no sinker. His back was turned to it. There came the sound of a fish jumping, then once more, and again they heard the splash of a big trout falling back in the water.

Hal shouted, "Charlie, I think you've got a fish on!"

Charlie looked around in surprise. The line jerked at his hand.

"FISH!" he yelled, and began to retrieve his line hand over hand as fast as he could pull. Taken by surprise, the fish had no time to resist, and in seconds, was out of the water and thrashing about in the bottom of the skiff. Charlie promptly dispatched it with a bit of branch kept for that purpose. He held the trout up proudly. It was a beauty, one of the big plump West Lake cutthroats about twenty inches long. The boys exclaimed in admiration.

"Not bad," judged Charlie critically. "Guess Old Indian keep." His face was one big smile of satisfaction.

He took the hook from the fish's mouth, inspected the lure, tossed it back into the water, and leaned back comfortably.

The brothers caught some more of the smaller fish, but Charlie disdained to comment. He merely splashed a bit of water on his fish now and them, ostensibly to keep it from drying out, but the boys were not so easily fooled.

And then the old man caught another fish, in almost exactly the same way, but slightly larger than the first. He held it up eloquently, his expression a mask of satisfaction. When it had been admired sufficiently, he placed it carefully beside the other one. He looked up at the sun, now approaching the mountains, and then at the end of the lake where they had started from, nearly a mile away.

"Time to go home" he said, and began to roll his line up around its stick. As the boys protested,

"Long way to go," he said firmly.

They knew enough not to argue.

When, on the way back home, they came to the little lake by the roadside, there was still an hour or more of daylight left to them. The boys put down their burdens of fish, (Charlie of course, carried nothing) and began to get their rods ready. When he heard no footsteps, Charlie turned to see what they were up to.

"Why boys stop here?"

"Don't you remember?" asked Cliff in surprise. "You wanted to stay here and fish, and we promised to stop on the way back. Are you too tired?"

"Charlie not get tired. Boys get tired." He gestured towards the lake.

"Little lake, have little fish. Old Indian catch big fish," he said grandly.

He turned and continued on down the road, not looking back to see it they followed or not. They hurried to catch up with him.

That night as they lay awake in bed, going over the happenings of the day, Hal asked his brother somewhat tentatively, "Did you hear what Charlie said when he got the big fish on? I mean how he said it?"

"Yeah" replied Cliff, and after a moments hesitation "I knew he could speak properly if he wanted to. I heard him talking to Dad. I didn't want to say anything to you. I thought you might not like it."

"I heard him too," laughed his younger brother, "and I didn't tell you for the same reason."

They never spoke of it again.

Chapter 18

Long Hard Winter

IN SPITE OF JACK'S ATTEMPTS to downplay its importance, the need for money was always with them. They were too civilized to be able to find satisfaction at the level of mere subsistence, and they were not far enough above the primitive to have any desire to go back to it. There were so many things they needed, things they had come to regard not as luxuries but as necessities.

Clothes and shoes and linens, sugar and salt, cocoa and tea, flour and dried fruit and spices. Fuel and harness, grain for the chickens, wire and nails and coal for the forge. On, and on, and on...

It was possible to make, find, substitute or do without these things, as Jack had once suggested, but at the cost of much time and tedious effort, and a mind-set that only dire necessity could instill.

Jack worked and schemed, schemed, and worked even harder, as if by sheer power of will he could transmute work into gold. For his scheming never paid off. He bought land, and couldn't sell it; it became a drain as taxes rose. He had chosen land he liked, but it wasn't farmland, and already the flow of population was towards the towns and cities. It would be generations before land of that sort would become valuable. He had owned land near what is now downtown Vancouver. He let it go rather than pay the taxes.

"That place will never amount to anything," he predicted confidently. "Why would it? All it is is mud, mosquitoes, and murky river water!"

There was no call now on Nelson Island for bridge-building or road making, nor was there money to be made as a carpenter. Most people did their own building, to save money. There was occasional work at the quarry in nearby Granite Bay, and he became friends with the quarry owner. But the work was sporadic. He handlogged from time to time. The work was hard, but he didn't mind that. The problem was that all the easy trees to handlog, the ones that would slide into the water as soon as they were felled, had been taken. The ones that were left, though often better timber, were on flatter ground, and required much work to get out. The only tools allowed were those a man could carry, which ruled out any form of winch or power. To get the trees to slide, the bark must be peeled off, leaving the hard, slippery surface of the wood. But this had to be done in the early months of spring, for in the winter, the bark couldn't be stripped off, as the new growth of wood had not yet loosened it. And as spring gave way to summer, that same new wood became sticky and glue-like, and the logs wouldn't move. And this period when hand logging on almost flat ground was possible, exactly coincided with the time when a farm needs all the work a man can give it. In short, you can farm in the spring, or you can handlog in the spring, but you can't do both!

And handlogging of that sort is brutal work. The tree must first be felled. Not easy for one man alone. The top part with the branches is then cut off. Next, perhaps most difficult, the spongy bark, as much as ten inches thick, must be peeled away from the wood. Heavy logging jacks are used to roll the tree, so that the bark next to the ground can be removed. Cross-skids are put in place, and the jacks are set in such a way as to give the tree a "start." If it doesn't slide, the jacks are re-set, to try again, and again. Finally the tree reaches the edge of the flat ground, where the land drops steeply to the beach. The tree goes down this steep slope with thunderous speed, to bury its top deeply into the flat beach, or the ground behind it. From there it must be jacked, foot by foot, until it is at last ready to slide into the water. This must all be done in one day. However tired you are, you may not go home and return to finish another day, for by then, the new jelly-like wood that makes the log slippery, will have dried to a sticky gum. The tree will then have to be covered from end to end on one side with soft

grease. But first it must be rolled with the jacks...No, better to keep working, though it means you must go home in the dark.

Even when the tree was finally in the water, there was yet more to be done. It must be cut into logs of certain standard lengths for that species, so as to get the top price. By hand bucking of course, and in the water.

There is a great deal more to it, but this gives some idea of the picture. (Handlogging has changed since then. Now, powerful boats, even winches and wire cable are permitted, and a different breed of men are involved. But it is still hard work!)

When all this was accomplished, then came the matter of selling the wood. Local camps and the odd small mill would buy the logs, usually at half their value. This was accepted. A profit must be made for the transaction to be worth doing. But it meant that the handlogger might get as little as fifteen dollars for his back-breaking work on a big tree (which today would be worth nearly a thousand dollars,) and for that he must deliver the logs, and accept the buyers measurement. Not always accurate, but never over value.

The alternative was to ship his wood to one of the mills on the Fraser River, taking his chance of losing it on the way, for the sixty-odd miles of water were mostly unprotected from rough weather. This was the course Jack decided on.

Logs were shipped on the water enclosed in squared units called "sections." These were standardized at one surveyor's "chain" in size, or sixty-six feet. Six sections usually made a boom, closed off at each end and held together by long logs pulled across and chained at each joint, called "swifters." This standardized form was insisted on by the towing companies so that many booms could be tied together, and corner would always match corner and joint meet joint, so there would be a place to chain it.

Jack found that a tug wouldn't stop to pick up a small boom unless it consisted of at least three sections. This meant that he would have to get more than a hundred trees into the water, as well as maintain the farm, in the short few months when the trees would slide!

Somehow, he did it. It wouldn't have been possible had not Cliff and Hal been old enough to do much of the farm work. Even so, he drove himself mercilessly. The bark stopped "slipping" before he had enough trees out, so he felled trees crosswise, bucked them into logs, and rolled the logs down to the shore. Even harder to do, for the least obstacle will make a rolling log swing off course, and it must be realigned with the big logging jacks. And it must still be peeled.

At last it was done; holes bored in the long containing logs and swifters with the big four-inch hand auger, chains in place, swifters pulled and chained.

He took the whole family in the *Lady May* to the sheltered cove where the boom was tied, so they might admire it.

There may never have been a more perfect boom of logs. Three sections of big, high floating logs, fine-grained, no knots, almost no taper. All peeled—no bark, fitted together so tightly that in most places you couldn't get your arm down between them.

As they stood or sat on the cabin of the *Lady May* admiring the sight, Jack said proudly, "Look well. What you see will be worth more than two thousand dollars to us when it arrives at the mill."

That made them pay attention! Until then, they had formed no notion of what his work was worth. They chattered excitedly to each other. So much money! Hal and Cliff raced each other across the logs, shouting

"Two thousand dollars! Two thousand dollars!"

A vast sum. More real, because more visible, than the timber claim Uncle Eustace had found and lost, for they had never seen that, and had only half believed in it.

Once again, they planned what they would like to have when the money was theirs, and they returned home to the farm in great excitement.

It had taken more time than he had expected, for there had been many days when the farm had required his presence, and others when neighbours needed his help. He could never refuse a request for help. And there were all the unexpected delays such a life, in such a place, entailed.

It was now August, and he set about arranging to have the boom towed to the Fraser River. It proved to be more difficult than he had anticipated. The number of tugs going by, never great, had decreased sharply. He had arranged with a mill to buy the logs, and they promised to have Jack's boom attached to one of the tows going by. But even three sections wasn't enough to interest them greatly, especially as they had little idea of its quality. And connections weren't easy to arrange between a tug with a tow and a farm in such an isolated area. No tug stopped. Sometimes they could hear engines in the night, and several times Jack took the *Lady May* and went out to intercept a tug. But the captains wouldn't stop, leave their tow and come back for his boom, and the *Lady May* hadn't power enough to catch up to them while towing it.

September came. Soon it would be the time of the fall storms. Even fewer tows came by, and finally none at all. He was informed that there would be no more until spring. The boom couldn't be left until then. The teredos, the infamous marine worms that sink wooden ships if they are not protected, and riddle logs with holes until they are worthless, would soon be hatching as the water cooled with the coming of winter.

Desperate now, he made the rounds of camps and communities, and at last, when he had nearly given up hope, was directed to a small tug, whose owner was going to take it into the Fraser River for the winter. The captain was a genial sort, one of those men who, after ten minutes of conversation, acts as if he has known you for years. After some discussion, he agreed to take the tow, but insisted on payment in advance. For, as he put it, "Once the logs are cut up, it's a long way back here to collect my money."

Jack pointed out that this wasn't according to custom; that he would arrange to have payment made on delivery. But the other said that he needed the money for the extra fuel that would be needed for the towing. Desperation is the enemy of caution. Jack gave in, and went off to borrow enough money to make up the sum, for he had not quite enough. They arranged to meet at the cove where the boom was tied.

The tug appeared right on time, to Jack's considerable relief. And there went the boom at long last, heading out of Blind Bay into the calm of a late September evening.

The weather stayed good for five more days, then a storm blew up from the south-east. And another, and yet another, in the familiar manner which signals the end of the good fall weather, and the approach of winter. The days went by. Jack kept saying, "Five days. That's lots of time. He can easily make it to the River in five days."

He was worried. No word came. He wrote to the mill. Had the logs arrived safely? Were they satisfactory? And, he didn't want to hurry them, but at their convenience, the money could be sent to...

No answer came, until just before Christmas. Then, "Dear Mr. Hammond. In answer etc., we have had no logs delivered to us in your name. We are not familiar with a towboat with the name you mentioned, etc.etc."

He wrote to a lawyer in Vancouver with whom he had previously dealt, asking him to investigate. The answer came surprisingly soon. The boat he had described was in the Fraser River at a dock in Steveston. It had recently been bought by a fish company, and was being converted to a fish packer. There was no trace of the man who had last owned it, but further efforts could be made to trace him, if it was desired. Of course, there could be no guarantee... A bill for services was enclosed.

It was a long, hard winter. Jack's back had begun to pain him while he was still working on the trees. It had bothered him from time to time for years. Always before he had forced his body to obey him, and it would eventually repair itself. This time, instead of getting better, the condition worsened. When he tried to work in spite of it, the pain increased until the nerves of his left leg refused to function, and it would collapse under him. His temper grew short, and he would flare up at things he once would have ignored. Christmas that year had not been very merry, nor was the coming of the new year a happy one.

They were not actually so badly off. Many people would have traded joyfully with them. There were plenty of good things to eat, and a warm house to live in. They lacked no necessities. There was even a bit of money coming in. Jack had a trapline, which he limped along with the aid of a stick. If the pain got too bad, his sons could tend it. And both of them ran a line of traps.

One memorable day Jack found a fisher in one of his sets. Not common in that area, it was the first one the boys had ever seen. The dark lustrous fur would be worth a good deal more than even an otter skin.

But it was a long hard winter, just the same.

February. With the approach of spring, though his back still pained him, Jack was able to work without his cane, and his temper improved somewhat. He took the family on an outing to Pender

Harbour. There was a big parcel of furs to ship out, and shopping to do. He asked the storekeeper if any boats had come from Vancouver lately. It seemed that one had, just last week, and he set off to find the owner. When he did, he wasted no time in idle talk for the sake of politeness.

"Did you happen to see, between here and Vancouver, a small boom of logs? Three sections, and not your ordinary sort of logs."

"Why, now that you mention it, so I did. Tied to the shore at Trail Islands. Funniest looking boom of logs I ever saw!"

Assuming this referred to their complete lack of bark, Jack was optimistically certain it was his boom. He thanked the man abruptly, and hurried off in a fever of impatience. He must see for himself, as soon as it could be done.

He had intended to take the whole family, but a look at the clouds showed enough movement that the trip might be uncomfortable. He made hasty arrangement to have them stay with friends, for Trail Islands were almost half way to Vancouver, a round trip of about fifty miles, and he couldn't make it back before well after dark. No problem. In those friendly days, even strangers would have taken them in.

And then he was off, his sons with him, the *Lady May's* long hull cutting the water cleanly. He was his old self once again, cheerful, talkative. Even the habitual limp had disappeared.

"The logs are bound to be worth something," he told the boys confidently. "Even if the teredos have gotten into them, they float so high that half of them should still be good. The worms won't eat much above the water line."

Down the coastline they went. Down Malaspina Strait, past Thormanby Islands, past Merry Island, all the places father would come to know so well, but was seeing now for the first time. Turnagain Island, Smuggler Cove, Halfmoon Bay. At last, the little group of islands off Sechelt called Trail Islands. It didn't take long to find the boom. And what a strange looking boom it was! Oh, it was theirs all right. There was no doubt of that. But where were the clean, high-floating logs they remembered? No longer tightly packed, there was almost as much water showing as wood. No longer high-floating, but some almost level with the water. And no longer smooth, but all lumpy and ragged. And finally, so pocked and riddled and pierced with holes, as to be scarcely recognizable as wood at all. Holes ranging from the size of a pencil to ones the boys could have put a finger in. Holes so close together that often only a thin shell of wood no thicker than a thumbnail remained between them.

Jack put the *Lady May* in reverse, then stopped the engine, and the boys jumped out with the tie-up ropes. Cliff jumped onto one of the riddled logs. There was a crunching sound, and one foot sank in up to the ankle. He jumped back on the side-stick, which still looked like a log, and his brother came up to stand beside him. They watched as their father walked slowly across the boom, keeping to the highest floating logs. He seemed stunned, walking with his head tilted down, not speaking. They stood there, apprehensive, not knowing how this disappointment might affect him.

He turned suddenly, and beckoned to them.

"Come over here." His voice was calm. "I want to show you this."

They ran over to where he was standing on a big log floating a hand's breadth above the water, flat and stable. He took out his knife, crouched, and with the point of the blade, picked something out of one of the holes and held it out for their inspection. It looked something like a tiny clam shell. He transferred it to the tip of his finger, and held it up.

"There you see one of Nature's wonders," he commented admiringly. They felt a sense of immense relief, which they could each see in the other's face. He was in his "Curious Naturalist" mood. He had been not stunned but observing. They wondered what he was talking about.

"It is truly a marvelous thing, that little bits of shell like this one, driven by a muscle about the size of the one in your eyelid, can by patient repetition remove all the tons of wood from all these tunnels. They begin to hatch when the water gets cold enough, and the minute larvae drift until they find wood. They can live on a rock surface, but that's a different process. In the wood, they bore a tiny hole with a speck of shell, but they soon grow larger. First one way they twist and then the other, and each time they scrape off a shred of wood. They have been excavated out of a log to a length of twenty feet or more that I know of, and the worm is as long as its tunnel."

He kneeled and ran a finger tip over the rounded end of an exposed tunnel, telling them to do the same.

"Feel how smooth the cut they make. See how they line it with walls of thinnest shell. And do you know, one never breaks into another's tunnel. Never. Truly marvelous," he enthused.

Years later, Hal would say, "I couldn't believe what I was hearing. Looking back on it, I still can't. What sort of man could see a year's work wasted, more than a year's wages lost, and yet admire the thing that was responsible? I know I couldn't."

Seating himself on a cross-swifter, their father continued his lecture.

"You can hear them, you know, once they're well into a log. If you put your ear down on the wood, you can clearly hear the sound of the cutting. Sometimes you can hear it in a boat, but by the time you do, it's too late. The bottom will have to be replaced." His manner changed from the somewhat formal one he used to lecture them into something more direct.

"You know what happened here, do you?"

"The worms ate the logs" said Cliff promptly.

Jack shook his head.

"It's not that simple. They can't eat out into the air. How did it get like this?" He gestured around them. They kept silent, shook their heads, questioned him with their eyes.

"Well, as I have it figured, it went this way. The teredos got in on the first hatch. It was easy for them, no bark, you see. They can't scrape through fir bark, but here they went in every inch of surface. They grew quickly; lots of currents here, lots of food drifting by. They ate to the water line, even above it. The part eaten out was probably lighter than the rest. At least, it would be when the side-swells from the storms bumped the logs together and knocked off some of the weakened wood. After awhile, the logs began to roll over. As they did, the gulls flocked to the feast, and pecked away the wood to get at the worms. See those red particles? They're the undigestable bits from the skins of starfish, the gull's chief food in winter. New teredos began to eat the other half of the logs. They're still at it." He pointed into the water. "See that white powder in the water? That's teredo 'dust.' The logs are worthless. He rose, saying to Cliff, "Get the peavy, we'll take the chains home. The rest of it can go up on the beach and make soil."

They were on their way home by nightfall. He would run all night. There was stock to be fed, they'd been gone long enough.

After this setback, Jack didn't talk as much. He spent even more time reading his books on philosophy. And his back never really got better. There were bad times with it, and not-so-bad times. But there were no more good times.

Chapter 19

Dead Deer

A T AGE TWELVE, Cliff had been judged mature enough to go deer hunting. He had gone out twice: once alone, and once with his brother. He had been allowed one bullet each time, in accordance with his father's views of what was proper in the circumstances, and had brought home a deer on each occasion. Now another fall season had arrived, and the brothers were out on a morning hunt. Cliff had used his one bullet to good effect. The deer being too heavy for them to drag all the way back to the farm, they had field-dressed and left it, intending to return later with the horse.

When they got to the edge of the farm, there was Charlie's boat tied to the dock. Cliff said, "Look, Charlie's here. Too bad we didn't know he was coming, he could have gone hunting with us."

For Charlie loved to hunt, and contrary to the popular image of the Indian woodsman, he liked to have someone with him to talk to. For the brothers, his knowledge made every trip a lesson, a schooling of which they never tired.

They started to run for the house, but then Cliff stopped and called urgently, "Hal, stop, wait! I have an idea how to play a trick on old Charlie." For Charlie was always teasing the boys and they could never think of a way to fool him in return. "Let's go back to where the deer is. We'll take Charlie hunting up there and he'll shoot a dead deer!"

Hal was awed. This seemed to him the best idea his brother had ever had. "Let's go."

Back they went to the deer. They dragged it down to a bend in the trail beyond which was a long straight stretch. Here they arranged the deception. Lying supported by the branches of a fallen tree, the deer—its head resting on a thin stick invisible against its neck—appeared to be looking down the trail. Its eyes were open, its ears up, its every feature arranged in a life-like manner. From fifty feet away it would fool you. From the next bend, more than twice that far away, it was perfect. The scene was set.

Back went the two brothers. Carefully they scanned the trail for tracks. It wouldn't do to have two sets coming and going. Charlie was smart. He would be suspicious. Fortunately, it was hard ground and they were soon satisfied that even Charlie wouldn't suspect anything as long as he had no reason to look closely.

A sudden thought occurred to Cliff, "What will we say when Dad asks us what we got?"

They thought about that for a moment. It was Hal who found the solution.

"We'll just say we know where there's a deer, and we'd like to try again this evening!"

Cliff whistled with admiration at this precocious example of deceiving while telling the truth, and they raced gleefully down the trail.

Back at the farm, Charlie was his usual happy self.

"Ho," he cried when they came into the living room, "Old Indian like to see good boys. Even like to see you two."

Chuckling merrily, he tousled their heads.

Hal and Cliff could scarcely keep from laughing as they caught each other's look, each knowing that the other was thinking of the trick they had arranged. When Charlie gave each of the boys a little animal he had carved for them, they almost felt guilty. Almost.

The rest of the day passed quickly. When there were only a couple of hours left until dusk, Cliff asked, "Would you like to go on an evening hunt with us, Charlie?"

The old man was delighted.

"Sure," he enthused. "Old Indian always like to hunt. Teach boys difference between deer and bear. Maybe if boys pay attention, learn difference between grouse and blue jay!" He chortled.

Greatly daring, Cliff said that maybe one day they would be able

to teach Charlie something. The old man thought that was a great joke.

"Boys will be so old by that time, Old Indian be long time dead. Ho-ho-ho!"

So Charlie went to his boat, came back with his old rifle, and they were soon walking up the trail towards the deer. The boys, with much cunning, had told Charlie, "There's a good buck living about half a mile up the trail. We've seen him but he's too smart for us. He always sees us first and jumps in the brush."

So instead of watching the ground with any great attention, Charlie was keenly scanning the trail ahead. He was leading the way, the two boys trying to step as silently in their moccasins as he did in his.

They could scarcely contain themselves. Conditions were perfect. Under the trees, the evening light was dim, but not so much so that Charlie wouldn't spot the deer.

Just one more bend. They didn't dast look at one another.

Charlie stepped silently around the last bend before the deer. He didn't disappoint them. He took only two steps, raised his rifle and said softly, "Deer." Then in the same breath, and with no discernible pause, "Dead deer," and lowered his gun.

Cliff and Hal were dumbfounded. They could just barely see the deer's head, and they knew where it was! They said not a word, but followed Charlie up the trail. He looked at the deer, then at the boys, then back at the deer. He examined the arrangement, glanced at the many footprints. He began to laugh.

"Ho, ho, ho, ho! Bad boys try to fool Old Indian. Bad boys try to get Old Indian to shoot dead dear! Ho, ho, bad boys. Oh yes." He was delighted. "Bad boys do good job. Almost as good as Old Indian, but not good enough. Not quite good enough!"

Hal was in awe at old Charlie's ability to tell dead from alive for the rest of his life. The old man couldn't tell them how he knew. He just knew.

The funny thing is, that I am sure from what I saw of the acuity of father's perceptions in the woods, that he could have done the same thing when he got older. And I don't know how he would have done it.

Chapter 20

Revenge

A T THE AGE OF TWELVE, Hal was five feet eight inches tall, the same height as his brother, who was two years older. He was already showing evidence of the heavy forearms, thick wrists and fingers, and thick curved nails that would appear so incongruous on his lightly-built adult frame. Also evident was that peculiar, almost unnatural reserve of strength that he seemed to be able to draw on when necessary. It was about this time that his older brother began to refuse to wrestle with him, or to engage him in the scuffles that usually mark the play of boys their age.

I've mentioned previously that Jack had theories about what was proper to the development of a healthy boy. Three of these goals were laid out as matters beyond dispute: that a youth should be able to do a standing jump over a bar that he could walk under without stooping, and a standing long-jump of twice that distance. He should be able to stay under water for a full three minutes, and swim there for two.

His sons managed it. At twelve years, Hal could hurl himself over a bar five feet nine inches high, and leap eleven feet ten inches, taking no run. A distance of respectively one inch and four inches more than Cliff, who could just manage what was required of him. Of course, Cliff was more easy-going, scorning to practice with the desperate determination brought to the task by his brother. But the underwater part gave neither of them any trouble at all, for they both took to swimming like the proverbial duck. In fact, as long as he swam for pleasure, father preferred to swim under water rather than above. (I once saw him stay under so long and swim so far that people on the shore started to launch boats to go out and look for him.)

One summer, they managed to find a way to profit from their skill. Having read in a magazine how travellers in the tropics threw money into the sea for native youths to dive after, they decided to try it themselves. They were given a day off from the heavier farm work once a week, when only the lighter tasks such as filling the wood-box were required of them. They would ask for the day when the Vancouver passenger ship docked.

Jack had acquired a long, rakish looking green rowboat in payment for a debt the previous fall. Not without misgivings. It was a "clinker" built boat, and, as he said, "old clinkers always leak." (Properly, "clincher," as the boards overlap, and are fastened by nails driven through and clinched, or bent over, on the other side.) He accepted the assurance of the owner that it was "dry as a bone," and when water trickled from the seams when it was launched, that "It's just dried out a bit. Leaks'll stop when the wood soaks up and swells."

But, as father said, "It wasn't likely that we'd get anything else for what he owed us. He always drank up every cent he got. So there wasn't really much choice. Dad hated the sight of it, because even with re-caulking and re-nailing, it never stopped leaking. The wood had rotted between the overlaps in some places; he'd never noticed it, and he hated to be reminded of it, I guess."

The boys liked it. It was fast, and with its two sets of oars, and a bailing can to take care of leaks, they could visit the various communities around them. They could even make one-day return trips to Stillwater and Madeira Park.

After much discussion of the details, they settled on a plan of action they thought should work, and which dock to try it out on. The next weekend saw them waiting on the float when the steamship docked. It had on a good load of people, as was usual on a summer weekend.

Time to try out their scheme. Their problem was two-fold. First, there was no tradition for this sort of thing in these coast ports. Second, they didn't think people here were likely to throw their money in the water quite as readily as travellers in the South Seas. But they had a plan, and they proceeded to act on it. Hal plunged in and began to swim around beside the ship. Cliff, fully dressed, made his way up the untended gangplank, and mingled with the passengers. Making his way to the rail, he chose the moment, and holding a twenty-five cent piece in the air for all to see, called down, "I bet you can't fetch this quarter back if I throw it in the water!"

"Sure I can. Just throw it out and see!" The clear boyish voices cut cleanly through the confused sounds of conversation. Passengers on a ship at dock are always bored unless they're ashore shopping. These, welcoming a diversion, crowded to the rail.

"What do I get if you can't find it though?"

"Oh, I'll find it all right," came the reply. "If I can't, I'll give you two quarters back."

Someone called, "Throw it out, boy. That's a fair bet!"

They'd taken the bait like a tame trout. Cliff tossed the coin; his brother retrieved it.

Father told me, "It's not hard. A flat piece of metal doesn't sink all that fast, and it rocks back and forth and glitters as it sinks. The water was really clear there, and I could swim down to the bottom if I had to. It worked like a charm."

The same voice that had encouraged Cliff called out once more, "Want to try again, young fella? Same deal?" And at the answer, he threw the coin as far as he could out over the water. It was deep where it landed, and Hal knew there was no hope of getting there in time, but he pretended to try. There were cries from the deck of "Too far!" "Shame!" and "No fair!"

But the boys had thought this might happen, and were prepared for it. After a time underwater that had some people shifting nervously for a better view, he came up holding a coin. Not the same coin; they had planned for this, for they had no intention of giving up their coins that easily. He carried some of each kind in the pocket of his swimsuit. I don't know whose nefarious idea this was, but it worked splendidly. Never in all the times that summer that they played this game did anyone think to look at the date on their coin!

There were cheers and clapping as he swam easily along, holding the quarter up between the fingers of one hand. Better still, several people threw coins down close to him, as a reward. He felt just a bit guilty, but not for long!

He swam over to the float and put the coin in a can placed there for the purpose, so they wouldn't be suspected of "finding" the same coin. People on the deck were already calling new challenges.

The take for the day was six dollars and ten cents, for beyond their expectations. They came back the next week, and as often after that as they could manage. If they had left their routine as it was... But they decided to add a "grand finale." When the offerings were slowing, and departure time not far away, he would dive deeply for a coin, one Cliff had thrown if necessary, far into the green water under the boat. But instead of surfacing this time, he would swim completely under the keel, to come up on the further side. Then he would swim along to the open door of the loading bay, clamber up and through into the hold, and scamper up the ladder to the deck. Cliff would be acting worried, saying, "Something must have happened. He should be up by now!"

The newly galvanized crowd would be lining the rail. There would be one or two young stalwarts with their shirts off. At just the right moment, Hal would push through to the rail, while asking innocently, "Is something wrong?"

It always made a sensation, and was always well-taken, especially by the young men who had been given a chance to show their courage, and their muscles. There would be applause, and sometimes money. Most people were pretty good sports.

It was too good to last. In the first week of August, there must have been a change of officers. A new man appeared on deck— burly, black bearded, and sour-faced. He leaned against the rail, and watched the show disapprovingly. Next week he was there again. At the grand climax, when the people were beginning to worry, he spoke out in a loud harsh voice,

"Don't let those young con artists put one over on you. He swam over to the other side, and (pointing) he'll be coming through that door over there any moment now."

So when Hal stopped in the doorway, they were all looking at him. There were derisive laughs, and no applause. And no money. He ducked out of sight and into the hold, slipped quietly into the water, and swam under the float. He pocketed the coins from the can, then swam to shore under the dock. Cliff was there waiting. He was furious. The man had collared him—literally. Too shocked for the moment to kick or struggle—he had been taught to respect his elders, and for a few seconds it had inhibited him—he heard the harsh voice snarl, "If I catch you here on deck again, ever, I'll give you the toe of my boot." And a couple of men nearby laughed. More than most boys, Cliff hated to be laughed at. Hal too, was in a rage. He had been laughed at by a whole group of people, and pointed at in derision. It would be war, they decided. Total, all-out war!

They were, essentially, savages, in spite of Jack's philosophy, and May's attempts to civilize them. They would have revenge, sweet revenge. But how? It wouldn't be as easy as the affair of the Chinese cook, where they could lurk around in the woods and pick their time to strike.

They sauntered down the length of the wharf. Hal went to where he had left his pants and shirt, put them on. Then they sat on the edge of the wharf, at a level with, and not far from, the sour faced man who still leaned against the rail. He glowered at them menacingly. He seemed to hate boys. They stared back insolently.

"We could hide behind the winch," suggested Cliff, "then rush him and tip him overboard." They considered this blissfully for a few minutes.

"Wonder if he can swim?" mused Hal.

"Hope not!" said Cliff ferociously.

But, attractive as the notion was, they decided it was impractical. As Cliff put it, "Someone would see us, and if he drowned, they'd put us in jail." It wasn't the chance of drowning the man that deterred them.

Their enemy stopped looking their way, likely feeling it beneath his dignity to engage in a staring match with a couple of boys. They studied him intently. It was Cliff who saw the answer, "Say," he whispered tensely. "Do you see what he's leaning on?"

"The rail, of course, you...oh. Oh yes!"

Never slow to catch on, Hal was excited now. "Don't let him see us looking."

They pretended elaborate indifference. For the bearded man was leaning on a gate. Directly across from the big winch, on either side, the railings had a gate, which would be opened if something heavy had to be loaded, or a gang plank run out at an awkward landing place. The gates had pin-and-socket hinges on one side, and heavy sliding bolts that latched into slots on the other, so that they could be either swung open or lifted out entirely. They weren't padlocked. The area around the derrick was out of bounds for passengers; a sign proclaimed the fact.

Besides, people in those days were expected to take some responsibility for their own safety.

Each time they had seen him, the man had walked across the deck and leaned over the rail in exactly the same place, the centre of the gate. They had seen enough; the plan was obvious. They spent the week in fevered anticipation, refining, rehearsing, elaborating and rejecting. Already they possessed instinctively what some strategists never learn: "Keep it simple." When the day came, they were on the dock hours early.

The ship was on time, and then there was the usual bustle and confusion. They waited until the gangplank was clear, and the doors of the loading bay open. When he saw his chance, Hal slipped through into the hold, wearing only his swimsuit, so he would be noticeable. Someone called out "Hey, kid..." but he ignored them. He was after bigger game. It took only a moment before he heard the hated voice call, "Hey, you there! What are you doing?"

Then, much louder, for Hal had made a rude face, "Hey there! Catch that kid. Grab him!"

As well try to grab an eel while wearing boxing gloves!

In the meantime, while everyone's gaze was attracted by the diversion, Cliff trotted up the gangplank and walked casually to the gate. He drew the bottom bolt, tried the top one. It moved fairly well, but he smeared on a little of the grease he had brought anyhow, and then drew it until only the tip was holding. With a quick hitch he looped the bolt handle with a piece of strong fishing line, then ran it along just under the rail where it couldn't be easily seen. Up two bents of railing, down a stanchion, and across the deck to a hiding place behind the winch, where he crouched, waiting. Dark green against black, the line was near-invisible.

The shouts had ceased. Cliff knew his brother would have dived over the rail and swum away. Any moment now...

He peered intently through openings in the machinery. There!

Walking with considerable dignity, the big man crossed the deck, went directly to the gate, leaned heavily on it. Cliff jerked the line, the greased bolt slipped easily. With a startled yell their victim clung to the gate, which swung out, and stayed there, as the brothers knew it would. For with all the activity being on that side, the boat always had a slight list in that direction. Desperately the man tried to pull himself up, but the top rail was flat and broad, a poor handhold. His hands slipped, and he fell into the water with a great splash—water into which Hal had just dumped a big container of sticky black, used engine oil, cadged from the local repair shop that morning.

Cliff ran to the rail, stood peering down, grinning. The man surfaced, spluttering. Disappointment. He could swim. He looked up, shouted something, shook his fist. He shouldn't have done that. Raising his arm out of the water pushed his head down; he got a mouthful of dirty oil. He swam over to the float using a clumsy breast-stroke, gathering more oil as he went. A couple of bystanders helped him onto the float. His clothes were oily, there was oil in his matted beard, on his face, in his hair. He was shouting, and the words fully justified the reputation sailors have for salty language. The men around him listened with admiration, the women with interest. He looked up and saw Cliff. Aware suddenly of danger, Cliff ran to the bow, leaped onto the rail, and dove cleanly into the water, clothes and all. He had used up a full two minutes of breath before he surfaced near the rocky shore. In an instant, he was up the rocks and into the trees. His brother was already there. They didn't come out until the ship was well on its way, and even then they were nervous, feeling that he might well be hiding in wait for them!

They never dove for money again. That ship, of course, was out, but there were others. No, though they probably wouldn't have known the word, it was the sense that it would be an anticlimax to do it again that stopped them. It was time to move on to other things.

Chapter 21

The First Job

AS THE STATE OF THEIR FAMILY FINANCES worsened, the boys—now virtually young men—did their best to contribute. Cliff had been working for a year or so by then, but never for long at the same job, and with not much to show for it. He was at home now, having been fired once again, this time for knocking the camp owner onto his back in a pool of muddy water. He had thought it best to leave without asking for his pay! He could manage all the work the farm needed, so Hal decided it was his turn to bring in some money. He petitioned his father to this effect one evening.

Jack looked up from his book, thought for a moment, growled, "Well, I don't suppose you could be any worse than Cliff at keeping a job," and resumed reading. Next day he took the *Lady May* and his eager son out to check a couple of logging camps. At the second one, they needed someone to cut wood for their new steam donkey. Hal was thrilled. These machines were quite new, and he had never even seen one, much less watched one in operation.

It was love at first sight! He was fascinated by the power and complexity, seduced by the music of metal moving on metal, attracted by the feeling of danger aroused by steam under pressure and the boiler full of fire.

The job was simple enough. He had to keep the fire hot enough to maintain the steam pressure valve at a certain level, and to cut enough wood to maintain the size of the pile near the boiler. He wasn't expected to use reject wood. There was a good fir log nearby meant for this purpose, and a sharp saw. The straight grained blocks split easily. Of course, there had to be a problem.

The engineer, or "donkeyman" was his direct superior. Actually, every man on the claim was his superior, even the whistle punk, but the man who operated the machine was the one whose orders he must obey. Florid face; a drinker's complexion, with a nose to match. Drooping moustache. Shortish sandy hair, with a bald spot kept covered by his engineer's cap. A bit of a paunch, caused about equally by beer, and sitting at his job for most of the day. A bit soft; strong enough, but not markedly so. (It doesn't take a great deal of strength to move the counter-balanced levers of a steam donkey—at least, none that I've seen.) And a bully, as the boy soon discovered.

Not too bad the first morning. The donkeyman set him to petty, unnecessary tasks, then cursed him because he didn't keep the pile of wood up to level. Gave obscure orders, then cursed some more because they weren't acted on instantly. Small things, at first. Even the very eagerness to please shown by his young fireman seemed to somehow irritate the man.

Cliff had told his brother that the youngest member of a crew would be subject to jokes and tricks at first.

His father had explained, "Hazing is a way that groups use to test the mettle of a new member. How you react will determine—to some extent—how they will treat you. You should do all right, you're not the sort to whine or complain. Get back at them if you can; they will respect you for it, if you're not sneaky about it."

Noon, and the men near the landing gathered to eat lunch. The donkeyman's voice rose above the rest. Hal sat off to one side a bit, as befitted a new boy. The donkeyman's eye rested on him. Pointing, he said derisively, "Look there, fellas, see what they've given me for a helper. They must be logging the second growth now, if that's the best they can come up with!"

There were no laughs. It was obvious that the man wasn't much liked. Stung a bit by the lack of response, he tried again, "That, God help us, is all we've got to keep the fire going, so if we run out of steam, you'll know the reason why."

Deciding he couldn't let that pass, Hal replied coolly that if the fire went out, it wouldn't be his fault. Innocuous enough, but it provoked the other.

"We don't need any lip from punks like you," he snarled, then added more reasonably, "Make yourself useful. Run over to my toolbox and bring me the left-handed pipe wrench."

It was an old joke, the kind of thing Hal had expected. He trotted off briskly, came back with a pipe wrench, handed it over. The man looked at it, at the boy.

"You little twerp. Didn't I tell you to bring me a left-handed one? This is just a common wrench."

Hal stood there grinning. "You're holding it wrong. Turn it over."

There was laughter. The foreman said, "He's got you there, alright. Makes sense to me!"

At the look on the man's face, Hal's grin faded. He knew he had made a mortal enemy. He turned away as casually as he could while expecting to feel the wrench on the back of his skull. But the blow didn't happen. He reached the woodlog safely, picked up the saw, and started to cut another block.

The afternoon shift came to an end. Surprisingly, there had been no tricks played on him. But whenever he looked, the sullen eyes were watching him unnervingly.

Back in camp, the evening meal brought no trouble. There were two bunkhouses; he was in one, the donkeyman in the other. In spite of this, he didn't sleep well. It helped none when the foreman stopped for a moment as he was walking by, saying seriously, "You've made a bad enemy, kid. Watch yourself. I'm afraid there's not much I can do to help."

But again, the morning was uneventful, though now when he glanced around covertly, there was a mean little crooked grin on that face he was beginning to hate.

Lunchtime. He sat apart on a block of wood just sawn, tipped up ready for splitting. Opening his lunchbox, he took out the top sandwich. Took a big bite out of the soft middle. At the last moment, it crossed his mind that it didn't smell right. It wasn't right. He spat out the half chewed mouthful, opened the sandwich.

Instead of meat, it was full of dead worms. Some of them had been dead for quite a while, which explained the wrong smell. He looked through the others. Each had something unpleasant in it. A wad of chewing tobacco in one, four or five big brown wood spiders in another. He looked sideways at the other men. His enemy was watching him, grinning largely. He put the sandwiches back in the lunchbox, took out the apple, checked it carefully. There seemed nothing wrong, so he sat there eating it. The donkeyman rose, walked over, stood, still grinning.

"You're not talking much, kid. No smart talk at all today."

When there was no reply, no acknowledgement of his presence, "What's the matter, worms got your tongue?"

Still no sign from the boy. Snickering, the man walked past him, behind him. His back prickled with nervousness, but he would die before he would turn. There were obscure sounds, footsteps nearing. Then his shirt collar was pulled out roughly, and he felt something powdery being poured down his back. He knew what it would be. When the inner layer of fir bark is dry, it can be crumbled easily into a dust composed of tiny sharp-pointed slivers. Bark slivers. When they get into wool, such as shirt or underwear, nothing will get them all out; the clothes are unwearable, and will have to be discarded.

He sat there frozen, needing to do something, not knowing what. From the corners of his eyes, he could see the silent men watching. It wasn't their place to intervene. He heard the footsteps approaching from the direction of the machine. He refused to look. Then his hat was lifted off, and something warm and sticky poured on his head. It ran down his neck and back, over his face, down his chest and stomach. It was thick black oil, and it smelled bad, as if something foul had been mixed with it.

Father said, "All of a sudden, I felt nice and peaceful, as if I was just going to sleep. Everything started to go sort of pinkish, and then faded into a warm red haze. I felt good."

The next thing he remembered, was voices, and hands pulling on him, on his arms. He resisted them. He was doing something he felt needed to be done, something he enjoyed doing. But the voices got louder, and he felt himself being pulled upright. His vision cleared. His tormentor was lying on the ground in front of him, very still. There was blood on his face, but his chest was moving.

Feeling somewhat foolish, he asked the foreman, who was holding him by the arm, "What happened?"

"Damnest thing I ever saw! You flipped around and climbed up on him like a cat up a fence. Knocked him over backwards. Next thing you had him by the ears and was banging his head on the ground so fast it sounded like a woodpecker on a snag full of ants! Not that I blame you. He deserved every knock you gave him. I wouldn't've stopped you, but I need him, and in a couple more seconds, he wouldn't've been good for much."

His voice rose, "Jesus Christ, what's that you've got in your hand?"

Hal looked, dropped what he was holding as if it was a poisonous spider. It was a human ear.

The foreman beckoned one of the bystanders.

"You, Matt, get a piece of rag or somethin' to put around his head. It's bleedin' pretty badly. Hekkova place to put a tourniquet! Then throw a coupla buckets of water on him, tell him he's slept long enough. We're gonna need him this afternoon. Guess he'll have a bit of a headache, and he won't hear much that side. But he was always talkin' so much, he only listened with one ear anyhow!"

He stood, thinking for a moment, then shook his head. "Guess I'm gonna have to let you go, kid. Way I see it, either you'll kill him, or he kills you. Either way I lose a good donkey-man, and they don't lie thick on the ground. Sorry to lose you, you looked like you could be a good worker." He fished a stub of pencil from a pocket, then tore a sheet of paper from a grimy pad he took out of his jacket; wrote something on it. "Here, take this down to camp, they'll give you two days' pay. And go get a rag from the machine, see if you can wipe some of that mess off. What a stench." He turned to go, saying loudly, "C'mon boys, what're you all standing around here for? Show's over, time to get to work."

Father used his shirt to clean himself as best he might. It couldn't be worn, although most of the slivers might wash out of the thinner material. The wool underwear were beyond saving. He bundled them up to take home, where some use might be found for them. Then he walked down to camp, collected his money, and set off across the island to Hidden Basin.

Jack had been mistaken. Cliff's first job had lasted a full five days!

Years later, father told me, "I did a lot of thinking, then and for a long time afterwards. It scared me, what had happened. I could have killed that man, and not known I'd done it. I made up my mind that it wasn't going to happen again. That the next time I felt that nice peaceful feeling coming on, I'd give myself a good swift mental kick. And it did, once or twice, and I did, and it worked. But, you know, the saying is true. You do see red, if you get mad enough!"

Chapter 22

Fire in the Iron

AFTER THE LOSS OF THE LOG BOOM, and the money they had hoped it would bring, the family's financial situation became desperate. Especially as his back had become too bad for Jack to handlog or do heavy work until it improved.

Cliff's jobs brought in very little money. He didn't take well to routine. He was happiest on his own, trapping, or fishing. Such things he was good at, but they were seasonal, and they paid poorly.

Hal's first real experience with logging went well, apart from the abortive first job, but when the camp closed, there were no others nearby who wanted such a young man on the payroll. Then Cliff came home with the news that he had been offered, and declined, a job at the quarry on Granite Island (on the charts as Kelly Island).

Next morning, Jack and Hal set out in the *Lady May* for Granite Island. It's a short trip, and they were at the dock before the quarry was at work. Jack knew the superintendent well, and the details were quickly settled. They chatted for a while, then Jack left for Hidden Bay, and Hal was taken to the foreman, who would send him on to wherever he was needed.

It was an interesting job. There were a myriad of chores in a place like that for an active, intelligent young man who could handle tools well. He was strong for his fourteen years, and didn't have to be told anything twice. The quarry was a very busy place just then. The Island granite split cleanly and was much in demand. In addition to supplying building granite for the fast-growing cities to the south, they had acquired a contract to supply granite blocks for the breakwater at Victoria.

The drilling was done by hand, using teams of three men on the vertical holes, two on the horizontal, one to rotate the drill, the others to drive it.

When the blocks were free, they were rolled out, trimmed if necessary, then rolled and slid to where the big derrick, made of a whole fir tree, could pick them up with its multiple block and tackle, and stockpile them on the dock—cut out of the solid granite of the island—until the barge arrived to take them out.

The new young helper got along well with almost everyone, and the range of things he was able to do grew rapidly, but one of the jobs he most wanted was denied him. He knew he was good with a hammer and he wanted to drive steel, but the foreman said he wasn't big enough for that job.

"No, no, Hal," he laughed. "It takes a lot of man to swing a hammer all day long. You're doing just fine where you are."

Hal bristled. He said hotly, "I can swing a hammer with any man out there!"

But it was to no avail.

"I'm sure you could," said the other, "for a while. Put on another twenty pounds and I'll think about it."

There was plenty to do—explore the island, for one thing, for it is a small island, and he soon knew every foot of it as well as the farm in Hidden Basin, except for one place—the blacksmith shop. He had been warned about the blacksmith and his temper before he had been on the island more than a few days, but it hadn't stopped him from wanting to investigate. The shop sat on a flat spot on a hump of rock above and behind the derrick. It was an important part of the quarry. The drills had to be constantly re-shaped and re-tempered, and the mushroomed ends trimmed. Hammers had to be squared and given new handles. Heavy hooks, shackles and all the articles of iron needed for the workings of a quarry were also usually made by the blacksmith.

Hal was interested in blacksmithing. There was a small forge on the farm, and Jack had shown him some basic elements of the art.

The blacksmith kept to himself. He had a little shack near his shop, and didn't eat at the cookhouse with the rest of the crew. They said he ate strange foods, with strange smells to be smelled if one was bold enough to go near at mealtime.

After a week or so, Hal's curiosity could be denied no longer. He invented an excuse in case he was accosted, and when he knew he wouldn't be needed for a while, sauntered up and along the trail to the blacksmith shop. A few yards before the door of the shop, the way led along a couple of planks that spanned a cleft in the rock. As he stepped on them, the planks dropped an inch or two, and a little bell over the shop door gave a clang. It seemed that the smith didn't like to be taken by surprise.

He took a few more cautious steps, trying very hard to appear as if he had business there, when suddenly the half closed shop door was thrown open, and there stood the dreaded smith.

Nothing that anyone had said had prepared father for the figure that confronted him. The smith was short, almost a dwarf. No more than five feet tall, but almost as broad as he was high! His head was huge, set on a neck that bulged with muscle, and he was totally bald, though he had, as father put it "enough hair in his ears and eyebrows to make up for it." But two things drew most of his attention: the great scar that ran diagonally across his cheek from ear to mouth, and the huge gleaming black moustache, curled up at the ends, that measured the full span of his great head. He was wearing a heavy leather apron over canvas pants that may once have been brown, and a black shirt with the sleeves cut off at the elbows.

Grimacing horribly, this apparition crooked a calloused, coal-blackened finger at him and croaked, "Come in my young sprig, come in. You come in good time. I have here that which must be tempered in blood!"

But his young visitor was not to be frightened off so easily. Willing his voice not to quaver, he said firmly, "No one tempers with blood any more. There are better ways to get a carbon surface on steel."

The ferocious looking gnome flung his head up. His great black moustache seemed actually to quiver as he mocked, "Ho, a lesson in iron-working is it?" Then ominously, "Do not be too sure. Blood still is used. But not, perhaps, here. But worry not, little one. There is not in you blood enough to temper the smallest blade!"

Big teeth flashed whitely as he laughed. (White teeth were unusual in a time when most working men chewed tobacco.)

Father decided he didn't like this strange creature. He was conscious of his slight build, and fiercely resented any reference to it.

Suddenly the smith's strange face took on a look of real menace, as he snarled at the startled boy, "Now begone. There is work, and I will not have spying. Sneak you around windows, I give you the red end of the iron to hold."

Father could never tolerate a threat. He flashed back insolently, "First you'll have to catch me!"

But the response surprised him. The strange man shouted with laughter

"There you are right, little one, built I am not, for running!" He

went back into the shop, still laughing, and closed the door behind him. Hal went lightly back down the path, avoiding the planks that rang the bell. He thought that he had come off rather well.

Most of the work, such as drill sharpening, the smith can do on his own, but some of the heavier jobs require the use of one hand on the tongs, while the other holds a shaping or swedging tool, so someone else must be there to swing the hammer. The tricky part of the job is not swinging the hammer, but following the smith's quick shifting of the tool. Some make this easier than others. This was one who gave no thought to making things easy for anyone. Men dreaded to be chosen as his helper, and no one lasted long at the job.

One day, when he had been there about a month, Hal was splitting wood not far from the blacksmith shop. There had been the rhythmic sound of a heavy hammer on iron, but suddenly the clang changed to the clatter of a mis-hit. He heard a yell of rage, and looked up just in time to see a man come running out of the shop door. Behind him came the squat figure of the smith. He didn't try to follow the running man, but stood there roaring, with a voice that could be heard all over the small island, "Go, dogspit! Go! No, no, come back, come back, I feed your head to the forge!" He was brandishing a heavy length of drill steel with one hand as if it was a stick he was shaking. With a last shout of rage, he went back in the shop, slamming the door behind him.

The running man stopped where the trail to the forge started, and waited there while the foreman came over from the drill site. As he drew near, the ex-helper turned and shook his fist up at the shop when he was sure no one up there was watching. He swung back to face the foreman.

"I'd rather hit for the Devil in Hell than for that man up there!"

"What happened?" asked the foreman tiredly.

"He doesn't give you warning when he moves the swedging tool. I missed and hit the iron." He grinned. "I think it might have fallen on his foot. I hope it did," he said viciously.

"How far did you get on the hook?"

"We were just starting to draw it out."

"Well, I need that hook. But I don't know who else I can send up there." The foreman's sharp eye rested on the young man not far away, obviously listening.

"You, Hal,"

"Yes sir?"

"You say you can use a hammer. Now's your chance to prove it. The blacksmith needs a helper. Right now!"

Father put down his axe, walked reluctantly up the path to the ogre's lair.

He told me, "I think I'd rather have faced a grizzly bear than go up there. But I thought to myself that the blacksmith would have to be mighty quick to catch me, and felt a bit better."

Approaching the shop, he trod heavily on the planks that rang the bell, feeling it might be best not to take the occupant by surprise. The bell jangled, but the door stayed shut. He went up to it and tapped gently, then stepped back a pace. Suddenly it was thrust open, and there stood the smith, wearing a scowl as black as his moustache. But it lightened a bit when he saw who was there.

"Ho-ho," he chuckled "It's the sprig that would teach me to temper iron! Is it tired of life you are, to beard the angry boar in his den?"

"I was sent up here to be your new helper."

Throwing his arms wide, the smith proclaimed to the sky, "They send me a twig, when the whole tree would be not too much!"

Father was getting angry. He'd heard quite enough about "sprigs" and "twigs." He came back evenly, "You shouldn't judge a man until you see what he can do."

His tormentor made a show of being surprised.

"Oh ho, a man is it now? Well then, let us see."

He went into the shop, returned holding a ten-pound sledge and some three-inch nails. Going over to a big block of wood to one side of the door, he put one end of the hammer-head on it, and placing one of the nails against the bevelled corner of the hammer, pressed it into the wood with a calloused thumb. He did the same thing at each of the other corners, leaving about two thirds of the length of the nails sticking out. Father tried hard not to show it, but he was mightily impressed. The nails had seemed to sink into the wood as if it was sand!

The smith now rocked the hammer a bit, so that the nail heads were just slightly clear of the hammer, which he then lifted out from between them. Turning, he stated solemnly, "This test we give the apprentice, to know if he is worth the teaching. Drive the block, but not the nails."

He tossed the hammer without warning. Hal caught it, with no show of effort. He looked along the handle. It was straight, the wide part perfectly in line with the hammer. He swung it gently back and forth, then went over to the block and took his stance. Driven by anger, he whipped the hammer around in a full arm swing and slammed it between the nails. The head sank half an inch into the wood, compressing it so that the nails leaned inwards, and the hammer, held by the nails, stayed in position when he let go of it. (It is difficult to do, but not as hard as it may seem). Turning to the smith, he asked innocently, "Like that?"

The smith said nothing for a space.

He reached up and tugged at the moustache on the scarred side, distorting his face horribly. Walking over to the block, he pushed at the hammer with his finger.

"I said that this way we test the apprentice. What I said not, is that no one I know ever passes this test! Sure I am not that even I..." He shook his huge head doubtfully. He peered up at the young man before him with clear eyes, grey as Hal's own, strange in that swarthy face, and it seemed that he was really seeing him now for the first time.

"Well boy, you have the eye, certain it is that you have the eye. Now we see if you have the wind. Come, bring the hammer." He went back into the shop.

The forge fire was banked. Coals glowed darkly, with a hint of brighter red beneath. A large piece of iron lay half covered in the heap of coal. Pointing to the bellows, the smith commanded, "Air."

Hal went to it. There was a handle, also a foot treadle that could be operated by one foot or both. It was still called a bellows, but was actually a gear-driven fan. He tried the handle. Gears whined, and a puff of ashes rose from the glowing coals. He turned harder. The gears resisted at first. He was used to this, and increased the speed slowly. Sparks flew, and the fire grew brighter. The smith drew more coal over the iron, looked at him, growled, "Faster."

Father knew that much arm effort would be needed to force the gears to go faster. He stepped onto the treadle and with his weight balanced, began to rock it, until the gear whine grew shrill. The iron began to redden, bright and brighter.

"Enough. Hammer." Plucking the big piece of glowing iron out of the fire with a tongs, the smith carried it effortlessly in one hand over to the anvil, and picking up a swedging tool that lay there, positioned the iron and placed the tool.

"Strike!" Father was ready, hammer swinging before the word was completed. The iron was large, he struck hard. After three blows, the smith grunted, "Harder!"

He struck harder, swinging into the easy rhythm that comes naturally if you let it, alert to the quick movements of the swedging tool; he knew the gnome was testing him, moving the tool erratically, unexpectedly, but always the hammer struck true and square.

"Faster" came the order. He quickened the swing.

"Faster" and again "Faster." The hammer blows made the very air ring; if you know how to catch the bounce, a hammer may be swung amazingly fast and Father knew. He was sweating now, sucking in gulps of air, his wiry body become a machine for hammering.

"Faster!"

He had reached his limit, physically and emotionally. He swung mightily, but as the hammer began its descent, he spun about and hurled it with a splintering crash right through the shop wall! He turned quickly, balancing there, alert, ready to flee the wrath of the enraged dwarf, only to be surprised once again. The smith stood there, tongs in one hand, shaping tool in the other, a look of mild inquiry on his face.

"Why hurt you the wall? It has done you no harm."

He seemed to be genuinely interested to know why. Father

answered, perhaps more honestly than cautiously, "I couldn't very well throw it at you, could I?"

The white teeth flashed, "Throw you could. Hit you could not!"

He went to the forge, placed the iron in the coals and covered it. He turned, and putting thick hands on hips, explained earnestly, "When we get a new tool, one we have not before used, we test it, we see if it is good. You will do. Yes, I think you will very well do."

Turning again to the forge, he said to the astounded young man standing there speechless, "Fix you the wall. There is too much light here."

And that is how Father began his new job.

He must have done well at it, because a week or so later, the foreman stopped him on the way out of the cookhouse.

"Well, Hal, how do you like your new boss?"

Father, cautious, said that he'd no complaints.

"Well, I don't know what you've done, but I hope you keep on doing it. I've never seen him in as good a mood. If you can keep him like that, you'll have earned your wages and more. The last one we had here quit. He said there was too much work for one man. Now we're running more drills and the smith waits for us to bring work. His drills cut faster and last longer. I'd hate to lose him!"

In truth, Father was enjoying what he was doing. For one thing, he found himself liking the smith more as he grew to know him better. In spite of his reputation, Father never saw him lose his temper. He had the gift of being able to explain things clearly, without using too many words. He was patient if patience was needed, and he laughed easily. Short he might be, but the broad frame held a giant's strength. He was the first really strong man Father had met.

As he said to me, "Dad was a husky man. He was well-built, and his work kept him in good shape. But he wasn't really exceptional, and the smith was. Not that he performed any great feats of strength while I was there. Oh, he had a habit of putting two fingers in the corner hole of the swedge block, and setting it on the anvil, (about 100 pound weight), but that's not so wonderful. It's just that, whatever he did, it never seemed to take very much effort.

You got the notion that he never came anywhere near his limit, no matter what he did."

The smith liked to work at night, with no light but that from the forge and the hot iron. He told father, "You have to see the fire in the iron, to make it work for you. In the day, you see it not, and the work goes less well."

He seemed pleased by the obvious interest the young man took in the work and in the smith himself. He didn't answer all of the questions put to him but he never seemed annoyed by them. He must have been a lonely man. It wasn't long until, after the work was done, he took to standing at the forge, staring into the fire, talking to the young helper, a few sentences at a time between long silences.

One night he seemed more reflective than usual.

"Respect the fire, boy," he said seriously. "Treat it well, and it will be good to you. Fire is life, and life is fire." He reached into the coals and took a brightly glowing one in his fingers, dropped it into his other palm, and held it for a long moment. Then he slowly reached out again and tipped it back from where he had gotten it.

Father knew that this was an old blacksmith's trick. Their hands became calloused from the hammer. A quick lick of the tongue to moisten the fingers; it wasn't hard to do. But the smith didn't lick his fingers, and he was certainly not doing tricks.

He spoke again, quietly, almost as if he was talking to himself, "From fire we come, boy, and to fire we go. In the sky is fire, and in the earth, fire." A long pause, then, "I have seen a mountain burn, boy. Like melted wax the rock flowed, onto the farms below. The people prayed, but the gods heard not. It might be, that at the last, stronger is the fire than they. Or it may be, that there is but one God, and He is Fire."

Another pause, then he turned to the door, saying cheerfully, "Come boy, the fire sleeps. We will wake it in the morning."

Father was given an increase in pay, and spent as much time as he could at the blacksmith shop, even when there was no hammer work to be done.

About this time, the quarry obtained an air-operated drill called a Raleigh drill, I think (though father pronounced it "Riley"). It could drill rock, vertically or horizontally, faster than eight men. On the strength of it, the quarry engaged to supply the granite blocks for the two majestic lions which were to be placed before the doors of the new courthouse in Vancouver. Weighing thirty or so tons, these would be the largest blocks the quarry had handled. A special scow would be sent up for them on a set date. It was rather rushed, but with the power drill there would be sufficient time, though not much to spare.

Now there was a new sound on the island. To the ring of hammers on steel was added the chatter of the air drill.

For a time, all went well. But when the first of the big blocks was rolled free, there was a flaw in it, and it had to be cut up into smaller blocks. The flaw continued into the granite, and a new face had to be started. The holes for this were half completed when, about two in the afternoon, the sound of the air drill stopped, and didn't start again. Then the ring of the hammers ceased, and the men began to gather in a tight group where the new drill had been working. Father joined them, edging his way into the centre where he could see what was going on. The drill was off its tripod, lying on the ground, the foreman on his heels beside it. A big crack ran right around the tube that held the moving shaft. The quarry owner had been sent for, and now came hurrying to see what was the matter. The men made way for him, as he pushed through to stand over the broken drill.

"How did it happen?" he demanded. The operator shrugged his shoulders.

"I don't know. It just broke when I was halfway through the hole."

The foreman stood. He said, "We'll have to get another one. That can't be fixed." His manner held no doubt.

The owner shook his head.

"There aren't any more, and I don't know when there will be. Even if we could find one, it could take a week to get here, and we haven't that much time." He sounded very worried. "And you know there's a big penalty if we don't meet the deadline. Can we possibly do it with hand drills? Double shifts?"

"No," answered the other decisively, "not if we work through the night on triple shifts, we can't put in that many holes."

Someone said "Maybe it could be welded?"

"No," replied the foreman. "It isn't possible. You see," he explained, "there's a spiral groove runs around the inside that matches one on the shaft. They fit tight, no play. When you weld iron, you have to hammer it, and it squashes together a bit. There's no way you could line up the spiral grooves. And what's more, if the two pieces don't go together absolutely straight, it'll just jam and break again."

Father spoke. He knew he shouldn't, a boy in a group of men, it wasn't done in those days.

"I bet the smith could do it. I'll get him."

The foreman said impatiently, "Don't go bothering the smith. There's not a thing he can do." But his words went unheard, or were ignored.

The boy raced across the draw and up to the shop. The smith was filing at something in the vise. He listened impassively to the hurried explanation, then replied calmly, "Well, I will come. But you should know, some things there are even I can mend not." He grinned, "But not many!" He put his file down and went to the door.

With nothing else to do, most of the men were watching as he came down the trail and across the open area. Some of them had never seen the strange creature who kept their drills sharp, but they had heard the stories about him. With his short legs and massive body, the smith's gait was not like that of other men. It could have been comical, but it was not. There was something about it, an impression of power barely held in check, that made the group draw apart as he came near. He went to where the drill was, squatted on his heels and studied it closely. He seized it with both hands, one on each side of the crack, and twisted one hand one way, the other hand opposite, to expose the grooved shaft.

"I told them," said the foreman, "that it can't be fixed. I didn't want to bother you, but the lad..."

The smith stood.

"It can be done," he stated.

"But how can..."

"I said it can be done. Need you not to know how." He stooped, picked up the heavy machine with one hand, and started back, ignoring questions as if he hadn't heard them. But he went only a few steps, then turned and said, slowly and impressively, "When the dark comes, I work. Until then, I prepare. No one is to come near. If a step I hear, if a face I see at the window, I stop. I will begin not again."

The owner spoke. "Did everyone hear that? No one goes up there."

The smith hadn't waited for a reply. Father caught up to him.

"Do you want me to turn the bellows?"

"No, boy." The reply was kind but firm. "This you should not see. Not even if you are apprentice. This is for adepts, none else."

He walked across the trail, up to the shop and in, closing the door firmly behind him.

The men returned to work, but without the air drill, there was no point in hurrying.

After supper, first one man, then another, wandered idly about the camp. Each one's course ended below the rock on which the blacksmith shop stood, until by dusk most of the camp was there, standing about, hands in pockets, talking occasionally, but very softly. The shop was perhaps thirty feet up and the same distance away. Not far, as sound goes on a quiet evening. For a long time, there was the sound of a file on metal. No one could understand this. What could need filing on this sort of job? (He may have been making flux, a mixture used to help in welding. Many blacksmiths devised their own flux, the secret of which was often closely guarded. Clean metal needs no flux, but the necessary cleanness is sometimes hard to obtain in a coal fire.)

Then came silence. It was dusk now under the trees, but no one left. Father went up the path as far as he dared, and settled in a notch between the rocks. The gears of the bellows began to whine, and sparks flew from the forge chimney. On and on went the sound of the gears, far longer, everyone agreed, than should be necessary to heat a piece of iron that size. But at last it stopped, and they heard a tapping, very faint, but definite. Not at all the sound they expected. They all knew something of blacksmithing, but this was a thing they could not fit to their knowledge.

Tap-tap-tap-tap. Silence. Tap-tap-tap-tap. And once again, tap-tap-tap-tap. Then nothing for a space of minutes. Puzzled whispers were exchanged, but no light came of them.

And then once more, the whine of gears. Had the weld not taken? Of course not, you can't weld iron that way. Even if it could be done, the thing would never work.

This time it seemed the whine continued for even longer than before. Someone grumbled, "This is ridiculous. We're just wasting our time standing around here in the dark. I'm going back to the bunkhouse."

But he stayed there with the rest.

Once more, the tapping, tapping. It stopped, and there was no sound. The men began to stir. They spoke in normal tones, and were aggrieved at the absence of anything to reward their patience.

Father couldn't imagine what they hoped for. Thunder perhaps, and the smell of sulfur?

The shop door opened, and the smith emerged, a black shape against the red light of the dying fire. He closed the door, and his strong voice came out of the dark, although he couldn't possibly see them there below.

"It is done. In the morning it may be taken." And then, soft voiced, so that only Hal heard, "Go to bed, boy. Tomorrow I will want you."

And that, to father, was the strange thing.

He told me, "I was scrunched down there in the moss. I never made the slightest sound after he came out of that door. I was afraid he'd think I was sneaking up to spy on him. Yet he knew I was there. I've sometimes wondered, was he so tuned in to fire, that he could see the heat I made? There was something uncanny about that man!"

Next morning, right after breakfast, and long before it was time to begin work, everyone was out at the cutting site. They had all looked at the welded place, not that there was much to see there. A faint line where the crack had been, barely noticeable. The drill was mounted on its tripod, the air compressor started. The consensus was that it would break again as soon as the drill hit rock. The foreman himself put it in the hole where it was working when it had broken. The familiar chatter began, and rock dust trickled from the hole. He pulled it out, fastened on the next length of drill steel and handed it to the operator.

"Looks great, go to it."

There was still a while until starting time, but that sort of thing wasn't given too much importance back then. Go to it, he did. The men went back to work, and the day went by much like any other day. The big blocks were cut out, and rolled down to the dock, well before the tug and barge came to get them. In time, a replacement cylinder arrived. Unneeded, it stayed in a corner of the supplies room as long as father worked there.

The next day, when work was done and they were standing in the darkened shop, looking into the dimming coals, he ventured to refer admiringly to what the smith had done the previous night. For a while, the smith made no reply. Father was used to this by now and waited patiently. At last it came.

"If you wish, you could learn: that, and other things."

"You mean, you'd teach me how to weld like that?"

The other chuckled good-naturedly.

"Not for a while, Oh no, not for a long while is this for you to learn. But when time, yes. If you want."

He turned to face the young man, put a huge hand gently on his shoulder.

"As apprentice I would take you. Young enough you are, and for your size, strong. But sure you must be. Hard it is, and for long."

"How long would it be until I learned to weld like that?"

"It is for the last year to learn that art. And there are seven years."

Shocked, Hal queried doubtfully, "Seven years? That's an awfully long time. I'm sure I could learn in less time than that!"

But the other shook his head firmly.

"Seven years must it be. No more, no less. But make no answer now. Think deeply on it." In the light from the forge, his teeth shone redly in a broad grin, as he ended with, "Your life depends, boy, on your answer." And again the chuckle rumbled from his deep chest.

Father thought. He knew the answer would change his life. He liked working in the shop. The smell of the coal is a good smell, and working with iron is fascinating. He liked and admired the smith, and longed to know his secrets. He felt that there was knowledge to be had here that went back to the making of swords and armour, back to and beyond the age of chivalry that drew him so strongly.

But he also felt that the art was dying, that the time for it was nearly over, And he would have to take orders, do as he was told, for seven years. To a fourteen year old, seven years is close enough to forever! It is a very tender age at which to make decisions such as that, but he knew what he must do.

A week went by, when at the nightly ritual of watching the waning fire, the smith asked him, "Well boy, and have you decided?"

He had, long since, but dreaded saying it, for he feared the smith would think that he didn't appreciate what, he was certain, was a very great compliment. And he liked the man more and more as he got to know him, and felt sure that the liking was returned. Almost, he changed his mind, but he knew he mustn't. He replied slowly, hesitantly and regretfully.

"Yes sir, I have. It's not for me. I mean, I'm too impatient. Seven years—I mean—it's too long to wait. I really like to work for you, but..."

The smith broke into the awkward stammers, and his voice was kind. He must have understood what was going through the boy's mind.

"Well boy, need you not explain. Right you may be. Our skill is needed less, and for the art is less respect than before. Go your way, boy, may you be happy on it. But for now, be here tomorrow after lunch."

This story contains an anachronism, and for those few who may realize this, I'd like to make a brief comment. The use of hammers and hand drills was by now, in most places, a thing of the past. Machines driven by air or steam were the norm. Yet, his account of the work at Kelly Island was circumstantial—containing much more detail than I've included here—and quite inarguably authentic. Something that is probably relevant: the contract for the big granite blocks required that they be "quarried, not blasted," presumably, so that there would be no fractures in the rock. But it wouldn't explain the use of hand drills. However, if the quarry was still using the old methods, it might explain why it was chosen, apart from the quality of the granite.

I've left the story the way father told it, as well as I can remember it. But I believe the reason that parts weren't available for the broken drill is that it had been superseded. It was likely too old, rather than too new.

Chapter 23

In All Directions

A T THE QUARRY, things were changing, the old ways going. New machinery was installed, new drilling machines took the place of hammers, and the hammer men went off to find other work. Bridge building, track laying—there still were jobs where a sure eye and strong arms were needed.

The new drill bits couldn't be sharpened because of their shape, or perhaps it wasn't worth the doing. They had four cutting edges, and didn't need to be turned in the hole. There wasn't enough work to keep the smith busy, and what there was presented no challenge. There were still times when he needed an assistant, but one day as they were watching the forge grow dim in the fading light of evening, he said, "The fire sleeps. It will not wake for me again in this place." At Father's questioning look, "I will be off, boy. There is nothing here to hold me. It was never meant to last for long. I will go where the old skills are needed, and wake the fire once more."

Father said, "I felt a sudden sting in my eyes. I hadn't realized until then how much I'd come to like the smith. I had a sudden impulse to tell him that I wanted to go with him. I almost did it, but the words wouldn't come, and the time for it passed."

The smith looked at him intently, grey eyes dark in the glow of the fading coals.

"And what of you, boy? Have you thought what you would do? Mind you, there is always the fire. You have a gift for it, and might serve it well, though I be not here to teach you."

The young man answered, though his voice came near to choking, "I like the fire, sir, you know that. But it isn't the thing for me.

Besides, if you have trouble finding a good job, and have to work in a place like this... well, I guess I'd starve to death!"

In the light from the glowing coals, the smith's teeth gleamed redly beneath the great black moustache.

"Do not be afraid of that, young one. There will be need for the craft yet awhile. So you would let the fire sleep, and choose water?"

Father was surprised that the smith remembered, but he replied, "Yes sir, I want to buy a boat when I can, and work on the water. I like the sea, there's something about it..."

The deep voice responded, "So you should, boy. It is one of the great things. People think water is the enemy of fire, but that is not so. Fire and air, water and earth; without air, fire can not live; without water, earth lies barren. Each needs other, and all make Earth and us. Think of the new machines. Fire, fed by earth, held in iron, make from water the air that gives the engine power. Go to water, boy, you will never be far from fire!"

A few days after this, Cliff came in the *Lady May* to take him back to the farm. The news he brought was strange and disturbing.

For months now, Jack had been unable to do any work. He couldn't even bend far enough to tie his bootlaces, and needed his cane with him constantly. In addition, a cough that had begun to bother him some months before was now habitual. He had consented at last to go to the old doctor who had cared for their various ailments for so many years, though he remarked testily, "I fail to see what good it will do. He was able to do nothing for me a year ago. How should he be expected to do more now that the condition has worsened?"

Nevertheless, he went. What he was told went something like this, according to Cliff, who had taken him there in the *Lady May*, and stood listening silently throughout the consultation.

"What you need," said the doctor, as he leaned back and began to fill his pipe, "is a doctor who can treat your head, for it's there the trouble lies."

At his patient's obvious indignation, he waved the hand holding the pipe.

"No, no. I'm not saying you're crazy, nothing like that. But nothing can be done for your body until you change your ways, and for that your head must take responsibility. What's happening is this, as I see it. You hurt your back. Forced it to do what it couldn't do. Then when it ached, you refused to rest it; you just forced harder. I know you, Jack Hammond, and I know just how you respond. You're not the man to lie around while others work. But now you have to. So you sit there, in pain, worrying, fretting. You get no exercise, and your health suffers. Worry like that can kill a man; I've seen it happen. Then the cough. Not much to start with. Now it's self-sustaining, as the irritated spot gets worse. It's not dangerous yet, but it's not far from it. I could give you opium, likely would stop it until your lungs heal. But at the first signs of the first dose, you would refuse it.

"There is a cure for you, the only one for the man you are. While you stay there on the farm, seeing what needs to be done, or even seeing someone else doing it instead of you, you will only get worse. You must leave, go away. Far away. I would suggest the South Seas, or New Zealand perhaps. In a warm climate, your lungs will heal faster. But leave, you must, or the consequences will be dire!"

Now, the decision must be made. There had been, according to Cliff, nothing else spoken of at the farm for the past two days. He had thought his brother should be there. Apparently Cliff was the only one to think so. Not that he could have contributed much, but he felt left out.

As he said to me, "I would have told him that he didn't have to go, didn't have to worry about the farm. Cliff and I could take care of it now, and even bring in enough money to get by. That we wanted him to stay and not to worry."

But the decision had been made by their mother before they arrived home. Some of the girls were crying. May had taken the news calmly. Jack had thought he would improve, now that he had a handle on the problem, but she said that he should follow doctor's orders. He had objected that there was no money for the fare, if he took every cent they had. She told him confidently that something would turn up. For the next two days, the boys heard these arguments and variations on them. It seemed to them that, if their mother didn't actually hand Jack his suitcase and push him out the door, she didn't stop far short of it.

It's not too difficult to understand her reasons. May was a strong-willed woman, and she expected those around her to do her bidding. But her misfortune was that Jack was not the man to do any person's bidding. He sought to please her, but in his own way, with little thought for her needs. She would be a matriarch, but must defer to one who was stronger than she. It was not physical strength that told. According to his sons, Jack could scarcely have conceived of violence to a woman. It was his strength of character that made others obey him. He overshadowed her, and she was not the one to accept that.

She painted pictures. He was an artist. She was religious. He considered it superstitious twaddle. His learning made her feel inferior, but she wouldn't make the effort, or had not the time, to acquire any herself.

And, a major reason, one with which I sympathize; she wanted no more children. She felt she had done what was required of her. Now she wanted freedom. But, if he stayed... She was frank about this to some of her daughters when they were much older.

She wanted to move out of Hidden Basin, to where there were people, and realize her ambition to own a store. The doctor's prescription was just the medicine she needed. Some thought that she arranged it, but only the doctor could confirm that!

And something did turn up. The quarry owner stopped by, heard the story, and offered to loan Jack three hundred dollars, enough to go to New Zealand, and to live there until he could work (and assured him that he could pay back the loan when, or if he could.) At May's insistence, Jack finally accepted.

When Father returned to the quarry, the smith was gone. He felt a sense of loss that lingered a long while, and a feeling that he had made, perhaps, a wrong decision. Added to that, the knowledge that Jack would now be well on his way to the other side of the world, and a rather glum young man was the result. But something happened soon that changed that.

The quarry now ran on steam pressure. Steam drove the drills, steam powered the machinery to move the blocks, steam pressure broke the blocks loose after the holes were drilled. And making steam takes water, lots of water. Granite Island and Hardy Island were too small to have much water. In fact, Granite (or Kelly Island) had almost none, being little more than a lump of rock in the sea. So the water for the quarry was brought there each day by a tank on a scow, towed by a gas boat. The water was pumped from the scow to a holding tank on the island. The scow and tank belonged to the quarry, but the boat was owned by a semi-retired fisherman.

There was a good deal of responsibility involved. If the water tank ran dry, work stopped until it was refilled. (Salt water can't be used for steam. The salt is very corrosive and forms a hard coating almost impossible to remove.) But the man who owned the boat hadn't retired just to work every day; his arrival times were erratic, and sometimes the scow failed to appear at all. The pay was good, though. Too good, for it allowed the boatman to buy enough whiskey to remain on the border between drunk and sober for weeks at a time. And sometimes, he crossed that border.

This day, the scow hadn't arrived, the tank was empty, and there were yet two hours until quitting time. The quarry owner was furious. After he had been pacing back and forth for awhile, Father approached him.

"Well, Hal, what is it?" His tone was sharp. He was in a foul mood.

"I can tell you how to get the water on time, and at the same time every day, and not miss a day."

"If you can do that, lad," said the owner skeptically, "you will earn your pay this month if you do no more work for the rest of it! What do you advise me to do, to make this wonderful thing happen?"

"Buy the boat," came the prompt answer. "Sell it to me. Take the money to pay for it out of my wages. I'll take care of the pumping and the equipment. In fact, you can make a mark in the tank two-thirds down. If the water ever goes below the mark, I'll give you a week's pay!"

The other man looked him up and then down, then looked into his eyes as if seeing him anew. He nodded his head, put out his hand.

"It's a deal," he said. "But what if the fellow won't sell his boat?"

"Oh, he'll sell," came the confident answer. "I've already talked to him."

At last he had a boat of his own. Never again in his life would he be without one.

The job was a dream. It was undemanding, except in its requirement that the tank on the island be kept full. He never had to pay the forfeit. The size of his first cheque, even after the deduction for the boat, was such that he was sure there had been a mistake. But the owner just smiled at him, saying, "It's worth it to me to know the water will be there when we need it. Besides, you have a family to look after now."

He was getting three hundred dollars a month, a vast sum for a young man in those days!

So now, for the first time in years, the finances of the family were no cause for worry.

The quarry moved to Hardy Island, and the job with it. May moved her family there as well, to a smallish house provided by the owner. She started a store, with her older daughters to run it, and seemed happy. The farm stock was sold, killed or allowed to run wild. The fields began to illustrate the Darwinian idea of "Survival of the Fittest." Jack would have been interested in the result. In the fall, it presented an opportunity for May and her girls to play at "hunting," for the deer came from miles around to gorge on the fruit that covered the ground under the trees, and they became quite tame.

Many letters arrived from Jack. True to his nature, he described the new country and its plants and animals. His health did improve quickly, especially the cough, which went away entirely, but he was very lonely, and missed his wife and children greatly. His letters were full of endearments and concern. But gradually, they became bitter. Always he pleaded to come home, and for her to write to him.

"I am in Auckland, and there is no mail for me. Surely there is a letter on the way somewhere? I wonder where it can be?..."

"My darling, I wonder how you are today. I worry a lot about you..."

"I think it better to go back home, or better yet perhaps, to die. There seems to be no place for me, and I am lost without you..."

"I am glad you are feeling so well. I can face the world better..."

"I wish I could go home, but am afraid I can't. Besides, you don't want me..."

"It's a long time since I wrote, but I don't suppose you care, judging by your letter. It certainly was short, and alas, not very sweet. You seem to have put me right out of your life. I wonder what is to become of me. I am very lonely..."

After a year and a half, he felt well enough to come home, thinking he could win her back to him if he could only be there to try. He arrived one day, tanned, but seeming to his son to be strangely shrunken. Certainly better than when he left, but as certainly not the man he once was. The visit did not go well. He was dismayed at the change in the farm since he had last worked on it two years before. The *Lady May* was gone, also the property on Texada Island. He had said in his letters that she could sell them if she must, for he seemed to have been unaware of the improvement in the family finances. He obviously had hoped she would not and so it came as a shock to find them gone. And May was not pleased to have him back.

Father was staying in the house at Hardy Island. Jack was not permitted to sleep there, and spent most of his time at the farm. In his letters, he had spoken much of the girls, how much he missed them too. But they had not been shown these. Now in total command, May had consolidated her position by convincing his daughters that he had left them to live in a place where the women went around wearing no clothes. Now they wouldn't speak to him. Still he would not give up, and there were arguments in the house on Hardy Island. And now there came another blow to his pride. It was his own fault.

He had been surprised to find his middle son now so mature, and was disconcerted rather than pleased to find him with such a well-paying job. They hadn't spoken much together. Then one evening as he was leaving for Hidden Basin, he stopped at his son's boat. They exchanged a few words, then he said abruptly, "I'll need the boat tomorrow. There's a claim up the inlet I want to look at."

Now, it is certain that Jack did not possess the gift of diplomacy. But I can scarcely believe that he would have done this. I think he was testing the extent of his authority, and would have rescinded the demand had it been granted.

His son was surprised and resentful. He tried to explain that Jack could have used the boat, and welcome, but there was a contract; he had given his word, and there was, besides, the matter of a penalty. His father took the refusal calmly.

"Then you won't let me have it?"

"I can't, dad. I haven't any choice. I just can't do it."

Jack merely nodded, said good night, and set off on his way home in the long green clinker rowboat, the only boat still left at the farm.

Jack remained away for several days, then came one afternoon and stayed for supper. After it was over, he indicated that he would like to be left alone with his wife. Father's room adjoined the small living room, and he eavesdropped shamelessly. Even so, much of what was said was lost to him. Jack spoke low-voiced, but with obvious feeling. May seldom answered him, and then only in short phrases or single words. After some time of this, his voice rose as his hard-held patience began at last to leave him.

"I may as well go back," he cried. "What is there here for me? You've turned my daughters against me. My son doesn't obey me. You've sold my boat, and my land. You've let the farm go to ruin while you sit here on this lump of rock and play at storekeeper. But it's not too late, even now. Say you'll take me back, even that there's hope that you'll take me back. We can start again, just the two of us, like it was long ago. Tell me, Molly, say yes. Tell me there is hope!"

There was a long silence. And then, at last, he spoke again, voice weary, resigned.

"That's it, then? Your answer is—no answer? Very well. I can do nothing more. I will leave in the morning, and you will not see

me again. But if you should change your mind, if that should happen...but I know it will not."

He left, bidding no good-byes. They never saw him again.

His sons, and perhaps his daughters, remembered him with respect, but no love. And May? She loved him yet, in her way. He was hers, and she was jealous of him. There are hints in the letters. And then, there were the paintings.

When Jack met his wife for the first time on his return, he presented her with a thin suitcase full of paintings he had done on his travels.

"They may bring you some money," he told her. "They should do well over here."

May opened the case, looked at two or three of the sheets it contained, then snapped it shut and stowed it away. A few days later, Father asked if he might look at them, only to be told firmly, "They aren't for you to see."

Some days after Jack left, Father was reading in his room when he heard the sound of flames in the little fireplace. It was late at night, the others in bed, the house silent. He went to the door. May was sitting on a low stool, the case beside her. She took out something, examined it, put it slowly in the fire, watched it burn. When it was consumed, she took another, and did the same with it. Cat-silent, he walked across the room, stood behind her. She took yet another picture from the case, held it in front of her for a moment. He could see it plainly in the lamplight. In warm browns and vivid greens, it showed a clearing in a forest of strange trees. In the foreground stood a young native woman, wearing only a piece of bright cloth around her hips. She was very beautiful; very exotic. She joined the others in the flames. The case was half full. One by one, it was emptied, until none were left.

"Why didn't you stop her?" I asked, angry that he had saved neither pictures or books.

"They were hers," he replied simply.

When the case was empty, she turned and saw him watching. Her face was streaked with tears. He had never seen his mother cry before.

Jack Hammond died in New Zealand in 1941, leaving a small legacy to his wife.

The *Mabel Brown*

NINETEEN FOURTEEN, AND THE "War to End All Wars." Cliff joined up, in spite of his mother's protests, and went overseas. Aside from the small amount of Cliff's army pay, Father was the only source of income for his family. He wanted to follow his brother, confident that the government would maintain the family of those men who joined the army, but May forbade it, and she was not a woman who could be disobeyed easily.

With the money made by her son's boat and the water-scow, they were better off financially than they had ever been. However, the European conflict could not be evaded so easily. Construction requiring granite blocks was halted almost completely, as all efforts were turned to war. The quarry closed, the water-scow was no longer needed. Gone was the magnificent salary it had brought.

When the stoneworkers left Hardy Island, there were no longer people enough for May to even pretend the store was profitable. She moved back to the farm, but made no attempt to maintain more than the house itself. She refused to give up her ambition, however, and caused her son to nail a sign on a tree near the entrance, with GENERAL STORE printed in big white letters, and an arrow pointing inwards.

Father found other jobs, but the income was uncertain. Many of the camps closed, and the store made no money. All the action seemed to be in the city. He decided to go to Vancouver and get one of the high-paying war jobs everyone talked about.

Boats fascinated him; he decided that building them would be the perfect job. And if he was going to build boats, he would build the best. He would go to the shop of Andy Linton. As long as he could remember, this was the name that stood for quality in design and workmanship. If you had a boat built by Andy Linton, you had the best.

Off he went to the famous shop on the waterfront near Stanley Park, troubled by few qualms, confident in his abilities. He went through the door, was asked his business by a clerk whose arrogance toward a young man obviously not a customer proved no deterrent. The shop was everything he had thought it would be, full of the scent of cedar and cypress, linseed oil and tar, with hints of others he couldn't name. He was shown the master of the shop, and accosted him as soon as he could without interrupting.

"So you want a job building boats, do you?" asked Andy Linton, a bit of a smile creasing his weathered face. "Can you use tools, boy?"

"I think so, sir," he replied politely.

He didn't like being called "boy." At age 19, he felt entitled to the respect due a man grown. But he knew that his slight frame and smooth cheeks invited the term, and the friendly tone in which it was delivered robbed it of sting.

"Think so? You should know. Don't be modest, boy. People may believe you! Well, you may be in luck. There's lots of work. I can use a good young fellow, if he's the right sort. Come along, let's see what you can do."

He led the way through the shop, past busy men working on boats in all stages of construction. He stopped at a pile of heavy boards about eight feet long, planed smooth, gleaming with the pale glow of flawless spruce.

"Here you are. We're behind on oars."

He took a handsaw and carpenter's hatchet from a bench and handed them to the young man. "Rough out the pattern with these. Just follow the line. I'll come by in a bit, see how you're making out."

Father examined the tools. They were good, and they were sharp. He set to work confidently. This was the sort of work he enjoyed, and he knew he was good at it. After a while, he felt a presence and looked up. Andy Linton was watching him. Picking up one of the roughed-out pieces, he looked at it carefully, then set it back on the pile. He smiled warmly.

"Not bad," he approved. "Not bad at all. You may do, boy. You may do. But there is just one thing." He tapped one of the boards with a finger. "Leave a little bit of the line, boy, so I know the cut is true. Leave a little bit of the line." And off he went. Father stood there, lost in admiration. A carpenter's pencil is wide in one dimension, but that is to give it strength. It is not used that way. The line it leaves when used properly is about twice as wide as that of a normal pencil. And Andy Linton had not said "Leave the line," but "Leave a little bit of the line." That was the standard of accuracy he demanded. No wonder his boats were famous! And for the rest of Father's life, it was the phrase he used when accuracy was required. "Leave a little bit of the line."

When he had roughed out enough oars, he was given the next phase of the operation, with the assurance that, in a short time, perhaps as little as a year, he might be trusted with the whole job from start to finish! As he felt quite competent for the task without any further delay, this wasn't quite the encouragement it was meant to be, but he wisely said nothing. He was accepted, and he was enjoying the experience. Andy Linton seemed to like him. One day he stopped by the bench where the young man was working, and after a few words of instruction, said unexpectedly, "It's a good job, boy. A safe harbour. Most of these men have been with me for years. If they want it, they have a job here until they're carried out. You could do a lot worse." And off he went on his rounds.

Father, remembering, said, "I had a sudden strange feeling that the walls were a little closer, and that the good-smelling air had got just a little stuffy."

One day, one of the older men was planing some yellow cedar planks with one of the big Jack planes. With each long slow strike, a wide coiled shaving, the full width of the plane iron, curled up and joined the heap on the floor. It was warm work. He took his heavy shirt off, and resumed his task in only a short-sleeved undervest. Father was shocked to see that his arms were deformed. At least that is how they appeared at first. A ball of flesh the size of a grapefruit filled the space on the back of his arm between elbow and shoulder. Then he realized that it was a ball of muscle. As soon as he could find a pretext, he stopped near one of the younger men with whom he had become friendly. He gestured covertly up the shop floor.

"Have you seen old Malcolm's arms?" he whispered, "they're all lumpy!"

The other man laughed. "It's from the planing," he explained. "All the old plane-men have arms like that. It takes a lot of power to push that big plane that smoothly. If he stopped half-way along the stroke, you wouldn't be able to move it. I'm heavier than you, and I can't move one of those planes set for a cut that deep. You couldn't find arms like that on a circus strongman."

Father went back to his bench, deep in thought. It disturbed him profoundly to think of a man working at a job so long that it distorted the shape of his body. It was a good life in some ways, he knew. No one hurried, the work went smoothly, and it was satisfying to handle wood, to watch it take shape beneath his hands. But he knew he wasn't suited for the even pace of this life.

Andy Linton listened sympathetically as he tried to explain why he was leaving. "I'm too young," he finished, "best I leave now before you'll miss me. You need a steadier man than me."

The other nodded his understanding.

"We'll miss you now," he said. "It's good to have young men around. Keeps us old fogies on our toes. But it's work that goes at a steady pace. It's not right for everyone."

So he left, with the promise of a reference if one was needed, knowing he was doing the right thing, but feeling very badly. He went to the Wallace Shipyards in North Vancouver, for much of the talk at Andy Linton's shop had been about the ships being built in the Wallace yards. Six ships in all, of a type called "auxiliary schooners," with five masts for sails, and two engines. At two hundred and forty feet overall length—almost as long as a football field—and forty-four feet in breadth, they were the largest ships the yard had ever built, and the largest, I think, to have been built in Vancouver.

He took his boat across to the North Shore, found a place to keep it, and set off for the Wallace works at the foot of Berwick Ave.

He had no trouble getting a job; there was a shortage of experienced men, and when he mentioned where he had last worked, his welcome was assured. He was assigned to the *Mabel Brown*, the first keel to be laid. He arrived at work next morning, a half hour early, which gave him a good start with the foreman, who had himself been there for half an hour already. After a few questions, the foreman decided, "I'll try you with a couple of the old ship's carpenters. They can use a lively young fella to run errands. They're slow as cold molasses, but they do beautiful work. Beautiful."

He shook his head sadly.

"They should be working on some millionaire's yacht. What we need here is speed, not beauty." The ships were a large investment for the owners who hoped they would be launched in time to take advantage of the wartime need for shipping, and the expected postwar expansion of trade.

"There they are," said the foreman suddenly. "Right on time. I don't know how you'll get on with the old coots. They're a bit odd."

Hal looked at the approaching figures. Old they were, and frail in appearance, each one with shoulders bowed under the weight of two chests, which they placed carefully on the ground as the foreman introduced them to their new helper. Their names were David and Sandy, one Welsh, the other a Scot. Sandy's hair, where it wasn't snow white, had reddish tinges, especially in his truly magnificent pair of sideburns. He was otherwise clean-shaven. David, equally white of hair, had once been dark, as his huge black eyebrows proved. His sideburns met under his chin, giving him the appearance of a man looking through a porthole.

They looked each other over carefully. The Welshman said in that delightful Welsh lilt that Father often tried to imitate, but always failed at, "Helper? I'm not in need of a helper. My partner here, Sandy, now, it is true he is getting a little feeble..."

The maligned Scot glared at him, snarling, "Feeble is it, man?"

He held out a huge gnarled hand. "I've more strength in one hand than you have in your whole measly body."

He also had a slight trace of his origin in his speech, and Father could never decide which was the more attractive to his ears, for the Scots accent at its best is one of the musics of the world. The two old men were glaring at each other like a couple of fighting roosters. The foreman had hurried off, so the young man thought that he should perhaps distract them while he could. He said, "Can I carry your tools up to the deck?" They transferred their glares to him.

"I am quite able, young man" said David the Welshman icily, "to carry my own tools." To which the other grunted assent. But Father was never slow for an answer.

"Of course," he said cunningly, "I can see that you're able to, but the thing is, should you have to?"

The eyes peering through the sideburns widened in surprise.

"There is a point there you have, which might bear thinking of."

To which his mate added, "Aye, there is indeed." And to his new helper, grandly, "You may carry my tools laddie, but, mind you, carefully."

"And mine also" came the Welsh lilt. They stood there expectantly,

an odd glint in each pair of eyes, which made him feel obscurely uneasy. He stepped to the nearest chests, those belonging to David, and lifted.

Years later, he told me, "I almost collapsed. Those things must have weighed sixty or seventy pounds apiece! I made up my mind in a flash that I wouldn't let it seem that they were too heavy for me if they pulled my arms right out of the sockets."

He took a half step for balance, set himself, lifted smoothly, and carried them up the stairs in the scaffolding to the ship's deck, took a deep breath, then returned for the other pair. This time, the old men followed him, after the slightest of grins to each other. He pretended not to notice. He discovered later that they were so protective of their tools that they took them home every night, where each one that had been used even slightly would be carefully honed and oiled. The two old men were the best of friends, but you wouldn't think it to listen to them working. They were constantly sniping at each other. David would select a tool from his box for a certain job, whereupon Sandy would exclaim, "What are you doing, mon? Ye're not going to use that, surely, for the work," to be met with, "I intend to use it, and I will use it. It is the right tool to use."

"Not a Number Seven, mon. Ye'll no' tell me ye're goin' to use a Number Seven gouge. Ye're not digging coal now, mon."

"If I was digging coal, I would be using the right tool for it, and I would have a sackful before certain horny-handed Scotsmen would have decided where to dig!" And so it would go.

They were fascinating to watch. Slow they were, and methodical, but every stroke counted; there was no motion wasted, The result was as near perfection as humans might approach. They never stopped for a rest. They both had a prodigious, if well concealed, sense of humor, although at times you were not sure if it was operating or not. Father came soon to like them as well as he had ever liked anyone.

When he began work, the decking was being laid, and though this was not really work for such as Sandy and David, they could not do their real work until it was in place. Besides, they told him, a proper shipwright can turn his hand to anything, and do it better.

The decking was of Douglas fir planks, four inches thick, in places doubled in a cross-pattern for extra strength. They were held in place with ten-inch spikes that were left sticking up a bit so that the hammer-head wouldn't bruise the wood. Father was one of the ones put to doing this, as the two old ship's carpenters didn't need him just then. He was happy; he liked using the long-handled hammer. It could have been boring, but he tried constantly to improve his technique, and to use as few strokes as possible.

After a few days had passed, the foreman stopped him.

"You're a pretty fair hand with the spike maul" he commented. "Can you use the other side?"

A spike maul has one face like a sledge, the other tapers to a point about half the size of the spike head, roughly the diameter of a person's smallest fingernail. On a smaller job, the hammer man will drive the spike flush, then reverse the maul and with one more stroke countersink it. But there are a lot of spikes in a deck 240 feet long, and 40 feet wide for most of that, and with the shortage of skilled men due to the war, there were not enough who could, or would, use the small face of the hammer, for it looks daunting. But is not as difficult as it may seem. Anyone competent with a hammer should be able to do it. But it takes confidence. A miss will produce a large hole in the deck. Father had that confidence. He hadn't done it, but he knew he could.

He replied, "Yes sir," and waited.

The foreman said, "Let's see you try it."

Father reversed his hammer and walked back along the line of spikes, driving them below the surface of the wood, one blow to each. "Good," approved the watching man. "That's your new job for now."

A couple of days later, just after lunch, he heard voices coming up behind him. It was a group of important-looking people being given a tour of the ship by the foreman—a dozen or so men and women. As they came close enough to see what he was doing, they exclaimed in awe at the accuracy needed for it.

The foreman said, "This is our best man at the job. He never misses."

Father laughed as he told me, "I was doing fine until he said that. Then my muscles all tightened up and I drove the hammer into the deck a full two inches from the spike."

He worked the point loose, set the head of the hammer on the deck, and stood there leaning on the handle. The foreman said with a smile, "I think he's trying to tell us something," as he led the group away. It was no big deal; the hole would be filled with a plug. He never missed again.

With one blow to each spike, he soon caught up to the deck layers, and was sent back to where David and Sandy were working to help in the monotonous task of filling the holes over the spike heads with sections of round wooden dowels, and trimming them flush with the deck. Any child could dab a bit of glue on the dowel plugs and drive them in the holes, but it takes a skilled hand to chisel them flush without gouging the deck or splitting the edge of the dowel. He was set to filling the holes, while the two old men chiselled the ends off. They had to kneel to do it; it was not a favoured job. Unusual for them, they grumbled, and sniped at each other more earnestly than ever. He went along with this for one day. Then, next morning, he asked, "Might somebody have an adze I could borrow for a moment?"

He well knew these men wouldn't loan one of their precious tools to the foreman himself, but the brashness of youth admits no barriers. They looked at him, then at each other. David said, "He wants to borrow your adze."

The Scot was silent for a moment as he considered this bit of effrontery, then, "Not mine. He was looking at you when he spoke, mon."

There was another moment of silence as they looked at him. As if a sudden thought had struck him, he said apologetically, "Oh, I should have thought. They'll be old, they'll break easily. I wouldn't want to take a chance with them. I'll get one from the foreman."

David said, "You may use mine. It is of razor steel, and cannot be broken."

He rose to his feet and went to his box of tools. Sandy said, "It may do, but if the job be a hard one, I will give you the real thing, made in Scotland of the steel they used to make the claymores."

His partner returned, carrying a leather pouch and an adze handle. From the pouch he took a gleaming adze head which he slipped onto the handle. Tapping it on the deck to seat it, he handed it silently to father, who took it carefully and examined it. The adze was his favorite tool, he was a master of it, even at that age. He often said that a good adzeman could take off a slice of wood so thin that you might read newsprint through it. (Unlikely though that may seem, I have seen him demonstrate this many times, though no job we had needed such accuracy, I'm afraid.)

David's adze was a tool of such perfection, such balance, and such design, that it almost seemed to live in his hands. He hefted it, leaned it on the deck, gave a trial swing or two, then cut off a protruding dowel with a single stroke so smoothly that the piece remaining in the plank seemed almost to be part of it. He looked at the adze admiringly.

"Now that," he approved "is an adze."

It was hard to be certain, but he thought that the weathered face of the old Welshman actually flushed with pleasure under the tan. They both looked at him with a new respect in their eyes.

"It was certainly an accident," said Sandy skeptically. "Better get out the plane. We'll surely have to smooth the deck if he tries again."

"No, the tool would not permit that, know you. But I wager he'll change his mind before he has done six of them."

Sandy grinned at that.

"Oh, aye, he will that, mon."

Father wondered what he meant. At the third stroke, a piece of dowel flew up and struck him on the cheek. Out of the corner of his eye as he rubbed the stinging spot, he saw the two old men grinning. Giving no sign that he had noticed, he did another two, but at the next stroke, a piece hit him on the chin with such force that it drew blood. He realized then what David had meant. The angle at which the blade must meet the plug would make the tool throw hard, sharp-edged bits at your face, which must surely become raw in a very short time. But he couldn't quit now. He thought for a moment, then he put the adze down carefully, and pulling his big square linen handkerchief out of his pocket, tied it around his head so that it covered all but his eyes. Then he pulled his hat down to meet it, leaving only the smallest possible slit for seeing. That done, he picked up the tool and proceeded methodically down the deck, stopping at each plug just long enough to take the adzeman's position, elbow on thigh. A single blow would suffice, and it was on to the next one. The foreman, who missed nothing of what went on around him, came over to watch. He said approvingly, "Good work, Hal. Your name is Hal, isn't it? That's the way to do it. But the old ones won't, and the young ones can't. Keep it up."

He turned to go, then swung back. "You know, don't you, there's a bonus for anyone that finds a way to speed up the work? No? Well, there is, and you've earned it, or rather, your team has."

When he had left, the two oldsters, who had been listening to this, moved closer.

"Do you get the feeling, " asked David gloomily, "that we will soon be the ones that will be carrying his tool-chests?"

"No, mon; it will be our own tools we will be carrying, and him that will be using them," predicted Sandy in the same tone. Then more cheerfully, "But hoot, if he gets us a bonus for each tool he uses, then more power to him!"

"Ah yes, there is that point to it, now that you mention it." And they went cheerfully along behind him, touching up with their chisels the odd high spot, for even father's strokes were not always perfect.

One day soon after, as they were setting in the plugs, carefully matching the grain direction to that of the planks, not for looks, but so the expansion and contraction would be the same, David complained, "A shameful waste of time is this. She is meant for the Australian run, and when the tropic sun dries these green planks, your hand you may put between them then."

"Aye," agreed the other. "And with those knees they are using, there'll be nowt holding the deck up anyhoo."

Now the "knees" they spoke of had already been an object of Father's interest. In a part of the yard nearby, there was a pile of stumps as high as a house, still with the roots on. These were brought in from wherever land was being cleared, and a good price was paid for what usually cost money to get rid of. From these stumps were sawed the roots, each with a section of stump, that would make a right-angled piece. These were called knees, and they were bolted to deck and sides to hold them together, and to support the deck beams.

"What's wrong with the knees?" he asked curiously. Sandy chose to reply.

"What's wrong, laddie, is that the grain runs wrong, and they will split. And that is because a stump off yon hillside is no the same as a root from an English oak. But they will use the old ways, even though they have not the old woods."

At the first opportunity, father went to where he could see some of the knees in place. To his horror, they were already splitting as the old carpenter had said they would. Some of them had spikes driven in to hold them together, and were splitting around the spikes. He waited for an opportune moment, and accosted the foreman, who was disposed to be friendly.

"What is it, Hal?"

"David and Sandy say the deck planks are too wet, that they'll shrink in the sun down there in the South Seas until you can put your fingers in the cracks."

"They will that," replied the foreman morosely.

"And the knees are all splitting, and they say it's because those stumps are no good."

"'Tis right they are. The stumps are not of oak."

Father had been thinking.

"Couldn't you glue and bolt some planks together and cut knees out of them that wouldn't split?"

"It's called laminating," said the foreman, "and it is the thing to do." He burst out bitterly, "I know that. The carpenters know that. A boy fresh out of the hills knows it. But the architect doesn't know it. The owners don't know it. And I'm damned if I think they care!"

"But can't you tell them? Surely they'd listen if you told them?"

The man turned on him intensely. "Let me tell you something, boy. I'm hired to do one thing—that is to see this ship gets built on time and to specifications, and if I don't do it, they will get someone who will."

He swung off up the deck, to snarl at some unfortunate worker who happened to be conveniently nearby. Father reported this to the two old men, who laughed at him.

"Now he's going to change the ways of the world," said David, "and finds that it has better to do than listen to advice."

And Sandy, "Ay, laddie, 'tis best to do your work as well as you can, and leave the wealthy to get wealthier," which was doubtless good advice, but it didn't sit well.

He thought of various schemes to set things right, but could devise no way of implementing them. There were too many layers of bureaucracy between himself and anyone with the authority to do something about it. It was a baptism of sorts!

Their next job was to trim the deck planks along the curve of the bow. The crew who put the deck in place made no attempt to fit them to the curve, but left them projecting over the side for the finishing crew. First they were sawn as closely as possible—his task—and then trimmed by the ship's carpenters to the shape of the curve. (All this was done about two stories from the ground, with no thought of safety measures.) It was a slow job. Fir planks that thick don't chisel easily. He thought he might just manage another bonus. After quitting time that afternoon, he went to a nearby shop that sold logging supplies. There he chose the best Sager swamping axe he could find, and spent most of the evening filing and honing it until it would shave the hair from his forearm. He oiled it and made a blade-guard for it with a piece of leather from a boot upper.

Next morning, early as usual, he concealed it behind a pile of lumber on deck and waited for Sandy and David to arrive. After he had carried their tools up, he stood around watching them don their canvas aprons and otherwise get ready for work. As the sawing went much faster than the chiselling, he was well ahead, and would be given other jobs to keep him busy.

The old men took out their gleaming tools and began where they had left off the day before, each one making derogatory remarks about the other's work. He went over and pretended to inspect it. They looked at him suspiciously. They had learned to be wary of their helper, who they had soon discovered owned a sense of humour similar to their own, and a wit as keen!

He said critically, "It's really quite good, you know, considering the tools you have to work with."

Any criticism of their tools, real or fancied, brought instant retaliation.

"It's an expert on tools he is now" said David mockingly. "It's lessons he will be giving us on the best chisels next."

But Sandy, more direct, asked ominously, "What the devil's wrong with our tools?"

Hal pretended alarm, "Oh, there's nothing wrong with them. They're the best set of tools I ever saw anywhere."

The Scotsman's face relaxed a bit. Not much.

"It's just that they're not right for this job. Too light for heavy planks like these."

"D'ye mean to say you could do better?" challenged Sandy truculently.

"Well," said Hal judicially, "maybe not much *better*. But much faster. What would you say if I could do five planks to your one?"

"I would say," replied David, "that it was time I woke up and got ready for work. But, just supposing it's awake I am, and not dreaming, what would you be doing the job with? For it's slightly curious I am."

Hal went to the lumber pile, came back with the axe, took the guard off and handed it over. David took it and held it out skeptically.

"And where are the trees you mean to chop with this bludgeon?" But there was interest in his eyes, and those of his partner, for they were men who knew tools, and it is likely that, common though it was in the woods, this one was new to them, for, though the double-edged axe is a tool as old as tools, and is pictured in Egyptian and Cretan wall paintings, the version as developed for logging in the Pacific Northwest may be unique. It is quite possibly one of the perfect tools. Sandy took it, hefted it, ran his fingers along the slim orangewood handle.

"Och," he said wistfully. "If we'd had these on the field of Culloden..." He shook his head, handed it back. "Show us, lad."

Father, remembering, told me, "I was pretty nervous. It felt right in my hands, but I'd not made even one stroke with it. I made a couple of practice cuts, well off the mark. I was afraid to look at their faces. But it went exactly where I wanted it to go, so I set to work in earnest."

He wedged a chip between that plank and the next, so that the last cut wouldn't split the wood, and went through that one as well. Then he stopped and leaned on the axe. They came and kneeled there, running calloused fingers over the smooth cut.

David said wonderingly, "There was a point there in the lad's words. It was the wrong tool we were using indeed."

And Sandy, "Och, aye. But it is a weapon of war, with other uses as may be, and we are men of peace. I will not have one." But he looked thoughtful.

An axe chopping fir timbers cross-grain is a noisy tool. The foreman had heard it and had come to stand there across the deck from them, watching but unseen. Now he walked over to examine the work. Then he looked closely at the tool used to do it.

"Sandy, David," he said abruptly "I've some work for you below deck. Hal, when you finish this side, go to work on the other. I'll send a man to do the sawing. Your wages just went up and there'll be another bonus for your crew."

He left without waiting for an answer. At his last two words, the two old carpenters looked at each other significantly. David made a comical grimace.

"Did I not foretell it? His crew; did you hear the man say it? Next, it will be his toolboxes!"

"Aye, and now he has his own helper. But it is not all bad. Did ye no hear the word 'bonus'?"

In vain did he expostulate that the foreman actually meant "the crew he belongs to." It did nothing to quell the headshakings and dire mutterings of the old men, who actually were quite content to put away chisel and mallet and go to work under cover of the deck. It was beginning to rain, and they hated to get their tools wet.

When the job was finished, he oiled his axe, put on the blade guard and sought out the foreman.

"Finished, eh? Good. You know, I've been keeping an eye on you, Hal. I'm taking you off the job you started on. I've got a better one for you."

Hal began to protest that he liked working with the two oldsters, but was waved silent.

"Those two, old David and the other one, Sandy. Welsh and Scotch. Double trouble. Stubborn as any mule. Do everything their own way. Never listen to what I tell them. I'm going to put you in charge of them. I'll tell you what I want done, and it's your job to get them to do it. That way I won't have to put up with them looking at me with those little grins of theirs. They make me feel like an apprentice again, and I don't like it!... Yes, what is it?" to father's desperate attempts to interrupt.

"I can't do that. That would be ridiculous!"

"Why not? And why ridiculous?"

"I couldn't give them orders. They'd just laugh at me. They've been doing this work for as long as I've been alive. I don't even know the names of some of their tools!"

"Twice as long. More than twice. They've been at it more than fifty years. What does that matter? They'll take orders if I say so. And you don't need to know what their tools are called to tell them what to do with them. So that's settled. Best idea I've had for weeks! You'll get a hike in wages of course."

Father thought swiftly.

"The only way I could do it is if they get more money too."

"How much?"

Swift thought, daring.

"A dollar a day more."

Thought; decision.

"Eighty cents."

It was a large amount.

"I'll try it," conceded the young foreman. He had been there slightly less than one month. "But you'll have to break it to them—when I'm somewhere else."

"Done." said the other. "I'll enjoy it!"

"But don't tell them about the eighty cents."

"Good thinking," approved the foreman.

But he wasn't finished yet.

"There's just one more thing."

"I thought there might be," sighed the foreman.

"Well, you see, I've been carrying those heavy tool chests of theirs up to the deck... It wouldn't look good now, but I'd hate..."

"I'll get one of the swampers to do it, if they'll let him. Now be off with you. Make yourself scarce for half an hour while I break the news to them."

And he was away with, father was almost certain, just a bit more spring in his purposeful stride than usual. And now, left to his thoughts, he dithered. There was no other word for it.

He told me, "I thought of quitting. I didn't see what else I could do. How could I face those two, and even think of telling them what to do? It was ridiculous. I cursed that foreman. If *he* didn't want to face them, how did he think I was going to do it?"

But he didn't quit. After enough time had gone by, he walked slowly up the deck past the piles of lumber, to where the two were finishing off a hatch. He knew they saw him coming, but they feigned not to have noticed him, as being deep in some discussion. He stopped a few paces from them; Sandy was speaking.

"Aye," he approved, "and d'ye mind the time they put that young pup over us on the old *Castlemain*? It was a bad end that one met."

"It was that," said David. "I've heard tell that his shade was seen to walk the foredeck when the moon was bright, with his neck all kinked awry."

"Aye, but that was no' as bad as he that slipped into the barrel of boiling pitch the very next day after he was put over us when we were working on..."

He pretended to have just noticed Hal listening.

"Wisht, mon, watch ye're tongue!"

They turned slightly, regarding him mockingly with eyes the identical shade of pale blue. He said musingly, "The foreman's looking for a couple of good men for the sanding detail."

Only the slightest change of expression acknowledged this riposte. Sanding the deck was one of the lowest of jobs, and one of the hardest. He shook his head wonderingly.

"I don't know what's got into him. Now he's got me carrying messages to tell you two what he wants done. I'd quit right now, only I wouldn't want you to lose your raise."

Sandy's expression became one of rapt interest.

"Raise? Did I hear ye say raise, lad?"

"Why, yes. Didn't he tell you? I suppose it was to make up for him not dealing with you personally."

"And how much precisely would this raise be, d'you know?" asked David.

"Well, he didn't actually *tell* me, but I think eighty cents a day was what he had in mind. But I don't know, I may quit. I wouldn't want you to think I was giving you orders..."

"Now, let's not be too hasty, lad," cautioned Sandy, "Let's not be too hasty here."

Abruptly, father abandoned the game.

"I can't do it," he said miserably. "I can't do it, and I won't do it. I'd rather quit, really, than make a fool of myself."

Sandy shook his head.

"Ah, but lad, the raise; you've forgotten the raise."

To which David commented, "Aye, there's the rub of it. The Scots are a practical race, they go straight to the point."

"Don't feel badly, Hal," Sandy said kindly. (He noted the use, for the first time, of his name.)

"D'ye see, we don't mind it. We'd rather you tell us what's wanted, than some jumped-up house carpenter. We don't mind at all."

And David, "We just want to do our work, with no bother. But when someone hangs about, hurrying us, why, we work a bit slower, do you see?"

And as they grinned slyly at each other, he felt an unexpected flash of sympathy for the man who might be so rash as to give them orders they disapproved of.

Next morning, the foreman showed him a spot on the deck marked with an X in black paint. "The main mast goes there. Take the taper of the foot and cut a hole to match it. Be careful. There's no room for a mistake."

Off he went in his usual abrupt manner, leaving behind him a very nervous young man. The mainmast was four feet through at the base, and fourteen stories high. Normally it would be a simple matter to cut a hole of the correct diameter in the reinforced deck, through which it would be lowered until it butted onto the keel, which would take the weight. But to keep the hold unobstructed, the five masts of the *Mabel Brown* were set into the deck itself, which here was seven feet thick of solid wood, built up of timbers bolted together. A cone-shaped hole must be cut into this, tapering from the full diameter of the mast to just a few inches. He went to his "crew," burdened with responsibility and the difficulty of the task, but they laughed at him.

"Don't worry yourself, Hal," David chided him. "It is what we do; it is what we are trained for; it is what we are good at."

And from Sandy, "And, d'ye see lad, the harder it be to do, the better at it we are. Just ye stand by and let us get to it."

And David, "If something you must be doing for your conscience sake, hand us the tools we call for, and keep the hole cleared of chips. We will cut the hole and the mast will fit."

And they did, and it did, and so did the rest of them, each with its particular name; fore, main, mizzen, jigger and spanker, in sailor's parlance. And the foreman was happy, or as happy as he could be with the job he had.

Time passed, and the *Mabel Brown* was ready to launch. There was still much to do, but it would be done on the water. It was to be a momentous occasion. The biggest ship, the first of her type, the pride of the Wallace yards. Every dignitary in the city, and some from outside it, would be there. Miss Mabel Brown herself would break the champagne bottle for the ceremony. Photographers were hired to cover every angle of the proceedings. A grandstand was erected to hold the important people, and provide a spot to swing the christening magnum. Father wanted desperately to be on board when she was launched, but feared to ask lest he be forbidden, but when he raised the subject with Sandy and David, he was astonished to hear Sandy proclaim, "On or off, lad, it's all one. The only way she's going to get wet is if it rains."

At his look of surprise, David explained matter-of-factly, "'Tis true, Hal, she will not launch. The slope is too little."

He went straightway to the foreman, who listened with unusual patience.

"Those two old gloomsters have been at it again, have they?" He shook his head. "It's never safe to dismiss what they say entirely; they make me feel like a green apprentice sometimes. The ways were laid out by a good firm, but I will admit that I've wondered if they may not have sagged a bit under the weight." He shrugged. "But we'll soon see, won't we?"

The day arrived, under a clear sky. He had never seen so many people in one place in his whole life. It seemed as if most of the city was gathered there for the event. There was a band, and, of course, speeches. And more speeches. But finally the bottle of champagne on its silken ribbon was set aswing by the young woman whose privilege it was, to burst satisfactorily against the bow. The band swung into a rousing tune, and the chocks were knocked free to the roar of the massed crowd. But the *Mabel Brown* simply rested there, like a ship carved from stone. The band faltered to a stop, and there came the buzz of many voices. Shouts were heard, and men brought jacks to bear against the bow. But the *Mabel Brown* was immoveable. Little groups of people began to drift away. The grandstand emptied of the jewels and the beards. From their vantage point on a pile of lumber, David and Sandy t'sked forebodingly.

"'Tis an ill thing," said David, "when a ship refuses the launching."

To which Sandy added, "Aye, a bad omen. There will be many who will not sail on her for this day."

Father scoffed. "You said the slope was too flat. How can that make the ship unlucky? That doesn't make sense"

"There has to be yeast," grinned Sandy, "before ale can be brewed." which elliptical insult Father found unanswerable.

Work went on. There was much to be done on cabins and rails, fit and finish.

The ship was raised a foot or so off the skidway. This seemingly immense task was done by only two men, and took but a few days. Long wedges were placed between the hull and track. One man started at the bow and went towards the stern, giving each wedge one blow with his mallet as he went. The other began on the opposite side at the stern, and moved towards the bow. Imperceptibly but surely, the massive vessel lifted. When the wedges were fully driven, new ones were placed on blocks, and the process went on. When there was room enough, the wood of the ways was charred with huge blowtorches to harden it. Barrels of paraffin were heated until they liquified, then brushed onto the wood with long-handled brushes. Then the wedges were tapped on the sides so that they backed out, gradually lowering the hull back to rest on the prepared surface. Now she was ready. But they were taking no chances on another embarrassment. A pair of one hundred-ton hydraulic jacks with a seven-foot extension were mounted on a solid footing to bear on a heavy pad placed across the bow. But that was only the beginning. This sort of thing had happened before at other shipyards around the world. There were traditional ways to deal with it.

When the big day came once more, a thousand people were assembled on deck, under the baton of a bandmaster. Three thousand more were set to pull on a tug's hawser attached to the bow. A series of bridles, or short lines, were attached to the big one, each bridle pulled by ten people. This time she would move!

The speeches were made, the bottle swung. It bounced off the hull unbroken. The crowd "ahhed"; the old men muttered direly. The bottle, hanging by its ribbon, was retrieved and given a roundhouse swing. This time it broke and the contents splashed and frothed on the hull. The band struck up. On the crowded deck the baton-master waved his wand. Two thousand feet marched in time.

Under that rhythmic tread, first the deck, then the hull itself began to move like a beating heart. A trumpet note sounded, the jacks were started, three thousand strong, the people on the hawser leaned into it.

Seven feet the great jacks thrust, their shafts gleaming. Seven feet the *Mabel Brown* slid toward the sea, but not one foot more. When she stopped moving, the sudden strain on the cable snapped it.

Father told me, "That was one of the strangest things I ever saw in my life. I was on deck by the rail marching with the rest. When the hawser snapped, all three thousand people fell to the ground at the same time! One moment a crowd pulling, the next a field of bodies flat on the ground."

The baton stopped, the hull stilled. The band stopped and the voice of the crowd rose in confused noise. Sandy and David, who, much to their amusement, had been marching on deck with Hal, found a couple of old sailors of a like temperament, and outdid each other in pessimistic prophecies.

"'Tis a jinxed ship she is, no doubt of it."

"'Twas bad enough the bottle didna' break," said Sandy ominously, "but twa launchings fou'ed! Na good will come o't."

"I wouldn't ship on her for double pay," vowed one of the sailors.

"Triple," said his mate.

"But why wouldn't she go?" Father wanted to know.

"'Twas the paraffin," said Sandy contemptuously. "Too sticky in this weather, which they should have kenned. Had it been midsummer, just maybe." He shrugged.

Now the yard was truly worried. What was to be done? Would she launch at all? They might have to dig a trench and float her out. It was a long way to the water, a colossal task, horribly expensive. A group of important men gathered by the bow, even before the crowd had dispersed, discussing these and other notions. The foreman was among them. Being greatly interested, Father had sidled up to overhear, but what he heard failed to impress him. Some of the ideas, often those advanced by the most impressive looking men, were laughably impractical. One of them suggested a system of giant rollers. He could stand it no longer.

Brash as ever (he had no respect for dignity without ability), he said, "The paraffin is too sticky," in that voice that compelled attention. "The loggers use cupgrease to make the skids slippery."

Everyone turned to look. A huge beard and moustache, with belly to match, asked the foreman indignantly, "Is this one of yours, sir?"

It wasn't the censure of irritated authority, or the eyes directed his way, but the look on the foreman's face that made father decide it might be prudent to leave.

"I just thought you should know," he said defensively, and retreated with what dignity he could muster.

They sent for an expert from the great shipyards on the Clyde in Scotland. Work went on, and in due course, the great man made his arrival. He was a short, broad, no-nonsense man with a soft voice and the air of one who had directed men for a very long time. He ignored the train of officials that trailed him, and called for surveyor's instruments. When they came, he took a sighting along the track. Then he took a child's ball out of his pocket and put it on the track timbers in several places. It rolled, wherever he put it. He ordered the ship to be raised once again with the wedges. While this was being done, he ordered seven barrels of soft cup grease from the firm in the city that supplied it for logging equipment, where, placed in pressure "cups," it kept the shafts of the machines lubricated. This was spread over the timbers under the hull.

Father and the two old shipwrights were working on the fore-cabin's trim when he felt a strange sensation of movement. He looked around, and his exclamation caused his companions to turn and they also stood and stared.

He told me, "It was the strangest feeling. The ship seemed rock-solid, but all the land around seemed to be moving past us, and it took me a moment to realize that the *Mabel Brown* was sliding down the ways towards the water. It didn't seem that we were going very fast, but as the stern hit the water, there was a hissing roar, and a great wall of water rose up higher than the deck, but it rolled away to the side and didn't come over."

Once on the water, their speed seemed so great, that it appeared as if they must cross the narrows and ram the shore on the other side, but the lines to the drag chains came tight and she slowed smoothly to a stop. The *Mabel Brown* was launched at last!

As they walked up through the yards after work, he turned for a good look at the ship, now tied at the dock for the raising of the masts and the finishing work.

"She doesn't look very graceful in the water," he said doubtfully. "Maybe when the masts are up and rigged..."

"She'll still," scoffed Sandy, "look like a fat duck squattin' there. She has na lines."

David added, "She is not made for grace or for speed either. She is built to carry cargo."

"She is not one thing," judged Sandy, "not yet the other. No good will come o't, mark my words."

The old Scotsman proved prescient. The *Mabel Brown* and her five sisters were obsolete when they were designed. Over-masted and under-engined, they were indeed not one thing or the other. A five masted full-rigged ship needs a large crew to operate it, far more men than would be economically practical. And unless the sails can be furled quickly, any sudden squall of wind could be dangerous. The two Bollinder semi-diesels were too small to drive such a heavy ship; they were undependable, and old fashioned before they were installed. The war had brought a surge of mechanical advances in its wake and although this was hardly obvious at the time, the day of the sailing cargo ship was over.

A couple of years or so later, long after he had left the shipyard, father came in to Vancouver. He decided to look up the two old shipwrights. He found them easily enough, working in mahogany and teak on a rich man's yacht. It was the first time he had seen what they could really do, and he realized at last why the foreman had thought them wasted on the *Mabel Brown*. He asked them if they had heard how she fared. They looked at him in amazement.

"Ye mean ye havna' heard?" asked Sandy. "Whar' hae ye been, mon?"

"The omens were plain to see," remarked David. "No man of sense who knew of them would sail on her."

The *Mabel Brown* had set off for Australia with a full load of lumber and a crew of twenty-one. A near-capsizing in a sudden change of wind made such an impression that they decided to set sails on only three of the five masts. She was very slow. The engines were balky and undependable. As the ship began to come under the tropic sun, the planking on deck and sides shrank until she started to leak badly whenever she heeled, and a sailing ship must heel to one side or another unless the wind is straight behind. She grew more sluggish, and the water in the hold began to rise as the pumps proved inadequate. It was impossible to plug the cracks; most of them couldn't even be reached. First one engine quit, then the other, and with them went the big pumps they drove. She began to list badly, putting more seams below water. The weight of the five tall masts tipped her more; too late they decided to cut them down. The *Mabel Brown* went over on her side and lay there. The cargo in the hold shifted and nothing they could do would bring her back upright. She drifted that way for months: five, six? Accounts vary. Much of the food was underwater, spoiled. The men began to starve. When she was at last sighted and towed to port, there were rumours of cannibalism, circumspect and obscure, and denied hotly by all concerned. For this was one of the tabu subjects, then and for long after.

"Damned nonsense, to make sich a fash o't. Sailors ha' always eaten their mates at need."

"At least," corrected his friend, "the sensible ones have done so."

"Would you eat a man?" queried father, fascinated.

"I would that," declared the old Scot positively. He grinned ferociously.

"Gin it walk on four legs or two, meat is meat when a man is starving, and I wad eat it with a will!" And old David the Welshman nodded positively in acquiescence.

The *Mabel Brown* was refitted and refurbished and sent out again on the world's waterways. But she was not a lucky ship. She ended her days in the Baltic Sea, wrecked during a storm, and was finally dismantled.

Chapter 25

Endings

THERE WAS STILL MUCH to be done on the *Mabel Brown*. The masts had yet to be stepped and rigged, and a thousand details waited finishing. In addition, ribs were already being attached to the keel of a sister ship on the same ways where she had been built.

Father stayed to see the masts go up, but his heart was not really in it. The talk was all of war, and he wanted to be there on the stage all the world was watching. England, it was said, needed help, and the traditions of his family were centered chiefly in England.

The letters from Cliff warned him to stay where he was. War, he had found, was nothing like what they had read in their books. Honour had no place in massed attacks against cannon and machine-guns, nor courage amidst clouds of poison gas. The soldiers from Canada were admired for both of these qualities, but the best among them tended to die unsung. But his brother's words had the opposite effect to the one intended. The worse it was, the more strongly he felt he should be sharing it.

He announced his intention to Sandy and David.

"Ach," said the Welshman, "the poor Germans. I'm not sure they deserve that!"

"The Boches," said the old Scot, "can be left to take care of themselves. Save ye'r sympathy for our generals. He will be telling them how to win the war ere he is a week overseas."

"It's telling them he will be, that it's the wrong tools they are using," grinned David.

"I didn't see that it was all that funny," remembered father, "but those two old billygoats chuckled and snorted until I thought they'd never stop!"

Not without a qualm at the defiance of his mother's orders, he reported to the enlistment office at Hastings Park. The recruiting officer asked his questions and noted the answers with the air of one who has done it all a thousand times before, until one bit of information made him look up in surprise.

"How many sisters?" And at the reply, nodding his head, "That's what I thought you said!"

He wrote at greater length than before, then indicated a door into another room.

"Go and get your medical exam, then report back to me."

The doctor was an affable sort, and talked continuously as he went through the rather simple routine. He was in no hurry; enlistment was slow at that time. He was the first, said the medic, and would probably be the only one, to apply that day.

"From Nelson Island, eh? That's right near Jervis Inlet, isn't it?" And on the assurance that it was, "Did you know a family up there called the Johnsons? Thought you might. One of them came through here, when the war first started. Frank Johnson. I examined him. Interesting case. I've been doing this job for nearly thirty years. In all that time, I never saw a more magnificent physical specimen than that man. Perfect body. I think he was a throwback to the old days before the human race became degenerate. Covered with hair, not like a hairy man, but a coat of it, like an animal."

"It was true," father said to me. "His whole body was covered with a pelt of short hair, thick as an otter's almost. I never saw anything like it. You looked at him, you felt nature had meant people to look like that, but something went wrong with the rest of us."

"Did you hear what happened to him?" continued the doctor. "Well, I did. I know everyone in the service that's a regular, and I found out, because I was interested. When they saw him shoot, they couldn't believe it. They made him a sniper and he was a natural. Gave him a rifle that could hit a man in the head a mile away. Sent him to France, to the trenches. First day there, he stuck his head up to have a look around, and a sniper on the other side put a bullet through it. Killed him instantly."

He shook his head scornfully. "Modern warfare. Just slaughter. A man like that should have ridden into the field between the armies, sword in hand, to challenge the other side's champion." With scarcely a pause, "You're as healthy as a horse. Report back to the officer you saw when you came in."

He did, but the result wasn't what he expected. The man behind the desk was kind, but firm.

"We have a note on you in the files," he said, much to father's surprise. "It seems that you are the sole support of your mother, seven sisters and a young brother. Your older brother is already with the forces in Europe. Is that true?" At Hal's affirmation, he went on, "Well, you will be of far more use to us looking after your family, and relieving the government of the obligation, than you would be in the army at the moment..."

At father's attempt to protest, he raised a hand. "No, no. No argument. You're a soldier now, you've been enlisted. Enlisted men don't talk back to their superiors."

His smile took the sting from his words. He pushed a paper across the desk. "This is your deferment. Keep it on you. We know how to find you if we need to."

The interview was over. He was in the army now, but there was no feeling of accomplishment. May had seen to it that her other son wouldn't get to war. Oh, there were ways he could have used to get overseas, as he well knew. But the whole attitude of those he had met at the depot indicated that there was no great desire for men at this time. He didn't feel needed, and he finally resolved that he would do as the officer had suggested. The war seemed to be under control, and the army probably could manage without his help.

There was no shortage of work for a reliable young man with a boat, and he had no difficulty in fulfilling the obligation imposed on him by the enlistment officer.

The war ended, and with the returning troops came the influenza epidemic of 1918, perhaps the worst the world has known. Over twenty million people perished. Father caught it, and went home

to Hidden Basin to die—as he supposed. He was delirious when he did so, or he would never have exposed his family to it. Strangely though, none of them caught it from him. In time, Cliff arrived back at the farm, with a foreign medal, and his lungs weakened by the poison gas that eventually killed him. I don't know what the medal was, but I remember that a retired English army officer seemed quite impressed when father showed it to him.

Like so many others, Cliff returned from the war an embittered and disillusioned man. Always something of a stoic, he now treated his body almost as an enemy, with no shred of sympathy for its weakness or pain. After much persuasion to tell something of his experiences, he related a story so terrible that his shocked brother never asked again, and Cliff never volunteered another.

The farm wasn't the same without the patriarchal presence of their father; they both left as soon as they could—Cliff to hunt and trap, and to do such jobs as he must to earn a living, and father to begin his restless exploration of the Coast, while working at various camps or handlogging. For a few years, his mother stayed at the farm with her children but as her daughters arrived at marriageable age, she wished to offer them a wider range of prospects.

Father bought them a store in the little community of Selma Park, near Sechelt, and moved them there with all their possessions. All, that is, except the books. May had no interest in her husband's library, and indeed rather resented it and the attention he gave it. She commanded that they be left there, on the shelves he had built for them. But father thought that Jack's books deserved a better fate than as nests for mice. A few months later, he returned to Hidden Basin and the now desolate farm. The books, however, were gone.

Eventually the properties on Nelson Island were sold. The family was no more.

Dick Hammond has lived on the Sunshine Coast
all his life and has been an independent log salvor
since 1955. To write this book, he drew on the
stories of his father Hal, who grew up on the
shores of Nelson Island's Hidden Basin. This is
Dick Hammond's first book.